THE MAN ON THE ENDLESS STAIR

THE MAN ON THE
ENDLESS STAIR

Chris Barkley

Polygon

First published in hardback in Great Britain in 2025
by Polygon, an imprint of Birlinn Ltd

Birlinn Ltd | West Newington House
10 Newington Road | Edinburgh | EH9 1QS

9 8 7 6 5 4 3 2 1

www.polygonbooks.co.uk

ISBN 978 1 84697 689 6
EBOOK ISBN 978 1 78885 731 4

British Library Cataloguing-in-Publication Data
A catalogue record for this book is available on
request from the British Library.

The publisher acknowledges support from the National Lottery
through Creative Scotland towards the publication of this title.

Typeset in Adobe Caslon Pro by The Foundry, Edinburgh
Printed and bound in Great Britain by Clays Ltd, Elcograf S.p.A.

For those who strive

'When writers die they become books, which is, after all, not too bad an incarnation.'

I

LOOK. LOOK CAREFULLY, PLEASE. The moment you turn away, everything changes and, when you look back, you'll have forgotten that for which you were searching.

First, let your eye be drawn to me: young, straight-backed and certain. I was peering over the edge of a ferry, Sea of the Hebrides churning below. It had become my habit to stand on the deck and watch for whales during the slow journey to the island. The trick, I had found, was to soften the vision, to allow the hem of the sky to fray into the sea, to take in everything at once. Then, when a fin bursts through, the landscape gathers about it and the eye cannot help but be drawn.

The little ferry seldom made this journey, due to lack of demand. On most of my previous trips I had been the only passenger. But on this occasion, my fifth visit since I'd returned from the war, there was another man with me. From inside, he flung open the cabin door and bolted across the deck, slipping on the spume-slick metal, crashing into the barrier. The column of vomit which left his mouth was thick and yellow, with the sour stench of a rich diet. It travelled in a heavy arc, out over the edge of the ferry and into the water below. Afterwards, the man remained clutching the barrier, chest heaving. He was hairless and resembled a gourd stuffed into an expensive suit, with folds turned down at the outer corners of his eyes, making him seem perpetually sombre.

I hurried across to him, held the barrier with one hand and, with the other, rummaged in my woollen coat for a cigarette to offer.

'All great introductions include the expulsion of bodily fluids,' the man said between gasps. 'Colm Hubert. Good to meet you.'

'Euan—'

'Oh yes, I know.'

I paused.

He stood a little taller and peered at me from under his solemn folds. 'We have the same patron,' he said. 'I am Malcolm Furnivall's solicitor . . .' He vomited again, dabbed the corners of his mouth with an embroidered silk handkerchief. 'Seasickness,' he said. 'Just seasickness . . .'

'Smoke?' I pulled out two hand-rolled cigarettes from my leather cigarette case.

He took one gladly, widened his eyes as I lit it for him. 'Liquorice papers,' he said.

After the war I'd started using these brown papers to handroll my cigarettes. A small luxury I allowed myself. I shrugged, lit my own, then tucked the cigarette case back into the inner pocket of my coat, watching the late-morning sun dance off the waves.

'I have read your books,' Colm said.

I watched him, hoping he would not vomit again.

'Very engaging,' he said. 'Yes, very engaging. You must be proud to have come so far.'

'What do you mean by that?'

'Oh, I meant it as a compliment. It is my business to pay attention to those closest to Malcolm.' Upon seeing my expression, he hastened to add, 'From humble beginnings to

Malcolm Furnivall's protégé. Tell me, is he as the rumours describe?'

'You haven't met him?'

Colm caught my gaze, held it, then laughed. 'Forgive me. I ought to hold my tongue. This journey has rattled my nerves.'

We smoked together. I tapped ash into the wind. 'If it's not too indelicate to ask, Colm . . . why are you here?'

He examined his silk handkerchief, grimaced, then, in a flourish, cast it over the side of the boat. With a look of exhaustion, he said, 'I don't . . . at this current moment . . . know.'

'You don't know?'

'I received an invitation to the island, a ticket for the ferry and a generous sum of money. Though my firm has represented Malcolm for many years, I have never met him. Never even spoken with him. He asked specifically for me in his letter . . . Perhaps he knew of my seasickness, wished for nothing more than to play a cruel joke.'

I laughed. 'Are you sure you don't know him?'

A wry smile crossed Colm's face. He took a deep breath, turned his body away from me. He scrunched his face, spat a gobbet overboard, stared out at the horizon. 'You visit him often?'

'Yearly.' I looked away from Colm, watched the seabirds circling, the waves being shorn apart by the ferry's bow. I wished I'd visited more often over the past five years, but I'd been working hard, dividing my time between writing, lecturing at Oxford and maintaining my empty childhood home on the coast of Edinburgh, which seemed intent on mouldering. Colleagues asked me why I didn't sell it. To them, my regular shuttling from Oxford to Edinburgh seemed absurd. But I was not like them; whenever I returned to that poor house, I was reminded of the gulf between us, which, I think, is the reason I kept it. On my way to visit Malcolm, I would stay overnight in the house, recalling the smell of my father's cigarette smoke, of mildew and grease. Those nights I would not sleep. I would lie awake, waiting for a knock on the door, for my past to come spilling in.

I pulled up my sleeve, glanced at the scratched face of my ATP wristwatch I'd received as a private and refused to upgrade. It read eleven o'clock.

Colm's eyes settled on the watch, a tightness in his expression.

'Malcolm wrote to me when the war was done,' I said. 'I'd begun lecturing at the university, writing on the side. One of my essays was published in *Horizon*, a piece about Malcolm's work. A week later, he wrote to me, asking if I had any manuscripts I was looking to publish. At first, I thought it was a hoax; one of my students seeking revenge after a particularly boring lecture.' I smiled at the memory. 'I just couldn't believe that he'd discovered my writing, let alone enjoyed it enough to contact me. After corresponding for a while, he invited me to his home, helped get my novels into print. We've stayed in touch ever since.'

'And you sensed nothing different in his invitation this time?'

'No.'

We smoked quietly.

'You want to say something,' I said. 'Say it.'

Colm straightened his tie, ran his hands down the front of his coat. 'I have it on good authority that he has summoned his children to his estate . . . He is gathering those closest to him. If something substantial is to happen, it might be an idea for you and I, the two outsiders, to become friendly. You understand me?'

'Yes,' I said, offering a smile. 'I understand you.'

Malcolm rarely spoke of his children, Clara and Lewis. They had moved to the mainland before the war, leaving only Malcolm and his wife, Anwen, behind. Malcolm had become increasingly absorbed in research for his new novel, separating himself from those around him. A month previous, Clara appeared at a lecture I was giving, accosting me afterwards and enquiring after her father. She said she feared for his health, that he was losing touch with reality. She demanded that I bring him back, said I was the only one who could. Though she had tried to hide it, I'd sensed her desperation. Clara, it seemed, was not accustomed to asking for help.

Colm patted me on the arm, leant in close. 'Are you sure there was nothing different about his invitation?'

I thought back to what Malcolm had written in his last letter. He'd mentioned his research, comparing himself to the physicist Werner Heisenberg, who had isolated himself upon the island of Helgoland to gain insight into the bizarre forces of the universe. Malcolm, too, had shut himself away to pursue his masterwork. Even in his writing, I sensed a change in him, a distance. Only briefly had he mentioned a 'troublesome' cough, but that line, over all others, gave me concern.

'There was nothing in his invitation that concerned me,' I said.

Colm narrowed his eyes, finished the cigarette I'd

given him, flicked it away. He watched the island as we approached it: vertiginous slopes black with pines. 'What has Malcolm promised you?' he asked. There was a sly note in his voice.

I tapped my thumb to each of my forefingers, turned away from him. 'If you need me, I'll be port side,' I said. 'I'll leave you to your ejections.'

'Wait—'

I stopped, turned back to him. His hand was outstretched, and everything about him was pitiable.

'I fear we have not been honest with each other,' he said. 'I think our experience . . . our *shared* experience, has taught us to be wary. I, too, was overseas.'

I rolled my eyes, moved to leave. Men like him sat in smoking rooms, laughing and dining as they sent boys like me to die.

'It is not seasickness,' he said.

'What?'

'I have been ingenuine. But my motive was only to save some discomfort.'

'Considerate of you.'

Colm gave a pained smile. 'When I was a boy, my friend and I would visit Cramond Island. You know it? We would race the tide, running there and back before the water swallowed up the path. One evening, we weren't fast enough. The tide took us, pulled us out to sea. I was a better swimmer so tried to keep him afloat . . . but I didn't have the strength. I saw him drowning. I couldn't pull him up and he started to drag me down with him. I wouldn't let go. I breathed in the saltwater, trying to shout for help . . . That sensation has stayed with me. A terrible way to die. I think the only reason sailors tell each other that it is warm and peaceful is to keep their courage up.' He paused, remembering. 'Someone pulled me from the water, but my friend was gone. I have felt nauseous around the sea ever since . . . Now I have been honest with you. Will you return the favour?'

I finished my cigarette, stubbed it out on the barrier, tucked the filter into my pocket to be disposed of later. After scrutinising the bulbous man, I spoke curtly. 'You want to know why I've come?'

He nodded.

'I've lost something. And I want it back.'

As he opened his mouth to speak, the nausea overcame him again, and he closed his eyes, lowered his chin to his chest, breath hitching in his throat.

I hadn't yet said it aloud, but it was true. My work had dried up, as had my life. In the past few months, memories of my time in France had plagued me and I had withdrawn, produced very little. When thinking back to when I was happiest, I returned, always, to bright spring days spent with the Furnivalls, to Malcolm's wild laugh and warm conversation. I think, as I stood upon that ferry, that I hoped to rediscover that joy.

I looked out over the water, saw waves crashing against the island. The spring sky was divine blue, the sun cold and bright. The smell of salt was on the air. Reinvigorated, I listened to the hymns of the wind, feeling, for the first time in recent memory, hopeful.

Colm muttered something, but his words swept past me.

I smiled, still facing outward, gaze drifting to a movement beneath the waves.

'What in God's name are you grinning at?' Colm said.

There, the pleated throat of a minke whale as it rolled in the wake of the ferry. I said nothing. I only watched as it fell behind, disappearing in the foam. Quiet. I kept my eye on the water.

The minke burst from the surface, hung in mid-air, then crashed back into the waves, leaving behind a column of briny mist.

'Did you see it?' I asked.

'See what?' Colm replied.

★ ★ ★

At the dock we were met by Lewis. He leant against a rusty Ford Prefect, rolling a strand of his long dark hair and whistling. He reminded me of his father, not in his looks, but in his sudden, unpredictable movements. This ensured that he held the attention of those about him – a useful trait for an actor, which is what he professed to be. He waved to us as we strode up the bay.

'I'll walk,' Colm said, shaking Lewis's hand, greenish pallor still on his face. 'A constitutional will balance the humours.' He took off before Lewis could give directions.

'Stick to the track,' Lewis called with a look of bemusement. 'You'll be at the estate in no time.'

Lewis turned to me, waited a moment. When I opened my mouth to speak, he thrust his hands out and pressed my shoulders. 'No need for introductions, Euan. It's a pleasure to finally meet the man I've heard so much about.'

I must have looked stunned, because he continued with a conspiratorial tone.

'In my profession, you must be adept at gathering and

distributing information surreptitiously.' He raised his eyebrows, the hint of a smile on his lips. 'Actors are terrible gossips.'

Though I had only known him for a moment, I felt close to Lewis. He had the ability to make you feel as if you were the only person in the world. He took my valise, swung it deftly into the boot. 'I've read *Ex Libris*,' he said, quite out of the blue. 'The bookseller told me it was their top seller.' *Ex Libris* was my most recent novel: a story about a son who tracks his missing father through the clues left in bookplates from his personal library. 'I can see my father's influence on you. And the twist . . . well—'

'You saw it coming?'

'I am a Furnivall; twists are part of my genetic make-up.' Lewis gave the impression he was joking, yet there was an edge to his voice; he seemed like the type to play the fool while slipping barbs of truth into his routine. He continued, 'Nevertheless, I was impressed. Your plaudits are well deserved.'

Face reddening, I thanked him. Despite myself, I couldn't help but feel proud.

He appeared to sense my embarrassment and looked at me warmly.

I found, once we were in the car, setting off along the track to Malcolm's estate, that Lewis had given up his most recent role when he'd received his father's letter. 'Tybalt,' he said. 'Much more interesting than Mercutio, which is the better-loved part. And with the same benefit of being able to slink out at the start of Act 3 for a few pints.' He laughed, but the expression on his face quickly soured. He was evidently bitter and conducted conversations as if he were still performing his role, onstage before an adoring audience.

'It must have been hard to give up the part.'

He drummed his fingers on the wheel. 'I had an understudy.'

I cleared my throat, then asked, 'What was the reason Malcolm called you home?'

Lewis took his eyes from the road, fixed me with a quiet stare. The smile on his face did not reach his eyes. 'Does a son need a reason to visit his father?'

'But the letter—'

There was a shout from along the way, and Lewis looked back to the track, swerving to avoid Colm. Lewis waved an apology, then said under his breath, 'I'll be honest with you, I'm glad he declined the lift. Solicitors set my teeth on edge.'

'Why has Malcolm sent for him?'

Lewis chewed his lower lip, drove on in silence. The track wound about solitary boulders, whose rain-hewn runnels seemed, in the late-morning shadows, like drooping jowls, or the hollows of sunken eyes turned to the sky. The track went on, through a dense forest of pine, rowan, downy silver birch. Streamers of flame-coloured flowers billowed from the branches of witch hazel, signalling the approach to Malcolm's estate.

'I hear you met my sister,' Lewis said.

'Yes, she slipped into one of my lectures. I was grateful she sat through and waited till the end to confront me. Perhaps she learnt something about Goethe's literary themes.'

Lewis laughed. 'Clara has always been one to take matters

into her own hands. And she can be dogged, can't she? She inherited our father's tenacity and . . . persuasiveness. When we were both children, she once convinced me to climb our mother's wardrobe and steal her jewellery box from the top shelf. All in the pursuit of a particularly pretty hairpin. She told me that if I did it for her, she'd play charades with me all afternoon. I managed to climb up, but when I reached the top, I realised the box was too heavy to carry down. She encouraged me to try . . . When the box fell on me, it cut open my head. There was so much blood, I passed out completely. But when I came to, I took the rap. If I'd blamed her, it would never have worked anyway. She has always been the favourite.'

'The things we do for family.'

He clicked his tongue against the roof of his mouth. 'You have siblings?'

'A sister.'

'She must be proud to have such a celebrated writer in her family.'

'She would have been.' I counted the trees as we passed them.

'I'm sorry.' He peered at me sideways and, when I caught his eye, looked forward again. 'Not far now.'

'You knew Colm was a solicitor,' I said.

'What?'

'He never told you his profession.'

Lewis turned the car abruptly, spoke from the corner of his mouth. 'I was told by my father.'

'Is he in good health?'

A muscle in Lewis's jaw twitched before he, again, affected his jovial tone. 'You can see for yourself this afternoon.' There was a silence before he continued. 'I've never seen him so engrossed in his work. He must have spoken with you about it.'

'Only briefly, during my last visit. He said that when we next met, he would tell me more. It seemed . . .'

Lewis's eyes flicked to me.

'I don't know.'

'What?'

'It seemed as if he wanted to tell me something, but was worried.'

Lewis fell silent again, and I could see, from the corner of my eye, that his lips were moving slightly, working to find the right phrasing of the next question. 'You're aware I am his son, Euan?'

'I am.'

'His interests are my interests.'

'Of course.'

'What I mean to say is, you don't have to be guarded with me. If my father has promised you something, I will respect that. He has invited you into our family . . . and as you know' – he pulled back his hair to reveal a scarred depression in his forehead – 'there is little I won't do for family.'

2

THE FURNIVALL MANSION WAS in the stomach
of the island. It rose from the bottom of a deep glen,
gurning against the wind which assaulted its crenellated
walls. Through the windscreen, I watched the mansion rise
before us: turrets, arches, cornices, arranged in a recursive
order. Every time I visited, it arrested my attention and so
my conversation with Lewis subsided while the mansion
interrupted in its language of angles. The longer I looked,
the more I had to wrestle with the dimensions, giving up,
starting again. It seemed to have been forged from a series
of disparate elements, balancing each other in a grotesque
symbiosis.

Many years before, Malcolm had moved with his
family to this Hebridean island, so that he might better
concentrate on his writing. It had taken three years to build
the mansion, using sandstone from a neighbouring island
and a few dozen craftsmen to whom Malcolm had passed
his intricate design. Yet, the mansion also could very well
have been created over time by deposits of living stone,
forming pockets which became rooms, crystals that became
windows. The essence of the place held the chaotic beauty
of something grown.

The western face of the mansion had started to crumble,
hunks of scarred stone sinking into the tangled weeds which

grew tall about the walls. Like a body shutting down, it was bringing the life force to its centre, allowing limbs to wilt away.

Lewis had grown up here with only his sister for company. I wondered, as he pulled the car into the drive, what a childhood in this place would have been like. What would it do to a mind, to live somewhere so solitary, to grow up in that intricate stack of empty rooms, surrounded by the encroaching wild?

A knock on the car window and the door opened. Mrs Gibson, the housekeeper, hoisted me from the seat and began to mutter to herself as Lewis left the car running and vaulted up the front steps. 'I'm starving,' he said, going inside without once looking back.

Exasperated, Mrs Gibson tugged at her long-lobed ears, which appeared to have grown longer since we'd last met. She was tall, imposing and increasingly haggard. 'Lunch is being prepared inside,' she said. 'I must get back so it doesn't burn. I'm afraid I can't show you to your room, but it's made up. You remember—'

'Where are the other servants?'

She pulled at her ears again, then swept around the car, taking my valise from the boot, thrusting it at me, then leaning in through the driver door, turning off the engine.

I peered in through the passenger door. 'Mrs Gibson?'

She checked through the windscreen, to make sure Lewis had gone inside. Then, we faced each other over the gearstick. 'Malcolm has fired all the house staff. It's only me now.'

I looked at her in disbelief. The mansion had never been particularly well cared for, and now, to fire all the servants but Mrs Gibson . . . Something drastic must have happened.

I began to understand why Lewis had been so guarded with me in the car. I searched Mrs Gibson's face and whispered, 'What? I . . . I told him I couldn't maintain it alone. He didn't care.'

'He gave no reason?'

She leant further over the gearstick, placed her red and calloused hand on the dashboard. 'One of my girls followed him out to his writing shed. He caught her, and . . . and the next day, everyone was told to leave.'

The writing shed. Malcolm had only taken me there once, by a convoluted route which I struggled to remember. When inside, he'd watched my every move. I recalled the look on his face: wary and searching.

Sensing something, Mrs Gibson turned her head from me and looked to the mansion. She glanced down again, then began to brush at the dashboard with her hand, as if dusting it. There was a change in her demeanour; her movements were sharp, her expression severe.

I looked through the windscreen towards the mansion, saw Clara in the drawing-room window. She was auburn-haired, cold-eyed and broad-shouldered, having swum competitively since the age of seven. The kind of person whose presence could be felt through windows, over large distances and possibly even through walls. She was watching.

I remained there in stunned silence as Mrs Gibson closed the driver door and hurried back up the main steps. 'The pheasant will be dry,' she said blackly.

I emerged from the car, looked again to the drawing-room window.

Clara raised her closed fist, then unfurled her long fingers and gave a curt wave. Each action was slow, deliberate, muscular. She turned on her heel and left me reeling in the driveway. By now, the midday sun was high and cold, gazing down like a stone eye as I made my way, alone, into the Furnivall mansion.

Standing in the main hall, I recalled how I'd felt like a stranger the first time I'd set foot in the mansion. Malcolm and Anwen had given me a tour, sharing stories about the place, laughing at little inside jokes, allowing me into their world. It had been overwhelming, to be welcome in the Furnivall household: a warren of curious and historied rooms. Before, I had wrestled with its complexity; now I surrendered, allowed myself to be swallowed. It was like hearing a poem: one had to succumb to its logic to know it.

Though the pathways within were difficult to remember, I had started to draw a vague map of them in my mind. My room was on the first floor of the western wing, and the turning which led to it was signalled by a great stag skull hanging from the wall. I stopped beneath the pair of branching antlers and cast about. A spear of light came through the stained-glass window, shining down on the recessed alcoves in which there were chessboards, all in various states of play. Malcolm would often walk the corridors, setting compositions for himself. I recognised the Scandinavian opening on one of the boards and smiled. Every time I had played Malcolm, he'd beaten me with some variation on that opening; moving the queen out early and decimating my carefully arranged pieces. How like Malcolm, to ignore fundamentals and move the queen early.

I sat down at the chessboard, rested my finger on Malcolm's queen. Since my last visit, a rough hide had formed about me, blunting all experience, keeping joy from coming in. But as I took the queen in my hand, held it tightly, I felt that hide start to flake away. From nothing, I had gained so much. There was happiness in my life; I had a job I loved and people who cared for me. It had taken twenty-nine years of life to find, but I had a family here. Anwen and Malcolm had welcomed me. A part of me still didn't believe it: who was I to deserve this? But as I sat there, holding the chess piece, I allowed myself to imagine a world in which I released the past from my grip, let it spin away in the wind. A world in which I sold my poor childhood house in Edinburgh, realised that this was my new home. A home I deserved.

I set the piece back on the board, made a move of my own and smiled. I imagined Malcolm's face upon seeing my subtle greeting. Perhaps it would only take that – a small, warm gesture, to call him back to this world.

When I came to my room, I found the door ajar. I set my valise down in the hallway and peered inside. There was Anwen: silver-haired, elfin. She swept about the room, straightening picture frames, dusting shelves, picking lint from the bedspread. The way she worked was frenzied. Though it felt impolite, I remained there, watching her through the crack in the door. It is a rare gift, to observe one's host before they can don their mask of hospitality. And though I had known Anwen for some time, I sensed there was much she held back from the world. She'd been a concert violinist in her youth and had performed with the most prestigious orchestras, though she refused to talk about her past. Sometimes, however, Malcolm would speak fondly of it when we were together. He spoke of her incredible poise and how, when she played, her face would stay completely still, as if frozen in time, while her body swayed and bowed along with the music. That poise had not left her: around others, Anwen moved with the fluidity of someone to whom each breath is a musical phrase. And so, I found it jarring that she, when alone, would move so feverishly. On her third round of the room, straightening and dusting, Anwen stilled. She stood in the middle of the room, as if all warmth had been drained from her. A single blue vein ran like filigree beside her eye. She stared at the far wall.

I leant closer, saw that her lips were moving. I could make out the shape of only two words. 'Just . . . so.'

She turned to the door, saw me, and her eyelids drew back to reveal raw, gleaming whites.

I turned my gaze away and muttered an apology.

She recovered and came to the door.

'Mrs Gibson told me the room was made up. I didn't know you'd be—'

She pulled it open, wide.

'Sorry,' I said.

'Not to worry.' A delicate smile formed on her lips, and she stepped aside, allowing me to enter. As I came to the end of my bed, set my valise down and removed my coat, she watched me from the doorway. 'I only wanted to make sure everything was in order. So little is, nowadays.'

We regarded each other from across the room, happy, despite the circumstances, to be seeing each other again. I think each of us sensed that our meeting, this time, was different – underscored by the unease of Malcolm's condition. We were both in need of some comfort. I said, 'It's good to see you, Anwen.'

The atmosphere softened, and I moved towards her.

'You too,' she said.

Then we were hugging. It was a brief embrace, and, when we parted, she brushed down my shirt, straightened my collar.

'It's a shame,' I said.

She raised a slender eyebrow.

'The servants.'

She inhaled quickly and some colour returned to her face. 'Yes, I was sad to see them go. Many were my friends.' She looked down, tilted her head as if considering a direction of travel, then she cast about the room. 'I hope it's to your liking. The draughts should be better; we painted the windows shut since your last visit.'

Just as she made to leave, I said, 'Where is he?'

She stopped, back turned to me. 'Busy.' Her black skirt swayed about her ankles with the motion of her halted exit.

'What's the matter, Anwen?'

She raised a long finger and used it to push the door shut. She turned to face me.

'I hear he's closed himself off, even from you.'

There was not anger in her expression, but rather pity. She looked at me as if I were naïve. 'The ferry will not have left yet,' she said.

'What?'

'You can go.'

'Why would I do that?'

There was a terrible stillness to her. The spaces between her words were vivid and withering. 'You do not know a single thing.'

'Then tell me.'

She straightened. 'The final *Gravitation* book . . . It has consumed him.'

It was Malcolm's *Gravitation* series that had catapulted him into the literary spotlight. They were intricate mysteries, but also much more. I'd read them many times, and, upon each reading, the novels had taken on new meaning. Like living things, they changed with time, grew wiser and darker.

'Consumed him, how?' I asked.

'There are some ideas which are better left unknown. Ideas which can turn a mind in on itself. He wrestles with something he feels but cannot explain, spends his days reading papers on the nature of time. He's become frail, hardly eats. He speaks for hours on the telephone to physicists, philosophers, mystics. When he comes away, he is not himself . . . I see it in him. He no longer understands the distinction between reality and his writing.' She ran her hand along the arm of her white silk blouse, took a long breath and fixed me with a clear eye.

I remained there, turning her words in my mind, imagining what Malcolm's final book might include. 'Has he shared any of his work with you?'

She smiled at me sadly.

I changed tack, sensing her concern. 'I want to help him,' I said.

She stayed still, the only movement being the slow rise and fall of her narrow ribcage. The longer she watched me, the more unsettled I became. In her expression was pity, affection, but also something sour. Something obscure. 'Why?' she asked.

'Because he has helped me.'

'In what way has he helped you?'

I regarded her for a moment, before deciding to give her the honest answer. 'Before I knew Malcolm, I was nothing. He plucked me from obscurity, showed me the path to a better life.'

She raised her chin, and, in that moment, I understood the sour note was fear. 'You speak as if he were a god.'

'He's an admirable man; don't you agree?'

She bowed her head slowly. She took a deep breath, then looked up at me. 'Of course I agree.' We drifted into an uncomfortable silence which I filled by opening my valise and laying the few clothes I'd taken with me out on the bed. It was a less than subtle gesture to convey that I would not be leaving. When I'd finished, I picked up one last thing and turned to face her.

She gazed at what I held.

'For you,' I said, pressing the burnished stone into her palm. 'I know Malcolm hates gifts, but this is only small. It's just to say how grateful I am for . . . for everything.'

She held it up, examined the hole riven through it. 'An adder stone,' she said. 'For true sight.'

'Recently I've been waking early, walking along the shore. I just saw it the other day and thought . . . Perhaps it was stupid.'

'No,' she said, looking at me through the hole in the stone's centre. 'Thank you. I love the old stories.'

Smiling, I asked, 'What do you see?'

She looked at me through the stone and embraced her role as soothsayer: 'You already have it all.' Bringing it down from her face, she furled her fingers about the stone.

Taken aback, I paused. I had come here to find peace, to

rediscover the joy I'd once felt with the Furnivalls. But, of course, she was right: I already had peace in my life, I only had to realise it. Anwen saw that. She saw most things. She looked at me lovingly.

I watched her, feeling she had something more to say. She sniffed, turned her head away from me.

I circled slowly about her.

Her eyes were pressed shut, and she breathed shakily.

'Anwen?'

She opened her eyes, placed a cold hand against my cheek. 'He has changed. He sees us as characters. He will hurt you. He will hurt everyone. Something is coming, and you will be at the centre. There is resentment in this family, Euan, and it will be directed at you. But you can still leave.' She paused for a long time, then said, 'I know you won't. But I had to say it.'

I touched her wrist, and she brought it down to her side.

'If things are so bad, why don't you leave?' I asked.

She pinched a pleat in her skirt, ran her eyes up and down my face. 'Because long ago, when he was a different man, I made him a promise.'

As she opened the door to depart, I said, 'Was he really so different?'

She said nothing, left without closing the door.

3

BY THE TIME I had washed my face and prepared for lunch, people were migrating to the dining room. I hurried down the central staircase and saw Colm lingering in a corner of the main hall. He was holding a photograph in his hands. His lips were pressed together, and his breathing was panicked. When he heard me approach, he drove the photograph into a pocketbook, looked at me as if I were a stranger. He blinked, rubbed his eyes, tucked the pocketbook into his jacket. Despite the vomiting, he had looked better on the ferry.

'Good of you to wait for me,' I said. 'How was your walk?'

'The track . . .' he said as I came to the bottom of the stairs.

'What about the track?'

'It was . . . I heard . . .'

I gave him a puzzled look.

He lowered his eyes, sighed, said, 'My nerves . . . My damned nerves.'

There was no time to interrogate him further, and I feared doing so would cause him further gastric distress. I chose to drop the subject. 'Come,' I said, giving him a comforting pat on the shoulder. 'You look like you need a meal.'

He nodded and, as we walked on to the dining room, kept his hand against his jacket pocket.

The pheasant was dry. After the niceties, we ate it quietly.

Colm sat beside me at the far end of the dining table, and at either side were Lewis and Clara. Beside Clara sat Tilly. Her hair was raven black and pulled into a tight bun. She wore a polka-dot dress and a periwinkle cardigan that had been patched in many places. Her first impression was a confusion of severity and chaos. She was older than I was, equal parts attractive and intimidating. I'd met her on my previous visits, as she resided in the house with the Furnivall family. Her personal history was cloudy, but I gathered that she'd known the Furnivalls for a long time. On my last visit, she and I had done some conversational sparring, and I'd sensed we'd left something unexplored. She interested me: her primary role was to guard Malcolm's privacy, to keep reporters and fans at bay, and to attend to all of his career matters that weren't writing. It was clear she held herself personally responsible for the commercial success of his most recent books. Which, in all fairness, was partly true – Malcolm hated self-promotion and regarded all journalists with disdain. He'd always had a reputation as a genius; however, it was clear that because of Tilly's fanatical dedication, Malcolm's work now reached more people than ever before.

Malcolm's seat was empty.

'He often arrives late,' Tilly said to no one in particular. 'Increasingly time runs away from him. He's devoted to his work, you see. I shouldn't say any more about it.' She was someone who enjoyed knowing things, or, at least, giving the impression she knew more than you. I could sense she was glancing across at me when I wasn't looking.

Beside Malcolm's empty chair sat Anwen. Now she wore her hostess' mask with poise. There was no trace of the woman I'd met only a half hour ago in my room. 'You ought to swim with us, Euan,' she said. 'It is invigorating at this time of year.'

On each of my previous visits, Malcolm and Anwen had invited me to swim with them in the lake, which was just a little way from the house. It was something of a tradition in the Furnivall household; Malcolm and Anwen would often spend their time there, shivering together and drinking whisky. Each time I had declined to swim. I could think of nothing less appealing on a cold spring morning, and instead would sit on the bank and watch them whoop and splash in the cold. 'Thank you for the offer,' I said. 'But I believe the better candidate to be sitting to my right.'

Colm gawked at me, then dropped his forkful of pheasant on the floor. He apologised and, attempting to distract from his faux pas, blurted, 'Is it true, the old story about Malcolm and G.K. Chesterton?'

At the other author's name, Tilly snapped to face him. 'What story?'

'The . . . incident with the sword.'

I held my head in my hands.

Colm fumbled on: 'I just read it somewhere.'

It was rumoured that, many years ago, Malcolm had come to blows with his old friend Chesterton after a dispute over who fully deserved the nickname 'Prince of Paradox' – or so the story went. This, alongside Chesterton winning the presidency of their writers' group, the Detection Club, apparently resulted in a young Malcolm stealing Chesterton's swordstick and beating him with it. Both authors had denied this ever happened.

Still, Dorothy L. Sayers, also a member of the club, had

written of the incident recently in a collection of published letters. I assumed that was where Colm had received his information. Though the story had become such a part of the mythology surrounding Malcolm, I'm sure most people who knew of Malcolm had also heard of the incident with the sword.

'Gilbert was a good friend,' said Anwen. 'We miss him dearly.'

'Of course,' said Colm. 'Sorry.'

We fell into silence.

I knew Malcolm and Chesterton had been kindred spirits; Malcolm often spoke highly of him. Though, towards the end of Chesterton's life, I gathered that he and Malcolm had grown distant: the other members of the Detection Club had taken offence at Malcolm's unreserved spite for the necessary constraints of the mystery genre, and since Chesterton had been the president, circumstance simply pulled them apart.

A slam as the door to the hallway shut, and Malcolm Furnivall loped into the room and stood behind his chair. The silence became even more silent.

Colm was the one to speak, rising in a cowed attempt to shake hands. 'What an honour—'

Malcolm slapped away the limp fingers and remained, steadfast, above his seat. He surveyed the room, meeting each of our gazes in turn. He was raw-boned and knotted. When he spoke, his lips hardly moved. 'Wet earth and beetroot.'

We folded our napkins, shifted in our seats, glanced at each other.

'That is what death smells like.'

We stilled.

He gave a raucous laugh.

Tilly immediately burst into her own frantic laugh, and the rest of us followed her lead, apart from Anwen and Clara, who looked up at him and waited.

Malcolm held up a hand and spoke again. 'It is well known to many of you that I despise administration, protocols and any kind of bureaucratic procedure. But there are times when one must organise. I'll be brief. I think I will be gone very soon.'

We were, all of us, balanced on an arête of levity, unstable and exposed. Malcolm danced along it, while we teetered, praying that we would not be the first to fall. With a forced laugh behind his words, Colm surprised me by, again, being the first to speak up: 'So this is the famous black humour I've been warned about!'

Malcolm turned his head slowly, like a stone monolith waking. He silenced Colm with a look. 'I am drawing up my will. Mr Hubert is here to assist me, provided he takes the matter seriously.'

Colm stuttered for what felt like a minute before tumbling into his next sentence. 'I only meant, Mr Furnivall, that you seem to be in good enough health. I do admire the foresight and preparedness, of course.'

All smiles had fallen from our faces.

'What makes you think you will die?' My voice was steady.

They glared at me, all but Malcolm, whose lip curled up at the corner. The question was impudent, but I knew Malcolm well. He liked plain speakers. I watched him, remembering Anwen's warning. Was this really a man who could no longer discern reality from fiction?

He regarded me from across the table. 'When a cat senses death, she leaves to find a quiet place to greet it. How does she sense when death is near? Why does she make such preparations? Our death is in us from the moment we are born, and we bury it like a bulb. It grows in us, and, if one pays attention, one might feel it pressing against the interior of the skin. I have not been well, Euan. I have not been at all well.'

Anwen rose to her feet, turned her back to us and whispered in her husband's ear.

'I've no appetite,' Malcolm said.

She spoke again.

Malcolm's expression softened, and he put a hand on her waist, before she sank back down into her chair.

He licked his lips and sighed, reaching out, spooning a mound of parsnips and pheasant into his mouth, chewing slowly. Once he had swallowed, he said, 'In this time we have together, I will be deciding what to give each of you . . . if anything at all. I am only certain of one thing.' He set his eye on me. 'The work with which I am currently engaged, the last book in my *Gravitation* series, will be finished by Euan . . . if he accepts.'

A moment, as the full weight of his meaning settled on each of us. Glances were cast across the table. I heard murmuring, cutlery clattering, a chair being pushed out. I could not take my eye from Malcolm. He held my gaze.

'There is only one copy of the manuscript, and I have taken measures to protect it, should anyone be tempted to steal my work.' He considered something, then spoke distantly. 'It is of great importance. Its effect will be considerable . . . but there is still work to be done.'

'Father, we've been wanting to say something for a long time.' It was Clara, standing and facing him. 'You aren't yourself. Do you know the strain you are putting us under, the people who love you? We want to help, but Mother says you never leave your writing shed, says you don't sleep. And then I hear that you have fired all the house staff, when the house was already falling apart. And . . . and *this*?' She pointed at me. 'Placing your life's work in the hands of an outsider. It's as if you're trying to sabotage yourself and cast your family into ruin. I'm not alone in thinking this, I'm just the one who fears you the least. Think of our futures. We're worried for you.'

Malcolm pressed his lips together, refused to meet his daughter's eye. A force built up in him. He began to cough violently, doubling over, eyes bulging from their sockets.

Lewis stood and moved to his father's side, holding a hand over Malcolm's back but never touching him.

The coughing ceased, and Malcolm wiped his lips, gulped from a tumbler of whisky which Mrs Gibson had discreetly set beside him. He surveyed every one of us. 'Is this the general consensus?' he asked.

Heads remained bowed, aside from Clara, who kept her gaze fixed on me. There was spite in her eyes, but also desperation. She'd given me that same look when she'd found me after my lecture, demanded I help her get through to Malcolm. I knew she felt pain at having to ask another for help; despite her pride, she knew there was a limit to her abilities. I felt as if she were willing me to speak up then, to relinquish any claim I had to Malcolm's legacy. Who was I to intrude upon this great family? I was no one. I had written my way out of the gutter, clawed and bartered my way to this seat. The war had given me a way to ascend through the ranks, not through acts of valour, but through simply surviving. My past was a skein of shame and survival. But here I was now, and I would not concede. I remained silent.

Malcolm cast about slowly, wiping his wet lips on his sleeve. He straightened, vertebrae snickering back into alignment. Grimacing, he walked about the table, stopped behind each of us. 'Does anyone else here doubt my faculties?'

Tilly picked at her pheasant, shook her head. Colm was a statue. Anwen watched her husband with a placid face. Lewis remained standing, toying with the hem of his shirt.

The air in the room was humid. It was the still, thick weather that precedes a storm. Malcolm stalked over to his daughter. He placed a hand on her shoulder.

Clara sat down slowly.

When Malcolm returned to his place at the far end of the table, Lewis remained standing beside him. He glanced across to his sister. I saw an almost imperceptible shake of her head. But then Lewis closed his eyes, took a sharp breath.

Malcolm looked sidelong at his son, bemused.

Lewis cleared his throat, then spoke in a measured voice. 'She's right, Father, you—'

A crack as Malcolm's open palm caught Lewis across the face, crumpling him.

We were, all of us, still. No one dared move, speak out, leave. We were fixed in an ugly tableau.

Malcolm's hand hung limp at his side, and he stared at his son, breathless.

This was not the Malcolm I had come to admire. I

understood then what Anwen had warned me of. Perhaps I should have left. But I was enamoured with his offer, believed that I could help him. Even then, in the wake of that awful scene, I understood Malcolm. He had lived here, separated from the world, separated from his children who rarely visited – and now they challenged him. Time had made him cruel, but I still saw the man beneath the cruelty.

'Have you ever had an original thought?' Malcolm asked his son.

Lewis was bent double, but slowly returned to his full height, eyes watering. He stepped away. He seemed, then, like a boy in man's attire; someone who must pace, or tug at his clothes, to find words that have not been rehearsed.

Malcolm was inscrutable. But when he, again, set his gaze on me, I thought I saw a shadow of pain cross his face. 'Euan,' he said, 'will you accept my offer?'

All eyes turned to me.

Just a few words, and a life can be altered indelibly. It is rare to realise these words at the moment of their speaking, but I knew then, pinned by the furious gaze of Malcolm's family, that I had been offered the rarest gift.

'I will.'

Clara stormed from the room, followed by her brother, who remained for a moment, watching his father, waiting for recognition. He received none. Once they had left the room, there was a brief thumping of footsteps before the front door slammed.

Slowly, Anwen rose and set her hand against Malcolm's jowl. She whispered again in his ear, nodded to all who remained about the table, and excused herself, saying she needed to rest.

It was just Colm and Tilly who remained.

Malcolm lifted the bottle of whisky, along with two tumblers. 'Come, Euan, let's move to the study. I have things I wish to discuss privately.' He glanced at Tilly, saying, 'Why don't you show Colm around? The glasshouse, perhaps?'

Tilly's face was red, her eyebrows drawn inward, but she didn't protest.

I rose and followed Malcolm, who stopped at the door, turned back to his stunned audience. 'Oh, and excuse the dry pheasant.'

4

MALCOLM FURNIVALL TURNED FROM the
fireplace and stalked towards me, holding a branding iron in
his frail fist. 'What is tradition, Euan?' he said.

Cornered, keeping my eyes fixed on the glowing metal, I
spoke carefully. 'Something which gets in the way of modern
thought.'

'But we must remember the past. Or we're fated to repeat
our old mistakes.' He gestured with the iron about his
study, lined with shelves of his old books. 'My books are
the product not only of me, but of my mentors. We must
honour those who came before us.'

I stood very still. 'Malcolm, we've been drinking for some
time. Why don't we take a minute, resume this talk in the
eve—'

'This must happen now.' Malcolm took a step back,
lowered the branding iron and looked over my shoulder,
out the window to the unkempt lawn of his estate which
stretched out into wild forest and, beyond that, cliffs. He
seemed to search for something, before returning his gaze
to me. 'You are a fine young writer, Euan. I wouldn't have
invited you here otherwise. Over these past years, you must
have realised I want you to become part of a legacy.'

'I . . . I'm grateful, Malcolm. I can't thank you enough—'

He brought the iron up, so the glowing square end

scorched the space between us. Sweat rolled down my face, collecting at the tip of my nose.

'I don't want your thanks.' He sucked air in through gritted teeth, rolled his head about his crooked neck. 'I want you to continue the work. That is all that we have, in the end.' He shook the branding iron, leaving a swipe of orange afterburn hanging in the air. 'This is a passing of responsibility. A tradition.'

I felt the glass of the window at my back, cooled by the gently pattering afternoon rain. Still facing Malcolm, I searched with my fingers for a catch to open the window.

'It has all been leading to this,' he said in a lullaby voice. 'The last coffin nail.'

That was how he lovingly referred to his final *Gravitation* novel; the one about which he'd been so guarded; the one I had agreed to finish.

'Malcolm, you say you want me to continue your novel, but I have no clue—'

'There is an order to this. A ritual.' The branding iron drifted down, level with my chest. Malcolm wiped his brow with his free hand, gave me a sad smile.

'I need some air,' I said and looked to the door on the other side of the study.

Malcolm stormed to the fireplace, flung the brand back, scattering embers across the carpet. He stepped back, cursing, spittle running from the corner of his mouth.

I ran to the door, put a trembling hand on the brass doorknob, then stopped. On my previous visits to the Furnivall estate I'd witnessed Malcolm's temper, but on this afternoon, there was something different. A note in his voice like wind over a hollow. I wanted to run, but something kept me there. I would have said pity then, but now I know it was fear. This man, double my age and sickly, had a gravity to him. Something inescapable. He stared at me, and I took my hand away from the door.

As a fit of coughing came over him, I went to his side, offered him whisky from the tumbler on his desk, which he quickly despatched. He apologised under his breath. Then, as I moved away, he caught my shirt and pulled me close. 'Do you smell it?'

'Smell what?'

He grimaced. 'Beetroot.'

He passed me the whisky tumbler and I returned it to the desk, not turning my back to him. I noticed his eyes had drifted to Anwen's record collection. 'You should have heard her play,' he said suddenly, in a low voice. 'That is the thing about music – it's gone the moment you've heard it. A recording is never the same.' He sniffed. 'But I suppose that's precisely what makes it appealing ...' Emerging from his thoughts, he beckoned me over.

'Why don't we get Anwen?' I said. 'Perhaps we've been alone together too long.'

'No,' Malcolm said, lips clamping around the word like a pair of pliers. 'I want you to roll up my sleeve.'

I walked to him, so we were both standing in the centre of the room on his threadbare carpet, scattered with cinders.

He held out his left arm, palm facing the ceiling. 'Do it.'

Propelled by the quiet force in his voice, I reached down, removed his cufflink and slowly pulled back his sleeve. There, under the fabric, was a snarl of scar tissue in the shape of a square, with eight lines knotting at its central point – the same symbol as on the end of the branding iron. I watched as he moved his fingers and the tendons danced beneath the parchment skin, making the knot twist. Malcolm spoke. 'This is our tradition; I marked myself long ago, just as you will mark yourself now. It is the symbol for the omphalos, the stone Zeus placed to mark the Earth's navel. He let fly two eagles from either end of the world and, where they met, he placed the omphalos. It marks the centre and origin of things. Those who have this mark will be like books from the same library. They share something vital. Do you understand me?'

I released his sleeve, stared at the mark. It was obscured by another, formless nebula of pocked, aggravated skin. Something else had scarred his arm. A burn, perhaps. He spoke again, before I could ask. 'But do you know what I find most enthralling about that story, Euan? The eagles find each other. In all the great expanse of sky, their paths meet.'

'Malcolm, I've agreed to finish your manuscript—'

'It's more than that. You are joining something bigger than yourself. If I wanted some hack to scribble down the last beats of a story, I would have given this task to one of my children. But I think *you* will understand, in time, what it is I have done. What it is I will do . . . Now, roll up your sleeve.'

'I . . .'

He smiled, placed a fatherly hand on the back of my neck. 'Do you want to be great?' His voice rang about the room.

In that moment, I felt myself carried back to my childhood, to nights spent staring at the mould-spotted ceiling, unable to sleep because of the cold. I heard, once again, the footsteps of my sister, creeping back into our shared room, reeking of sour sweat that wasn't hers. I traced in my mind the pattern I would walk to avoid our father, sitting and smoking in the kitchen. I remembered when I'd set pen to paper and known, for the first time, what it was to have power.

I answered quietly. 'Yes.'

'Then you'll do as I say.' He moved to the fireplace, pulled the branding iron from the flames. As he spoke, his voice began to slur, and his eyes stayed fixed on the iron. 'This is a small price to pay. There are others, people close to me, who would do anything to take this final novel. It is the most valuable thing I have. I have written . . . secrets. Things I have discovered and carried with me.' He barked a laugh. 'It's a fool who believes writers make things up. The important things, anyway. Euan, I have written something beyond the conception of most. It is the most urgent and shocking idea . . . and it must be completed. Do you believe me when I tell you this?'

I looked over, saw him swaying there, eyes dark and hooded. After a moment, I said, 'I do.'

'And?' Malcolm said.

'I believe the *Gravitation* series to be woven with clues, pointing to something.' I stared at him, and, for a second, his eyes flicked to meet mine. In them, I saw pride. 'Yes,' he said. 'You wrote that in your *Horizon* article.'

Embarrassed, I went on, 'I believe it to be something which crosses the border between fact and fiction. That is why I fell in love with your work, Malcolm. You were always able to make me believe in things at the edge of possibility. But now, I suspect, you have written of something very real. Something most will dismiss as fantasy, but you know to be true.'

'And why do you think that?'

'Because I have come to know you. And I know what you love most.'

Malcolm raised an eyebrow.

'Trickery.'

There was a long silence as he looked me up and down. 'If we're assessing each other, I shall tell you what I think of your work,' he said, lingering on each word. 'In your mysteries, every character shines, apart from the main one. They walk around, discovering beauty and strangeness in everyone they meet, but they themselves are lacking. I think this is because you are hiding something in yourself. Perhaps that's why you accepted my invitations? You thought I might be able to help you?'

A memory came and went, enduring long enough for Malcolm to see it on my face. He inclined his head and, when I refused to speak, moved over to his desk, motioning for me to lay my arm on it.

I stayed still, waiting for the feeling that had risen in me to subside. I focused on the things about me to remain calm. There was a two-tone, red-and-white record player. There was a glass cabinet filled with little figures. There was a column of exposed stone over the fireplace.

'Euan.'

I looked to him. He was beckoning me.

I walked over and stood at the end of the desk, but kept my arm to myself.

'What is it?' he said.

I reached across the desk, poured myself another tumbler

of whisky. I closed my eyes, drank, felt the warmth spread down through my chest. The rain outside was subsiding. The fire chuckled behind me.

Malcolm watched me, a knowing look on his face. He held the branding iron out to me, like a surgical tool. 'I think you have endured worse than this.'

'What do you mean by that?'

He opened his mouth to speak, then paused, smiled and said, 'I meant no offence.'

'Let me ask you something, Malcolm.'

He straightened, rolling back his shoulders and still clutching the branding iron.

'Was it worth it?'

Malcolm understood what I meant. This life of his, this legacy, had cost him dearly. He had lost himself in his work, that was plain. His family had drifted from him, and he was left occupying a ruin. He seemed to coast into thought, before looking up and watching me calmly. 'You will have to be the judge of that. Only time will tell.'

I looked down at the desk, at the dark knotted wood, at the smooth, ink-stained inlay of leather.

I unbuttoned my cuff, rolled up my sleeve.

As I did so, Malcolm returned to the fire, nestled the branding iron in the flames. As he held it there, he said dreamily, 'I often think of our mornings by the lake. Maybe you will swim this time? It is so refreshing.' He then came back to the desk to find me bare-armed and waiting.

'Hold it to your skin for five seconds,' he said. 'Prove to me that you want this. Prove it to yourself. You will count with me.'

He smiled, revealing crooked teeth, like those of an old

comb. His face took on a febrile gleam. He raised the iron so it was inches from my forearm, and I could already feel the heat of it against my skin.

I took the iron from his hand.

'Once this is done, you will share in everything I've built. My manuscript will be yours to complete. You will know, and guard, its secrets.' He stroked my hair, moved his hand down to my shoulder, squeezed. 'I trust you, Euan.' He stepped back.

My fingers tightened around the metal. I would have to fight the urge to pull away. This man, standing beside me, had given me a chance. He'd seen something in me that no one else had. He had brought me into his closest circle, been a mentor, a father, a friend. Perhaps he had seen something of himself in me – that quiet fire which fills those at the edge, which burns any who might dare to come close. We were not good men. We were survivors. If this was the price of legacy, the price of Malcolm's love, so be it.

He spoke with a faraway voice. I recognised his words as the opening line of his first *Gravitation* book: "The place we start from guides us to our end . . ."'

I clenched my fist and pressed the scalding iron to my skin.

'One.'

A burning, so fierce that my body could not determine heat or cold, only pain.

'Two.'

I forced myself to look at the glass cabinet, at the models inside: animals, people, monsters, carved with precision.

'Three.'

My body screamed at me to pull away, but I would not.

'Four.'

There was Malcolm's face, lines mapping years of furrowed brows and frowns. Under heavy lids, his eyes were cloudy and cold.

'Five.'

I looked down at my arm as Malcolm took back the iron, saw the burnt skin blackened and swelling red. Smoke rose from the wound in white wraiths. The smell brought bile to the back of my throat.

I looked beyond the cabinet to a painting on the wall. It showed a polyhedron, filled with small doors, through which creatures emerged. They seemed to be sharing the shape as a kind of shell.

Malcolm walked across the room, set the branding iron beside the fireplace, watched the flames for a moment as I breathed through gritted teeth. Then, he moved back to my side, kissed me on the forehead, and said, 'There's some ice in the sitting room. I'll fetch it.'

'Thank you,' I replied.

'Not for you,' he said with a grin. He reached over and picked up his whisky, swirling it before my face. Then, with a chuckle, he left the room.

5

AS THE DOOR SWUNG shut behind Malcolm, I stared down at my arm, to the sign of the omphalos. It was black and swollen. I didn't feel any different. I believed magical thinking to be the domain of the child and the old man – a desire for significance in an unfeeling world, a way to control the overwhelming tide of being. This was the reason I supposed Malcolm had built this estate. It was a spell, wrought of plaster and stone, to hold him long after his death; it was furnished with scenes from his books, curiosities, strange paintings and puzzles. You could walk through the mansion with a *Gravitation* book in your hand and see references to every chapter. During my visits, Malcolm had proved to be a man obsessed with making his mark. And now, he'd made it on me.

Trying to distract myself from the pain, I moved away from the desk to the record collection, flicking through till I came across one of Anwen's first performances: Mendelssohn's *Violin Concerto in E minor*. She'd performed it at Carnegie Hall with the London Symphony Orchestra. I took out the vinyl, set it on the record player and waited, closing my eyes as the first notes of Anwen's violin sang over the low thrum of the orchestra. Her violin was a cold mist encircling the orchestra's dark and looming island. I let the record play as I moved through the study. On the walls were more images which, when looked at briefly, seemed unremarkable, but when examined, revealed a discordance. There were tessellations in which simple shapes interlocked and wove until they created a greater creature, nebulous and strange. There were images of endless waterfalls, and prisons of perspective which trapped those inside in an impossible maze.

As Anwen's singing mist whipped into a flurry, and the dark island of the orchestra rose, I found myself drawn to one image. It was of two faces, turned to each other. They were unravelling together, and under their skin was not muscle and bone, but rather a swirling system of planets and stars.

Again, unwanted memories rose in me. I recalled my sister's voice, gentle but strong. And then I felt her, resting her head on my shoulder. I recalled what Malcolm had said about me lacking something.

Bringing my hand to my shoulder, the feeling went, and so I turned my attention back to the room, walking over to the glass cabinet of little figures. I looked inside and was struck by their beauty; some of ivory, some of wood, intricate and polished to perfection. There was a sleeping cat, and, in its ears, I could see each of the individual hairs. Beside it was a stag, with antlers that branched like forked lightning. There was a man, bending over a well, staring down into the depths as if he had lost something and forgotten what it was. As I turned my gaze to another figure, I wondered who in Malcolm's family collected the little sculptures. Malcolm had never told me.

Anwen's playing conjured a sense of motion, as if every

particle in the air were livid and sparking. I saw, in the jade eyes of a sculpted mouse, a fire which flickered over the patinaed hides of the other figures. Then, those eyes seemed to turn to the window. I followed their gaze.

There, watching me from outside, was a girl.

I stepped back, tripping on the carpet, steadying myself on the adjacent wall.

She blinked, making no move to run away. The long grass was up to her waist and the gentle misting rain had caused her dark hair to cling to her forehead in lank strands. Her face was heart-shaped, familiar . . .

'No,' I said. 'You're gone.'

The girl wore a white gown, torn and muddy at the sleeves and hem. She looked serene. The wind mussed the grass about her, but seemed to leave her be, as if she, herself, were an element to be feared.

Moving over to the window and placing my hand against the glass, I watched her and waited, the same way you might wait for a beautiful dream to fade. She seemed to look through me, but when I waved for her to come inside, she met my eye. And there was recognition, I could sense it. But it couldn't be my Julia . . . She would be older now.

The girl in the white gown shook her head. I saw her clenching and unclenching her fists. Her eyes flicked behind me, to the cabinet of sculptures. She seemed to be more interested in them than me.

'Do you want one?' I said, pointing to the sculptures. I went to the cabinet and ran my finger along the shelves, stopped when I saw her eyes light up. She gazed at where my finger was poised: a pair of otters, forming a circle with their sinuous bodies. 'This one?' I said.

She looked back at me. Fear marked her face.

A sound. I turned in its direction; it had come from the other side of the house. Time seemed to slow as dread sank through me. It was a shot. A single one, followed by silence.

I looked back through the window to where the girl had been standing, but she was gone. In her place, only the afternoon gloom and long grass, stippled with white wildflowers. Had they been there before?

I left the study with the record player still turning, rushed out into the hallway, across a wide foyer, weaving between staircases. I still found it difficult to orient myself in the house Malcolm had designed; like his books, it was near impossible to hold its entirety in your mind; rather, you had to let it pull you where it willed.

As I ran, I felt my blood coursing to the wound on my arm, pounding at the symbol, as if trying to beat it from my skin. I was the first person who came to the tall oak door of the sitting room, where Malcolm had gone to get the ice.

Facing the door, I froze. My gaze ran across the woodgrain as my thoughts drifted to the last time I'd heard gunshots. They had been all around, setting the wind alight. But now, this single shot had its own kind of horror. The silence about it had put the terrible sound in sharp relief. It held a meaning. A gunshot in silence is a scar on the face of a child.

I reached out with my good arm and held it inches from the doorknob. What would I find on the other side? I stepped back from the door, began to breathe deep and ragged breaths. No one else was coming. Had the wind

and rain obscured the sound? Or perhaps I'd misheard,
panicked over nothing?

'Malcolm?' I said.

Silence.

Wind against a distant window made me flinch. I
resumed my breathing, called out for Malcolm again.

This time, when he didn't reply, I gripped the doorknob,
turned and pushed.

The door jolted in its frame.

'Malcolm!'

Someone had locked the door. I pushed again but it
didn't move.

'Malcolm, open the door, for God's sake.'

Stepping away, I cast about for help of any kind, but
found only the vaulted ceiling, dark plum carpets, stained-
glass windows. The house swallowed my voice, regurgitated
it throughout its many rooms.

I pounded on the door, in the vain hope the oak might
crumble away and leave me face to face with the man I had
admired for so long. He would laugh and tell me this was
another of his tricks, and I would sigh with frustration, but
also love. Because I did love Malcolm. He'd given me more
than he knew.

I put both my hands against the door, pushing despite
the pain in my arm, calling for Malcolm to answer. When
I knew it was helpless, I rested my head against the wood,
trying to cast away the grim images which washed up like
flotsam in the tide of my thoughts.

He'd been drunk. He was not himself.

Anwen's violin reached out across the hall, ran delicate
fingers down my spine. It was as if she were here with

me, asking me why I'd let him go off alone. Why hadn't I stayed with him? Her playing became frantic, then sank under the crashing orchestra, only to surface again, wilted and full of sorrow.

I smelt burning. It was faint but unmistakable, and, as I stepped back, cast about, I saw tendrils of dark smoke seeping under the front door, unfurling through the house. Though I did not want to leave Malcolm, I thought the smoke could be related to the sound I'd heard. So, I hurried to the front door, heaving it open and stepping out into the damp afternoon.

There, a short distance away, was a well of churning flame. It choked and billowed in the rain but refused to die. Like a strange plant, it surged upward, chasing a dormant sun.

I ran to the fire, slipping as I approached and landing on my branded arm. I cried out and cursed. The long grass bent over me, dropping tears of rain as I scrambled back to my feet. My crisp white shirt was nearly soaked through, and my woollen trousers were streaked with dirt. The world narrowed, like an aperture closing.

I looked into the flames, which glowered under the gathering clouds, and felt as if the ground had opened up beneath me.

Someone had collected my novels, piled them up before the house and set them alight. Each time I visited Malcolm's estate, he had shown me his library, taking me to the shelf where he kept my published works in a variety of editions: hardcover, softcover, translations. He'd ask me to sign them for him, the way a father might ask his son to show what he'd learnt at school. He'd watch me as I signed for him, a look of pride on his face. I'd always been embarrassed, but had done it anyway because, somehow, it felt important; another ritual to bond us. And now, the evidence of that bond was burning.

I reached down into the fringe of the flames and picked up the charred remains of my third, and most recent, novel. Flicking through, I saw that not only had the person burnt these books, they had also scratched out pages. I backed away and threw the damaged book in the fire.

I was a character in an absurd dream. I'd lived my life certain of most things; but in that moment, I was shocked by how quickly my critical mind dissipated in the churn of panic. I began to see shapes in the gloom, figures lurking in the long grass, watching me, waiting for me to move. All about, the grass and thistles murmured. Malcolm never wanted his lawn cut as he liked to watch the deer from his study window. I felt, in that moment, like one of Malcolm's deer: oblivious to my observer.

Movement at the border of the forest. Not an illusion, but something solid. It was hard to see detail, but I knew it was the shape of a person. They were running into the trees.

I glanced towards the house, saw the window to the sitting room, obscured by creepers and long grass. No light came from the room. It was impossible to tell from where I was standing who, if anyone, was inside.

I looked back to the forest's edge, saw the shadow escaping.

The gunshot, the girl, the fire, the figure; they twined like roots of symbiotic plants. I followed the shadow, out across the sea of wild grass, under the woven canopy of firs.

6

CREAKING BOUGHS. WHISPERING STREAMS. Insect hum. I doubled over, listening to the forest's breath as I caught mine. I had been smoking too many cigarettes. Coughing up phlegm, I spat into a bolus of scrub and stood straight, casting about for the figure in the grey patched treelight.

The smell of wet earth. I remembered what Malcolm had said, about death's scent. But here, there was no distinction between decay and growth; they were interlocking parts of a strange and wild whole. Rotting leaves became fungus, fruiting bodies. This canopy concealed another world. A world where shadows lived. Then, the sound of dry wood cracking, echoing between the boughs.

Branches snagged at my clothes as I pushed through the dark undergrowth, into the mess of twining trees, towards the sound. I called out after them, but the only reply was a flurry of wings. Rooks rising. Running till my throat was raw, I slid down a bank of pine-needles, skidding to a stop at the bottom. As I regained my balance, I saw a streak of muddy skin. A dark eye. Then, the watching figure vanished into the woods, and I was alone.

I chased, but soon became completely lost. In the trunks of trees, burls became bulging eyes. They seemed to hold some secret knowledge – something that would seem obvious if only I knew. Wind laughed through leaves.

I saw the light of a lantern coming towards me. The sound of men moving through trees. The lantern light grew, shimmered, lit the face of a man between the branches. The hollows in his cheeks were darkened with grime, and his eyes, which peered from under an oversized helmet, were delirious. I looked away, telling myself that it was false. I'd seen my face, younger, thinner. I was a ghost to myself, using the lantern to track my way through time, to find myself here. I couldn't look up. Not again. I knew what I would see. So, I kept my gaze fixed on the forest floor, telling myself it was imagined. A child was crying. The sticks around my feet turned to blackened little bones. The lantern light faded, and the sound of mortars that had been ringing all this time grew quiet. In the past months, these irrational moments had become more frequent. I'd thought, naïvely, that here I would be free of them.

Another sound: a crack and then dull thudding. I could tell it was real, and, like a parched man moving to water, I pushed my way through the bracken towards the noise. Before long, I noticed the trees were thinning, and the forest floor was bare. Up ahead was a glade and a small cabin. I was approaching from the rear, but as I circled around the edge of the glade, I realised the source of the noise: Lewis was chopping wood. He stood before the cabin, sleeves rolled up, axe slung over his shoulder as he placed another log on the block. Then, like a creature cocking its tail to sting, he raised the axe, held it at the peak of its arc, brought it down and split the log. A crack as axe met log, a thud as it followed through and stuck in the block.

'Lewis!'

He turned to me as I walked out of the trees. Sweat gilded his skin and stained his shirt. Fibres of bark clung to him. His eyes were wide, and he stepped back, before collecting himself. 'Really, Euan, you're like a bad smell. Just when I think you're gone, I get another whiff.'

We drifted into silence, each man regarding the other, like stateless ships passing.

Lewis laughed. 'I'm about to get a fire going – you can come inside and stink up the cabin if you like?'

'How long have you been out here?' I asked.

'Since I lost my appetite. Why do you ask?' He turned the axe head-down and leant on it like a staff. Wiping his brow, he narrowed his large brown eyes at me.

'Something happened,' I said.

'Things happen all the time.' Lewis grinned with a well-rehearsed charm. It was as if the events over lunch had not occurred.

'I heard a gunshot, and then there was a pile of my books . . . burning. I saw someone, chased them—'

'It sounds like you've been drinking with my father.' Though his tone was light, the corners of his mouth had sunk, as if his face were recognising before anything else that something was wrong.

'He wasn't himself.'

Lewis rolled his right shoulder, wincing as if sore from the chopping. His bare bicep twitched. 'I know him better than you. Believe me, the moment you think you understand my father, he becomes someone else. I think he watches everyone very closely, determining how close they are getting. Then, when they are within touching distance, he sheds his skin like a great fucking lizard.'

Exasperated, I stood and stared at Lewis. 'We need to get back,' I said.

Lewis watched me, sucked air through his teeth, turned and set his axe down by the door of the cabin. He stood for a moment, looking through the cabin window. There was a large Turkish rug on the floor and a bottle of wine. 'This afternoon is going from strength to strength,' Lewis muttered. 'I can guarantee this is all part of a scheme. It always is.'

'He didn't answer, Lewis. He locked the door and . . . the gunshot—'

'All right. I'll come with you. Though I'm certain you're being toyed with.'

As Lewis tossed the last pieces of chopped lumber onto a pile, the image of the girl at the window came to me. 'There's something else,' I said.

'Yes?'

'Have I met everyone here?'

'How could I know? I believe you have, but—'

'There was a girl, wearing white.'

Lewis collected his coat from where he'd draped it over the deck's railing. Putting it on slowly, back turned to me, he asked, 'What girl?'

'She was young. She looked scared.'

'I don't know of any girl.'

Tallying up the glasses of whisky I'd consumed with Malcolm, I began to wonder whether I had in fact seen her. Could the pain and the alcohol have caused me to hallucinate? She had looked remarkably like Julia. The image of my sister was never far from my thoughts.

Lewis bounced his shoulders, adjusting himself within the coat. Then, he turned his face up, examining the roof of the cabin. 'I built this when I was sixteen,' he said. 'Back then, I was a fragile thing, enamoured with stories and songs. But my father wanted to change me, so he gave me a task – to build this. I hated it at first, but after a time, I learnt to find satisfaction in the work: creating something . . . solid. Before long, this cabin was all I thought about. I'd work all day and even sleep out here, between the roofless walls. I know every corner.' He turned to face me, all levity gone from him.

I stood, rooted to the spot as he approached and placed a hand on my shoulder. I felt one finger touch the skin of my neck. Lewis spoke softly. 'My father's greatest strength is to convince those around him that his desire is also theirs. Remember that, Euan.'

He tapped me on the cheek, then strode past me, on to an imperceptible path through the trees, back towards the mansion.

'Are you often haunted by strange girls?' Lewis said, weaving through tall firs. When I said nothing in reply, he looked over his shoulder at me. 'Well, there are worse things to be haunted by. I think we both know that.'

A pause, as his meaning settled over me like silt.

He spoke again, almost tenderly. 'I took you for a soldier the moment we met.'

Something hardened in my chest, and my words came out slowly. 'I could have been behind a desk.'

Lewis stopped under the bough of a pine, gave me a look, then said, 'No, you weren't behind a desk.'

Lewis held himself like a soldier. I'd spotted that, though

never said anything. Not even then, in the shelter of the trees. He understood and let the subject lie.

'One thing about this place,' said Lewis, trudging on, 'is that after a while, you start to perceive its language. You'll feel as if the universe were reaching out, using patterns to convey something. I believe my father has dedicated his life to understanding these patterns.'

'And what has he found?'

Lewis veered to the right, slipping under a fallen branch. 'Interesting,' he said.

'What?'

'No one knows what he's found. And nor, it seems, do you.'

I chewed my lip, wondering if I'd just been manipulated. I was stupid to think that Malcolm's children would not have inherited some of his guile.

Lewis spoke quietly. 'I don't know what you intend to do here, Euan, but perhaps, if you are looking carefully, you might read a sign hinting at the end: birds flying low before a storm.'

'My only intention is to help Malcolm.'

'Well then,' Lewis said with a hint of mocking, 'we'd better hurry.'

We padded over the soft bed of fallen needles, through a haze of rain. My arm again began to throb, and it was all I could do just to keep up with Lewis. Silence swarmed about us. Afternoon was setting down its instruments and we were in the pause, the tuning, before evening began its movement. We strode through the interval, through the unfurling wind, towards the house.

Someone approached from elsewhere in the forest. Just

as I noticed, Lewis called out. 'Clara, over here! Our guest has fallen for one of Father's tricks!'

Clara turned, and I saw, between the mossy boughs and bloom-stippled scrub, her tangled auburn hair and flushed face. She looked just like the pictures of her mother printed on the jackets of her old records. She met my eye, then began to walk over to us. 'It seems like you've both been caught in the rain, as well.'

Before I could ask, she said, 'I was just on my way back from the cliffs. What's this about a trick?'

I watched her as she pulled her coat about herself, leant against a tree. She, like her father, seemed to have sprouted from the earth; in the woods, she behaved as most would in their sitting room.

'Our writer friend was drinking with Father,' Lewis said. 'Then he heard a gun, and what was that about burning books?'

I walked over to Clara, and she straightened, pushed her hair behind her ears, and met my eye with an unwavering gaze.

'Have you been at the house since lunch?' I said.

'Why should that matter?' Behind Clara's every word was an implied eye-roll. She had the ability to make anyone feel small. It was quite a feat, to remain in her presence for more than a minute without feeling the need to justify yourself.

'Please, Clara,' I said. 'Were you at the house?'

'No. I was out at the cliffs, as I just said. I was watching the guillemots.'

'We need to get back,' I said, pushing through the branches now that I was oriented. As we went, I told them how Malcolm had gone to fetch ice, but locked the door behind him.

'Wait . . .' Clara said, as we passed the crooked sentinel trees bordering the wild lawn.

I stopped, turned to see her panting.

'Let me go first. Whatever nastiness he might be putting you through, he will stop if he sees me.'

She was right. Malcolm spoke to Clara as if she were a baby bird. This was particularly amusing to the family, considering Clara was both taller and broader than her brother.

'Go on then, let's get this over with,' said Lewis.

And so, we trudged together across the wild lawn of quitch grass and rattle, back towards the house where I had left Malcolm, alone.

When we passed the pile of cinders that had once been my books, Clara stopped and toed the ashy pulp. Lewis picked up a half-burnt cover, examined it in the gloomy light. 'Everyone's a critic,' he said.

Clara stayed quiet, raised her chin, looked towards the sitting-room window, narrowed her eyes. She walked closer, stopped, turned towards us. 'It's broken. Looks like someone threw a stone or . . .'

Lewis laughed nervously, then trailed off into silence. Without another word, we rushed to the front door, heaved it open and moved through the quiet hall towards the sitting room. When Clara came to the door, she laid her hand on the doorknob. She shook her head, as if dismissing a silly thought, then turned and pushed.

The door swung open.

'I thought you said it was locked,' said Lewis from behind me.

'It was.'

Clara said nothing. Breathing heavily, she turned and set her back against the doorframe, as if she, alone, were in the midst of an earthquake.

Lewis pushed past me and his sister. He stood, blood draining from his face. He reached out to steady himself, found the wall, slid down on his haunches, stared at his hands.

7

THE HOLE IN MALCOLM'S neck was like the mouth of an obscene creature; deep and wet, it belched blood so dark it was almost indigo. Reflexively I looked to his face, as if I'd seen something private. I saw the webs of burst capillaries in his nose, the heavy jowls drawing his lips down into a frown. His eyes were closed. Whatever had once been Malcolm Furnivall was gone.

The room smelt of blood, gun smoke and dust. In Malcolm's hand was a revolver and his knurled index finger hooked the trigger like a vine growing about an obstruction.

A noise came from behind me, and, when I turned, I saw Lewis had pushed himself into the corner and wrapped his arms over his head. Clara was trembling but standing. 'Police,' she managed to say, before running out across the dark hall.

I moved closer, felt the soft give in the carpet, saturated with congealing blood. I crouched by my friend's side, put my hand on his chest. Again, my eyes were drawn to the wound. It was not made by a gun. A bullet makes a brutish mess, and this was a delicate, deep gash. Why, then, had he fired? Perhaps at the person who had threatened him? The person who had carved the grim maw in the tender flesh between his jaw and collarbone.

I took three deep breaths, feeling as if heavy walls were

sliding into place about me. I would never escape that moment. *This* moment. It has hardened into an eternal present.

The revolver was an Enfield. Its slim dark nose snarled as I looked at it, like an animal aware of being observed. Malcolm had never struck me as a man who would keep a gun, and I wondered where he'd kept it concealed. He'd shot in the direction of the window, which was now a mess of vicious glass teeth.

I cast about the room for more signs of a fight. There were bookshelves holding hundreds of yellowed, dog-eared books. Some lay horizontal across the others. This was Malcolm's habit; he would take a book from the shelf, thumb it and set it back cover-down atop the row. I thought of Malcolm's insistence that work is the only thing that endures. Perhaps he was right. These horizontal books would be tidied, and his habit would fade like a footprint in wet sand. Yet his *Gravitation* series, which I saw there on a shelf, would remain.

The *Gravitation* books took place on an archipelago of islands, and each novel was set on an individual island, some expansive, some minuscule. The islands were divided into thematic groups: Dream, Memory, Sight, Death and so on. The books could be read in any order, and the series was organised according to a rigorous mathematical structure, which Malcolm had often described as a polyhedron. There were conclusions written along all of *Gravitation*'s edges. I had speculated in my *Horizon* article that the books were filled with hidden divisions, and pivoted around one central book which had yet to be written. This was the book Malcolm had entrusted me to finish. As I crouched over his body, I felt like one of his characters, here on my own island, searching for the conclusion.

Tasselled lampshades, bohemian drapes, taxidermy birds, the bucket of half-melted ice. Rather than paintings, Anwen's old sheet-music hung on the wall. In a large glass-fronted cabinet, her violins were arranged. Their wood was rich, with a grain that coiled like smoke, and they were stained about the strings from unwiped rosin. I got up and moved over to the cabinet, noticing the latch wasn't quite shut. The inside of the cabinet had not been cleaned in some time, and a heavy carpet of dust lay over the shelves and the violins. It was then that I saw the outline of a revolver in the dust. How many other weapons had he kept hidden about the house? I recalled what Lewis had told me, about Malcolm's changeability. I thought I'd known him, but perhaps he'd presented me with a character – someone he thought I'd want to follow. I moved back to his body, crouched beside it.

The room became like a word looked at too long – an incomprehensible shape. So, I gazed at Malcolm, set one hand on his chest, the other on his forehead. Why? I asked him. And then, as if in reply, the last thing Malcolm said returned to me . . . He'd gone to fetch ice. I looked up slowly, noticed how his left arm was outstretched slightly, in the direction of the ice bucket.

I shifted over to it, just a little way from his body. Blood had come all the way to the bucket's edge. Lifting it up, there was a circle of clean floor, and there, in the centre, a small, sealed envelope. On the front was the same sign that now lay branded on my skin. The omphalos.

Everything slowed. From the corner of my eye, I saw Lewis still sitting, head in his hands.

I stuffed the envelope into my trouser pocket, put the bucket back in its place and stood, moving away from the body. Again, I felt a sense of enclosure, like an insect caught in a jar. And there was Malcolm's face contorted by the curved glass, smiling at me. I could have told someone about the envelope; I could have gone with Clara to call for the police. I could have left that room and never returned. But Malcolm knew me. He knew I would keep his secrets. He knew that I loved him. I held my hand against the envelope in my pocket. This was for me. Only me.

I had to open it, but Lewis heard me moving about and was now looking up at his father's body. I couldn't leave. Not yet.

'Is he . . .?' Lewis's voice trailed off. He already knew the answer.

'Yes,' I said. 'But the wound . . . It's not from a gun.'

Lewis kept his gaze locked on his father. 'He can't have . . .'

My words, to Lewis, were radio static. There was a look of incredulity on his face, like a mortal witnessing the end of a deity. Malcolm, though sickly, had possessed the kind of manic energy that seems impervious to time, as if there were a vital part of him native to a land stranger than ours, where nature's laws don't apply.

I still pressed my hand to the envelope in my pocket. I imagined Malcolm crawling across the floor in his last moments, tucking the envelope under the bucket.

Footsteps, coming from the hall. Then Clara in the doorway. She paused, steadying herself before saying, 'The telephone won't work. I can't reach the mainland.'

'What do you mean?' said Lewis.

'The line's down.' She looked at her father, then bowed her head and swallowed hard. 'Is someone trying to hurt us?'

I began to feel like a bystander pulled into a spinning dance. A part of me knew the steps, but I had never made them. 'We need to gather everyone,' I said.

'This . . . this can't be real,' said Lewis.

Clara moved to his side, crouched next to him, stroked his hair.

I watched them and couldn't help thinking that this image was summative of the Furnivalls: Malcolm, departed, leaving those behind to piece a life together from his glorious wreckage. Clara and Lewis remained there, staring across the room at his body, too afraid, or too reverent, to touch him. I would have found it strange in any other case, that the children didn't run to their dead father, but this family was not like others.

'Did he leave anything? A note?' asked Clara.

I felt the envelope pulsing in my pocket. It was mine. I would read it first, before deciding to share. 'No,' I said. 'You're welcome to look.'

She pressed her forehead against her brother, whispered something in his ear, then rose and said, 'I thought you said the door was locked.'

'It was.' Then, as meaning clicked like a joint in a socket, I said, 'His eyes are closed.'

'What's that got to do with anything?' Clara said, stalking across the room, standing over her father's body. Stoically, she touched a long finger to her cheek, spiking a tear.

'When someone dies like . . . that . . . their eyes tend to stay open.'

'How do you know?'

I turned my face from her, relieved that she didn't press me. I did not like talking about my past. It seemed she respected that, and I was grateful.

Clara crouched slowly, began to press her hands against her father's pockets, like a child searching for sweets.

'The unlocked door, the closed eyes,' I said. 'Someone was here before us.' I went to the living-room door, stopping when Lewis stretched out his leg.

'Where are you going?'

The paper of the envelope was clammy from the sweat of my hand, and at the corner I felt the soft paper giving way. 'I'll be back with others,' I said.

Lewis rose slowly, a look appearing on his face that I hadn't seen before. 'What did my father tell you when you were in the house together?'

Heat rose in my cheeks, but I stayed very still, spoke slowly. 'Would you like to say something, Lewis? Bear in mind that *I* came to find *you*.'

He breathed through his teeth.

'I'll be back here soon,' I said. 'We need to gather everyone.' And before either of the Furnivall children could speak, I was gone. I had to be fast. It was only a matter of time before others would begin to search for Malcolm's manuscript. Over lunch, he had alluded to the value of his work, and I had no doubt that there were people on this estate who would rather the manuscript be in their hands than mine. These next few hours, before news of his death spread, would be the only time to search unhindered.

I hurried along the hallway, to the stag skull turning and the alcoves of chessboards. I noticed that the compositions had been changed. Someone had come here and rearranged the boards while Malcolm and I were speaking in the study. It was a small thing, but following what I'd just witnessed, it disturbed me. Someone was playing games.

I hurried through to the western side of the house, where disparate rooms were stacked in a jaunty hive and gusty hallways whined, as if bemoaning the state of the crumbling walls. I burst into my bedroom, threw the door shut behind me, fell back against it. I closed my eyes, trying to slow my hammering heart, trying to focus my breathing into a regular rhythm. Snatching my coat from where I'd laid it on the bed, I wrapped it about myself to stop my shivering. I reached into my inner coat pocket for the cigarettes, lit one, took a long deep drag. The familiar liquorice flavour was comforting. Feeling steadier, I brought out the envelope.

The sign of the omphalos was drawn in black ink on the front: small and deliberate. I traced it with my finger, as if that might cause the pattern to open like a chrysalis and reveal a hidden meaning. Taking another long draw on my cigarette, I thumbed the edge of the envelope, prising up the adhesive fold. Inside was a letter, written in Malcolm's spidery hand:

Dear Euan,
When faced with death, it is our essence that guides us. Some fight, some run; I, it seems, write letters.
There are many things which lie buried on this estate. Some might call them treasures; others, obscenities. I think there is not so much difference between these things. Why do we bury treasure? Perhaps out of intuitive shame: who am I to possess something so valuable? One treasure I will let you glimpse, because without it, you will not arrive at your end. On this

land, Euan, Time is different. It is in conversation with itself, and, if you know how to listen, you might understand.

I know that I will be killed. It is a sad realisation, but one I have used to my advantage. Euan, this is a test for you. No mystery is stranger than that we live ourselves. The novels we write are filled with artifice, fabricated logic. But this novel, this last book of ours, will be different. I want to capture the strange forces of this world. You will come to understand me. Find who has done this. Then, perhaps, you will have earned the right to finish my book.

Whether you knew it or not, the moment you set foot in this place, you began a transformation. There is nothing to do now but accept it. Take me up on my offer and immerse yourself in the water. Emerge changed.

Sincerely,

Malcolm

P.S.

To arrive at being all,
desire to be nothing.

I read the letter three times before I could make any sense of it. How far in advance of his death had he written this? I could hardly imagine the toll it would take, carrying around a letter like that, waiting for the time it was needed.

I folded up the paper into a little square, tucked it back into the omphalos envelope and pushed it into the inner pocket of my coat, beside my cigarettes.

There were noises coming from about the house. A metallic wailing made me flinch. I saw, again, the impression of my younger self, laid over the room like a photo negative. Bombers were coming over, wings shearing through the negative, obliterating all. Darkness, for a moment, then the world returning . . . The noise was just a pipe. Unease prickled through me.

I touched each of my fingers to my thumb. When I was a boy, my sister had taught me to spell the word 'safe', saying each letter as the digits touch. She'd said it would protect me. Catching myself, I wiped my hands on my coat, took a sharp breath and straightened.

There was so much I didn't understand about the letter, but Malcolm's sentences loomed like a fog about me. What had he meant about time being in conversation with itself? And that final line in the postscript . . . It made me shiver. Knowing Malcolm, every sentence would hold a deeper significance. But I could not, for the life of me, determine any. My head was pounding, my arm throbbing. *Oh God.* With every breath, that phrase pitched up in the back of my throat.

I heard footsteps from the hall. Turning my ear to the door, I waited for them to grow louder. When I was certain they were close, I pushed open the bedroom door and found, standing alone in the hallway, Colm Hubert.

'Christ, Colm, what are you doing?'

He looked at me with a bemused expression. 'Ah, Euan, I thought your room would be close. I'm just down the hall . . .' His face slackened, and his eyes grew hard. 'What's the matter?'

'You didn't hear? The gunshot, Colm.'

'What?'

'Malcolm . . . He . . .' I told him haltingly what had happened, saw the colour drain from his face, saw his fat lower lip fall open to reveal spiky teeth.

He spoke in a frenzy. 'I grew tired of looking at orchids, left Tilly in the glasshouse and I . . . I came in through the back entrance, went straight to my room to read. I felt rancid, only read a few pages before drifting off. But I saw nothing – you believe me, don't you?'

I saw he was trembling. Sweat rolled from his temples, dripped onto the shoulders of his expensive jacket. He looked pathetic, and I thought that he would not be capable of killing a man like Malcolm. There seemed to be no trace of blood on his clothes, and he hadn't changed since lunch. I also felt somewhat close to him; we had arrived together on the ferry and we were outsiders, bound by our strangeness. He had a sycophantic way about him – the kind of man who would say what he supposed you wanted to hear. I had known people like Colm before, and I found him easy to read. In a strange way, I was fond of him – the way one grows fond of a stray dog. But I knew that Colm was holding something back, that he was not presenting himself honestly. I searched his face for traces of deception, then said softly, 'When I came downstairs for lunch, you were looking at a photograph. You tucked it away in your pocketbook when you saw me.'

Colm pawed at his sweaty temple, wiped the wet fingers on his lapel. 'Is there a question?'

'Why were you so quick to hide it?'

'Because it did not concern you.'

'You seemed upset at the time.'

'It is a photograph of my family. I miss them.'

'You can show it to me now?'

He sagged, shook his head. 'Perhaps I will show it to you some day, of my own free will. Not out of coercion.'

'I only want to—'

'No, Euan. I . . . I won't.' There were tears in his eyes. 'There are things – every man has them – that are personal, private. Things they do not allow others to see, or even know of. Sacred objects, as much a part of themselves as their limbs. Please, understand.'

I sighed, seeing his trembling, his teary eyes. 'Then you must tell me what you saw on the track.'

He pressed his lips together in a tight line.

'You were muttering to yourself about the track. You saw someone, didn't you?'

He backed away from me as my voice became frantic.

'Was it a girl wearing white? Did she look scared?'

'Euan . . .'

'Who did you see?' I took him by the arms, held him fast.

He could not meet my eye, speaking into the fold of his second chin. 'This place . . . for some reason it's pulling at my memories. Dredging the dark ones up. I saw someone from my past, but not a girl. I'm sorry. Until now, I thought I was the only one seeing things, but perhaps' – he peeled back his lips to show a narrow smile – 'perhaps you, too, are seeing ghosts.' He paused, considering whether he should continue. His tongue flicked the corner of his mouth, and he said suddenly, 'Tell me, did they ever find your sister?'

I struck him with the heel of my palm, sent him across the hallway. The search for my sister had been reported in the papers: he'd evidently researched me. I thought he would shrivel and skulk away to his room again, but to his credit, the man came flying back at me with an attempt at a rugby tackle which he had evidently learnt in school many years ago and not used since. He brought me to the ground, but hit his temple on the doorway and lay there on top of me, snorting for a moment before regaining consciousness.

Perhaps I could not read Colm as well as I'd supposed.

I gave him a fraternal thump on the back, scooted away and helped him to his feet.

'I must . . . apologise,' he said. 'I shouldn't have mentioned—'

'No bother. Are you all right to stand?'

'Yes, yes.'

There was a long pause. We looked each other up and down, oddly brought closer by the scuffle. I was about to speak, when Colm said, 'Look, there was something.'

I raised my chin, tried to slow my racing heart, take in his words.

'When I returned to my room, I found, lying on my bed, a will.'

'What?'

He tapped his jacket pocket. Then he swayed from side to side, steadying himself by leaning a hand on the wall.

'Impossible. He was with me since lunch.'

'Someone could have placed it there for him.'

'Or—'

'It had Malcolm's signature.'

'Signatures can be forged.'

'What's more, there is an addendum to the offer he made you over lunch.'

'Christ. What—'

'I can't say any more. Please, I've already said too much.'

'Then promise me you won't speak of this to anyone . . . not until we are all gathered. In return, I will say that I saw you return from the glasshouse after the gunshot. I told you to go to your room and stay there. Understood?'

He nodded, though I was uncertain whether he'd taken in what I'd said.

'Now you should fetch Tilly,' I told him. 'Gather everyone, but do it slowly. I will need some time.'

Colm shook his head in bewilderment. 'What are you intending to do, go for a bloody swim?'

Silence fell between us.

I remembered a line in Malcolm's letter. It was from the last paragraph: *Take me up on my offer and immerse yourself in the water.* Of course, there was the offer to finish his novel, but perhaps he was also alluding to another offer? The offer to take me swimming in the lake out in the surrounding woodland. Was I seeing meaning where there was none, or could he be reaching out from the page, telling me where to go?

'Fetch Tilly,' I said to Colm, closing my bedroom door and dashing off down the hallway. 'I won't be long.'

And so I clung to my suspicion, tucked my hands into my long woollen coat, pulled it tightly about myself and set off, hearing stirring throughout the house, which I assumed to be Clara and Lewis searching for others. I slipped through the front door, out again, into the wild grass, towards the water.

8

I FOLLOWED THE TRACK which led north, and then I veered east, away from Lewis's outhouse, through the woods and on towards the lake. The last time I'd visited the Furnivalls, it had been late spring. Pine fronds had lain on this path, dewed with golden pollen, which would rise and float through the air as we tramped across them. We had walked together, Anwen, Malcolm and I, along this path to the lake. As we'd walked, Anwen had held me by the arm, asked me about my upbringing, had not pried when I'd left sections of my story blank. I think Malcolm had told her, or perhaps she had just sensed, that there were swathes which I just did not share.

Malcolm had marched on ahead, singing to himself, turning to us every so often to ask us what we made of a story he'd recently committed to memory. I remembered him recounting the words of the Russian poet Osip Mandelstam, whom he had decided to translate as a way of learning Russian. He'd asked us each our opinion on whether he'd captured the beautiful clarity of image in the Russian's work when describing the entity of time. In his translation, he'd named it a 'shy chrysalis' and a 'cabbage butterfly sprinkled with flour'. Both Anwen and I had applauded his accuracy, despite neither of us being familiar with the piece. Malcolm had laughed in triumph and strode on, leaving me and Anwen to our complicit snickering.

When we'd arrived at the lake, they had stripped down to their underwear, gooseflesh rippling over their skin as they toed the water's edge. Though it was nearly summer, the air was still cold. I remember how they'd looked at me, laughing and taunting me for staying on the bank, wrapped in my coat. I'd watched them enter the water, noting how each of them moved: Malcolm throwing himself into the cold; Anwen striding carefully behind, till the lake, clear as glass, slipped around her neck.

It was there, as I watched them swimming, that I'd opened my notebook and written the first lines of my third book. Sitting with my back against a silver birch, I remember noticing a foreign feeling come over me. I felt safe. Until then, my books had been anaemic – deeply researched and cunningly crafted, but lacking in spirit. They were just feats of planning. Whether they knew it or not, Malcolm and Anwen had given my prose, and my life, fullness. I let the music of their laughter guide my pen across the page, wanting, as the sun traced its lazy arc across the sky, for time to stand still.

But now, as I pushed through the overgrown track, the pine branches swiped at my calves, the sky was roiling and grey. It was like returning to an old friend, only to find them bitter and half-mad.

The trees seemed to be frozen mid-fall, clinging with black limbs to the land which dipped into a churning rocky bowl. And there, at the bottom, a dark body of water, fed by streams which ran like white threads stitching the earth. It was just when I'd started to feel foolish for reading a deeper meaning in Malcolm's words that I saw what looked, at first, like drifting weeds, lost in the lake's still water. But, as I neared, I saw that beneath was the shape of a submerged body. What I'd thought was riverweed was, in fact, long silver hair.

Veering off the path, which wound about the bowl to the water, I ran down the steep bank, sending scree and clods of earth flying.

The body floated in the black water, hair curling about the delicate slip worn by the woman, who I knew now was Anwen. By the time I was at the water's edge I'd thrown off my coat and shoes. I waded and thrashed over to her, turning her thin body over so that her face looked up to the purple-hued clouds and the gleaming silver sky. Her eyes opened slowly and she turned them to me, like someone weary after being woken. Someone who would rather stay asleep.

'Malcolm?' she said.

'It's me, Anwen. How long have you been here?'

Her skin had taken on a bluish hue, and her lips were grey. She blinked and whispered, 'I thought it would wash away.'

'Let me help you,' I said.

She planted her feet on the bed of the lake, stood there in the freezing water like a creature from a fairy story, her slip clinging to the runnels where her delicate muscles joined with her long thin bones. She looked at me the way you might look at someone across a great distance.

I knew who had unlocked the sitting-room door, who had closed Malcolm's eyelids. The gunshot must have woken her; she'd discovered him while I was in the forest. 'You found him,' I said.

She didn't speak, but something vanished behind her eyes.

'Come on,' I said, being careful to avert my gaze. 'It's freezing.'

Expressionless, she tucked her long pale hair behind her ears and moved away from me, back to the bank. When she reached the shore, she removed her slip and wrung out her hair, which dripped silver onto the stones. Then, she put on her black skirt and silk blouse, wrapped a green woollen shawl around her shoulders. She coiled her hair up, held it in place with a pin, and slumped down on the bank.

When I tried to offer her my coat, she looked straight ahead, saying nothing. I expect she thought I needed it more than she did, now that I was soaked. I wrapped it around myself and sat on the bank beside her.

The mineral song of water against stone. Leaves rustling. The slow thrum of rich earth.

'We couldn't reach the mainland, but Lewis and Clara are gathering—'

'He prepared me for it,' Anwen said. 'But how can you be ready for that? How could anyone?'

'Prepared you?'

She seemed to break from her trail of thoughts, said, 'Not one person here deserves your trust. No one, do you understand?' She grimaced, closed her eyes and moved her lips in what seemed to be a silent prayer.

'We need to get back,' I said.

A smile flickered on her face. 'Do you want to know something about my husband?'

'What?'

'When a magician performs a trick, there are those

who desire wonder, and there are those who see it as a personal offence, who will not rest until they understand the mechanics. When Malcolm talked about dying, he was a man possessed – as if death were just another puzzle.'

'Who wanted him dead?'

'By the end he was willing all of us to do it. Do you know what I think, Euan?'

Shivering, I sat and waited for her to go on.

'I would rather be stupid and mystified. Life behind the curtain is a joyless thing.' She rubbed at her eyes furiously, then opened her mouth and looked up at the sky. 'You're in danger here,' she said. 'You can end this for yourself if you just go.' She turned to face me, and there was anger in her expression.

'Malcolm gave me a task—'

'Forget his damned tasks. Just . . . just leave, Euan.'

'But I saw someone. At the window, a girl . . . and then a figure running into the trees.'

Anwen hardly moved as tears fell from her face. 'Please, go.'

I thought of the bond I had made with Malcolm. I thought of the letter, still there in my coat pocket. Malcolm had told me to come here. If I hadn't come, what might have happened? If I left now, what would be left undone? I didn't yet know the real reason he wanted me here. There had to be something about the lake, something that would help me find who had done this.

And then, the more pernicious thought . . . What would become of Malcolm's unfinished manuscript? If I were to leave now, there was no knowing who might find it. What secrets would they learn?

Anwen spoke with a soft voice, almost to herself. 'Malcolm played piano.'

I held my tongue, waited for the slow movement of Anwen's mouth, for her words to emerge, strained at first, then tumbling.

'I met him in Duino, at a private recital just after the Great War. I remember he sat with two men, one older and one younger. They had a wild look about them, a sort of hunger. Malcolm later told me their names were Niels and Werner.'

I looked at her, incredulous. She gave a small nod, confirming what I'd thought: that Malcolm had known the two physicists: Bohr and Heisenberg – men who had dedicated their lives to understanding the most subtle mysteries of our universe.

'When the recital was done, they all asked for more. My accompanist had left, so, Malcolm offered to play for me.' Her lip quivered as she smiled. 'He was quite useless. Afterwards, we swam in the Adriatic, and he told me . . . He spoke to me about a man named Ludwig Boltzmann: the grandson of a watchmaker who laid the groundwork for quantum theory. He said . . .' She closed her eyes in dreamy recollection. 'He said our understanding of entropy is rooted in bias; that the difference between past and future refers only to our blurred vision of the world. What if we could unblur our perception? Boltzmann was made an outcast by his own ideas. They haunted him till the end of his life. And Malcolm spoke of him with such admiration. It was intoxicating, the way he talked about those things. I know you understand. He had an incredible gravity, an ability to inspire, so that even the dullest person, if left with him long enough, would begin to shine.' The smile dropped from Anwen's face and she looked out across the lake, eyes wide and watering. 'What he didn't tell me was that Boltzmann later hanged himself, there in Duino, not far from where we had swum.' She broke down, balled herself up and wept.

I reached out to comfort her, but she glared up at me, and I saw blood returning to her cheeks. 'I . . . I didn't even see him. The weeks before you arrived, he was working in his shed, pushing us all away. He's spoken to you more than his own family. What has he told you?'

It would have been so easy to pull the letter from my pocket, to pass it to her and let her read her husband's words. But a selfish force kept me quiet. I said nothing.

Anwen laughed desperately. 'Of course,' she said. 'You're just the same.'

I sat there, her words percolating through me, like lead in my veins. I spoke softly. 'You haven't accused me.'

Her long white teeth emerged from behind her lips. Closer to a snarl than a smile. 'Because I know you . . . perhaps better than my husband did. I saw the way you looked at him.' Pity marked her face. 'And how he looked at you.'

I rose, stepped away from Anwen, who lingered on the bank.

'We have to get back,' I said. 'The telephone's down and we'll need to send for help. Maybe a boat to the police on the mainland—'

'Tell me something, Euan.'

I stilled, watched her expression become stony. Her jaw trembled.

'If you knew the person you loved would consume you, till you were nothing . . . would you regret knowing them?'

My answer came to me, as if someone had whispered in my ear what to say. 'If a thing is worth doing, it's worth doing badly.'

Anwen held my gaze, then wiped her cheek and stood. 'I think writers will believe anything, so long as it sounds pretty.'

'I'm sorry, Anwen.'

She looked up, as if that might stop her tears. After a silence, she said, 'I can make my own way back.'

'But—'

'I know what you want,' she said. 'No need to pretend with me.'

We regarded each other, as another veil between us fell away. 'You said he was in his writing shed in the weeks before I arrived. He only took me once, and I don't recall the way.'

Anwen toed the rocky earth with a bare foot. 'Are you asking me to tell you where it is?'

'It was your husband's wish for me to finish his book. You know that. If there's a chance the book is in that shed, I need to—'

'The other side of the lake. Beyond the silver birches, you'll smell wild garlic. Follow the scent, and you'll find it.' She didn't meet my eye; rather, she looked across the lake at the dragonflies, the pond-skaters, the midges, all painting drowsy patterns over the still water.

'Thank you,' I said.

'Go, then,' she said, beginning to walk back. 'Chase whatever you think needs chasing.'

Just as she was leaving, I said in a hurry, 'They come back to you.'

She turned.

And in that moment, all I could picture was the little girl at the window. The one in the white gown. 'The ones we lose,' I said. 'They come back.'

Anwen bowed her head, and her hair fell in silver stripes across her face.

★ ★ ★

In the stillness of the woods, I felt time fall away, like a creature sloughing its skin to become new and pliable. Seconds might have been hours. I thought of what Malcolm had written in his letter, about time being different here. Was this what he'd meant?

Just as I was about to go looking for the writing shed, an idea struck me. What had Malcolm wanted me to find at the lake? He'd told me to immerse myself in the water. I recalled how I'd first seen Anwen, floating face-down. Perhaps she'd been staring at something, there beneath the surface? Something Malcolm wanted me to see. I felt as if I had missed something.

And so, I remained there on the bank, slowly disrobing as flashes of that happy spring returned to my memory. I remembered Malcolm padding about the rocky edge of the water, arms winged out to balance, watching Anwen swim back and forth across the glimmering surface. I remembered how they had dived down together, resurfaced with wide smiles and gleaming bodies. What was there beneath the water? Had it been there, even then? I had to look, before I searched the writing shed. I had to know.

I waded into the black water, feeling the cold punch the

air from my chest. I swam out into the lake, a little further from where Anwen had been. Numbness prickled across my limbs. Just as the cold reached my bones, I stopped, took a deep breath and dived down.

What I saw was obscured by darkness, but there were shapes down there on the lakebed, ragged pillars in the gloom. A stone circle. Swimming deeper, I reached out, touched the top of one of the taller stones. It was smooth, slick with a skin of lake weed which ran like a mane of long hair from the stone's pate. In fact, the stones seemed like the bodies of men who had lived so long on this island that their bodies had petrified. Now, they stood together, lichen-spotted, drowned to the world.

My breath was running out, but I stayed there, trying to piece together what Malcolm had wanted me to glean from seeing the stones. I pulled myself down so that my feet were almost on the lakebed and stared into the face of the tall stone. I laid my palms against its smooth surface. As the weeds coiled around me, I heard voices, calling out across the years. They were telling me something urgent. Just a few seconds more, I thought, but already I was fighting the urge to inhale.

Something spined and tensile touched my foot. It weaved about my toes, advanced up my leg, palpating the soft meat of my calf. I thrashed at the water, silt spinning. I had to surface. I raked the stone, fingernails cutting through algae. The voices in the dark became as indistinct as currents clashing, and my fingers, pressing to the body of the stone, twined with those of another. They were cold, muscular, dominant: the fingers of my father, holding me down in the dark. I spasmed, freezing water filling my mouth as the stone grip softened, warmed. Julia was here. I felt her holding my hand, as she had when I'd left her, standing on the railway platform. Dressed in my military uniform, I'd watched her through the train window as we'd left the station, Father's fingers wrapped about her narrow shoulders. I could see our lives, splayed across time like a half-dissected creature. Then, my mother's fingers, caressing my head, moving down over my eyes, erasing her image from my memory. Fingers about my throat. I heard Colm's words again: *A terrible way to die.* It is a lie, the peace of drowning.

With the last of my will, I ripped my hands from the stone, fell back through the dark water, felt the weeds slip from my skin. I kicked, rose back to the light.

Coughing and gulping air, dread gnawed at me. What I'd just witnessed was impossible. I thought of what Lewis had said, about the language of this land . . . Ashamed of myself, I swam back to the bank. The events of the day had begun to unravel me. I rubbed my hair dry and put on my clothes, hurrying away from that place, towards Malcolm's writing shed.

9

I LIT A CIGARETTE and reminded myself of who I was, and why I was here. Malcolm had given me a task. I had to find his manuscript. But, whoever had killed him – and he *had* been killed – was out there still, and I had reason to believe they also wanted to do me harm. They had burned my books as a warning.

I looked out across the lake as I walked its border, thinking of Malcolm's final moments, of the panic that would have gripped him as he searched for the Enfield he'd concealed in the cabinet. Still, it had done him no good.

And there were the drowned stones in the lake. Why had Malcolm wanted me to see them?

The cigarette in my mouth went out as something whistled past. Beside my head, a tree trunk burst open. A bullet, its voice echoing like that of a dreadful forest creature. I turned to see who had fired but saw only trees and still water. I ran, clammy clothes making me clumsy as I rushed up the bank to where the trees grew thick. I thought then that the figure I'd seen running to the woods must have waited here for me to return, watched me till they were certain I was alone. How stupid I'd been, to leave the safety of the house. I rushed through thickets and scrub, feeling a tightening in my chest. I clawed my way through the silver birches, bark falling away like dead skin as I went.

When I came to the end of the gathering of birches, I stilled, pressed my back against a wide trunk and closed my eyes. Things were returning. Smells, sounds. Moments compressed, like a concertina contracting: I was lost in the trees; blood soaked the bed of pine needles; mines threw daggers of shattered trees; the screams of my friends. I noticed I was, again, tapping my fingers against my thumb: the charm my sister had taught me.

Opening my eyes, I counted the trees about me. Seven birches, all with ghostly bark latticed with thin dark cracks where burls emerged. I remembered what Anwen had told me and breathed deeply, the scent of wild garlic coming from nearby. Making towards the scent, I kept low and out of sight.

I could see, behind me, the northern edge of the lake, and could hear the little waterfalls gushing into it. It hid the sound of my footsteps. I moved in a loping crouch, spotting the grey outline of a building up ahead.

Now my panic had ossified into a single intention. I weaved through the remaining trees, the waterfalls at my back. The building ripped through the gathering dark. It stood secluded on an open stretch of ground which was carpeted with clusters of wild garlic flowers, small and white. The woodland here felt ancient. Ivy twined up the shed, and its roof was crusted with lichen, the slates jutting out like petals of an old pinecone.

I wasn't certain I'd lost my pursuer, so I crept around the glade, towards the back of the shed, seeking another way inside. Perhaps the person who'd shot at me knew that this was where I was coming? Perhaps they were waiting, rifle trained on the front door? I went round to the back, suppressing the urge to cough, breathing in short bursts so that even the cloud of my breath could not be seen.

There was no entrance at the back of the shed, but as I moved away, concealing myself in the trees which overhung the wild garlic, I saw a flat area in the woods. It seemed out of place, among the thorny tumble of undergrowth, so I moved towards it, looking over my shoulder every time a branch crunched underfoot.

I stepped into the flat area and found myself walking on blankets of moss and fungus growing over dark rotting wood. There was something about it that didn't seem natural, but it was too late to turn back. In my haste to evade the shooter, I'd moved too far, and the ground beneath me groaned. I leapt for the edge of the flatness, but the rotten wood floor gave out underneath me and I plummeted into darkness.

I crumpled in a heap. There was something soft beneath me and I reached down to feel delicate fabric. Looking up, I realised that I had fallen through a mouldering ceiling to a basement. The cracked mouth I'd created from my fall dribbled light into the little room, but hardly enough to illuminate my surroundings.

I sat there, breathing quietly, feeling as if I'd fallen into an adjoining world, a place of absence. It was calm. I wondered if Malcolm had felt the same as darkness swallowed him.

Malcolm's book. The thought brought me back. I stood, took the cigarette lighter from my pocket, flicked it open, held it out. The basement was small and seemed to have been used as a storage space. Rough brick walls arched about me. In the light of the flame, I saw piles of dresses, folded with care. These had broken my fall. There were tennis racquets, tea sets, jewellery. Things belonging to a child, all left to moulder here beneath the earth.

Malcolm had written of buried things . . .

I thought of the little girl. Visions of my sister came to me, but I pushed them away, warding off ghosts in the dark. There was an explanation behind this. Something rational. I walked through the room, finding three candles perched about and lighting them with my cigarette lighter. In their flickering glow, I searched through the clothes and toys for Malcolm's manuscript. I wanted to be thorough, before I allowed myself to walk up the narrow stair at the end of the basement, which I assumed led to Malcolm's writing shed.

Just as I was about to give up and move into the room above, I saw something I recognised. It would have seemed to anyone else like just another child's toy, but to me it held a unique meaning. Though I was beneath the earth, I felt the kiss of sea breeze against my skin, the salt drying my lips, the gentle pressure of her hand in mine. I recalled the scuffed knees, the brave face, the quiet shared at the end of a day. I was with her again. I stood, silently, and stared.

Leaning up against the corner of the room was a hobby horse. It looked just like the one my sister had owned. She'd lost it on a trip to Wardie Bay, the little beach at the north end of Edinburgh. She'd set it down by the shore, left it there, and when she'd returned it was gone. I'd told her the tide must have taken it. That was the last memory I had of my sister, unclouded by pain. As if borne by a deep current, her name came to me, and I spoke it under my breath. 'Julia.'

I had memories of chasing her as she rode the hobby horse, its wooden end scuffing against the pebbles of the beach.

I went over to the hobby horse, picked it up and immediately dropped it. There, on the bottom, were scuff marks. It took me a moment to collect myself and realise I was being stupid. Any hobby horse would be scuffed like this. I bent down to collect it and put it back, but then heard a creaking from above, in Malcolm's writing shed.

Staying very still, I listened. Footsteps, quiet but clear. I went to the bottom of the stairs. Suddenly realising I had nothing with which to defend myself, I reached across and took a candlestick from a shelf. Whoever was up there, I couldn't let them leave. Not without seeing who they were. I left the hobby horse lying on the floor and made my way, slowly, up the narrow stairs.

The door was ajar, and, as I peered through into Malcolm's writing shed, I saw a heavy man wearing a tweed suit, with a crop of hair that made him look as if he'd just walked through a nest of cobwebs. He was rifling through Malcolm's things, and he opened a drawer in the desk, pulled out a stack of papers, thrust them into a shoulder satchel. When I barged into the room, candlestick raised, he whirled and faced me with his hands in the air, his jaw working but no words coming out.

'It's . . . Jim,' he managed to say.

I lowered my impromptu weapon. Malcolm had spoken about Jim, his neighbour on this island. I'd not met him, but I knew they were close.

'Clara told me what happened,' Jim said.

'Did you follow me here?'

'What?'

'I was chased. There was a gunshot.'

Jim lowered his arms and held them awkwardly by his large waist. 'I did hear something.'

I watched him, hoping the silence would suck more words from him.

'You're Euan,' he said. 'You came up in the last conversation I had with Malcolm.' At his dead friend's name, he grimaced, paused.

'So you know why I'm here?' I said.

'I do.'

Jim stiffened. I realised then that he was a foot taller than me and, though old, had a physical dominance which made the conversation feel as if I were walking through a bull's field. He raised his chin, breathing deeply.

'Malcolm and I were here in the wee hours of yesterday morning. I left my cane,' said Jim.

'Your cane?'

'Aye.' He moved over towards a large green armchair positioned in the corner of the shed, beside a wide bookshelf.

'Hold on,' I said.

Jim held his palms up, said, 'You're paranoid, Euan. Clara found me, asked to use my telephone but—'

'The line was down.'

'Aye. Someone here is—'

'Why did you come here? Why now?'

Jim flared his nostrils, reached over the armchair and picked up a long burled wooden cane. 'I wanted to be sure of something.'

'What?'

'I think you know.'

I met his eyes, which were so dark they looked to be one large pupil. I saw in them that he also knew. 'Malcolm's manuscript.'

Jim gave a faint smile. 'I don't want it to fall into the wrong hands.'

'And the right hands . . . I suppose they're yours?'

Jim smirked, pointed his cane at my candlestick. 'Why don't you put that down?'

I steeled myself. 'Why don't you empty your satchel?'

Jim grimaced, shook his head and said, 'You don't know—'

'Empty it.'

My heart was hammering as Jim put his large hand into his shoulder satchel and brought out the papers. He walked slowly across the room, set them on the desk. He looked down at the papers with a look of dismay across his broad features. He spoke in a growl. 'This is what we were discussing this morning. Well, arguing about, more like.'

Cautious, I moved over to the desk. Keeping my eyes fixed on Jim, I set down the candlestick and picked up the papers.

'It's pure shite,' said Jim.

It took me a moment to register what I was looking at, but I soon realised that this was not Malcolm's writing. It was a typewritten sheaf of papers, an attempt at a story using the characters from Malcolm's *Gravitation* series. I looked up at Jim, saw him smirking at me, then looked back to the papers. I read the first page, then sat at Malcolm's desk and finished the opening chapter with Jim pacing the floor behind me. It was all exposition, listing family names, locations, histories. There was no doubt the writer of this work had an encyclopaedic knowledge of Malcolm's series;

however, their ability to tell a story left much to be desired. When characters did appear, they spoke in convoluted paragraphs, and all with the same voice. The story had no tension, aside from the tension that built up in my neck the longer I read the piece. To write anything is an achievement, and I, more than anyone, know the struggle it takes to compose even the worst of work. But it was just a simple fact that this would not even fill the shadow of Malcolm's masterpiece. This was an imitation.

'It's by Malcolm's assistant,' said Jim. 'Matilda MacArthur.'

'Tilly?'

'Aye.'

'And when you were here this morning, this is what you discussed?'

Jim grimaced, and I could see his grip tighten around his cane. 'I told him he needed to fire her. *This* – he hit the papers in my hand with his cane, 'is unacceptable. I told Malcolm to destroy it then and there, but he refused.'

'Why?'

Jim raised his exuberant eyebrows and said, 'The man had a soft spot for her. I suppose he thought he could mentor her ...'

A thought struck me then, as I hadn't taken Malcolm for the sentimental type. 'Or, perhaps, he feared what she might have done if he spurned her. She must have known things few others did about his business.'

Jim tapped his cane on the wooden floor, looked at me with narrowed eyes. 'Whatever the case, I intend to destroy this imitation. It would be a tragedy if people thought this was Malcolm's final book.'

I set the papers back on the desk and tried to comprehend

the full meaning of what I'd seen. Tilly MacArthur had written her own manuscript, her own ending to Malcolm's series.

'It seems she wanted your job,' said Jim. He sighed, moved closer to me, so I could smell the bitter coffee on his breath, see the bush of hair sprouting from each nostril. 'You should be thanking me, Euan. And trust that Tilly will be looking for the real manuscript. She may have already come here.'

I searched his face. His lips were wet and he habitually licked them. Little moles were scattered like buckshot across his cheeks. He smiled at me, broadly, as if to say, *What will you do now?*

I recalled the ferocity with which he'd rummaged through the drawers. He wanted the real manuscript for himself. Perhaps he knew what it contained.

'I have a question for you now, Euan,' said Jim.

I waited, arms folded, aware of the cane in the large man's hand.

'I'm sure we're both aware of Malcolm's penchant for trickery. Whatever he's written in this final novel will no doubt hold some kind of mystery. He alluded to a great secret. My question to you is . . . what if you do not like what you read? What if you are not a mentee, but a target? What if you are everything he despised, and his final act on this earth was to torment you?'

I broke away from his gaze and looked out the window of the writing shed, across the field of wild garlic. I felt the letter in my pocket grow heavier, as if Malcolm's words were amalgamating into a deadweight. I had not considered this.

'Do you know how I met Malcolm?' Jim continued. 'For thirty years, I composed cryptic crosswords for *The Observer*.

And every crossword, without fail, would be returned almost immediately after publication, solved, by a reader who signed their letters "Sestina". They were so good that we began to suspect it was someone I knew, a colleague or the like.'

I recognised the word: '*Sestina*. It's a poetic form . . . devious to compose. Nightmarish to read.'

Jim laughed. 'Yet the beauty lies in its elusiveness. In the repetition and recycling of patterns that cannot be quite held in the mind all at once. To read a sestina is to feel some greater power laughing at you. To hear a language of signs which are just beyond your grasp.'

I nodded. Yes, that would be Malcolm.

'He delights in deception, does Malcolm,' Jim said. 'When eventually he revealed his identity to me, we had been writing threats and jibes to each other for many years and had, quite by accident, become great friends.' Jim's grip tightened about his cane again, and he raised his face to the ceiling. 'When he invited me here, to this island, I thought it was because of our friendship, but . . . perhaps he has left one final puzzle for me.' He lowered his chin, met my eye. 'Tell me, have you found anything?'

I considered, for the slightest of moments, showing Jim the letter in my pocket. Perhaps he would be able to discern some cryptic clue in Malcolm's words? Would he understand the haunting postscript, *To arrive at being all, desire to be nothing*? But still, I said nothing. How could I trust this man? Jim could have his own motives for finding Malcolm's manuscript. He seemed to me a man possessed. He and Malcolm were similar in many ways, the one main difference being that while Malcolm swam, Jim drowned.

Puzzles had consumed his life. He had a look of madness about him. If I were to give him the letter in my pocket, I knew no good would come from it. It would drive Jim deeper into the labyrinth.

These were the reasons I used then, but I would be lying now if I said my own selfishness had not been a cause. Malcolm had promised his manuscript to me. Not Jim. Not anyone else. It was my puzzle to solve.

'There is one thing,' I said to Jim, gesturing to the door through which I'd emerged, the one leading down to the basement. 'Have you been down there?'

Jim retrieved Tilly's papers, drove them deep into his satchel as if they were radioactive and required containment. He licked his heavy lips and peered through the door which I'd left ajar. 'Malcolm used it as a storage room,' he said. 'Keepsakes from Clara and Lewis's childhood. He wanted them close to him while he wrote.'

I looked at Jim, tried to read him. Nothing. 'By all accounts, Malcolm was not a sentimental man.'

Jim grinned, yellow-patinaed teeth behind wet lips. 'We all hide parts of ourselves, do we not?'

Again, the thought of Julia crossed my mind. I had abandoned her, left her to live alone with our father. I had welcomed the chance to fight in the war. Had welcomed the chance to leave her. If I was honest with myself, the main reason I would not sell our childhood home was because I'd hoped, someday, for her return. I maintained the little house, kept her room as she'd left it: they hadn't found her body.

Jim and I stood there in the quiet, neither willing to give any further ground, until finally, I offered, 'Neither of us will be satisfied if we leave without searching properly.'

He gave a grunt of agreement, then said, 'What happens if one of us finds the manuscript?'

'Then,' I said, 'we will talk.'

He rolled his fingers over the head of his cane, then reached out to shake my hand.

I shook it, and we began to search together for the manuscript, each of us keeping an eye on the other as we scoured from floor to ceiling, finding nothing. When we were content that neither of our efforts had been successful, we decided silently to leave the writing shed and walk, together, to the house and Malcolm's body. And as we made our way back along the rainy, darkening path, I think we were both relieved that we had not, in fact, needed to talk.

10

ANWEN ADJUSTED THE SILK covering which now cocooned Malcolm's body, stopping when we walked into the sitting room. She looked up from where she was holding him, as if we were disturbing his sleep. Then, she blinked, gestured for us to take a seat on the chairs which had been arranged into a rough circle about her.

We rubbed the rain from our hair, dried our hands on our coats. Before sitting, Jim went to Anwen, put a hand on her shoulder and whispered in her ear. She bowed her head, acknowledging his words, then she peeled the silk away from her dead husband's face, and Jim stared. 'We'll find who did this,' he said. 'I promise.' Then he reached down with his heavy hand and delicately pulled the silk back over his dead friend's face. 'Come, Anwen, sit with me,' said Jim.

She shook her head, still cradling Malcolm.

Jim stood and watched her for a moment, before deciding it was not worth an argument. He moved across the room, muttering, 'I'm sorry, son,' as he passed Lewis.

His words didn't register on Lewis's face.

'My telephone is down as well,' Jim announced to no one in particular. 'But we will get help. Believe me.' He took a seat by the broken window and sat, examining the shards left from Malcolm's bullet, breeze mussing his thin hair.

After a minute, he drew the thick velvet curtain, slumped and just looked at the floor.

I had been lingering in the doorway, but eventually roused myself and removed my coat, hanging it on the back of a chair beside Lewis, who was sitting with his legs folded, glassy-eyed, trembling. I sat down slowly. 'Where's Clara?' I asked.

Lewis was far away. He pulled at a thread coming from the hem of his untucked shirt. Then, suddenly, he said, 'She's . . . she's taking care of things. Like she always does.'

'Euan,' said Anwen.

I looked to her and saw she was beckoning me over. Leaving my coat on the chair beside Lewis, I went to Anwen, crouched beside her.

'Tell me, did you find what you were looking for?' she asked.

I lowered my gaze to the silk which covered Malcolm.

A sound came from the back of her throat like laughter. 'Of course you didn't.'

I shook my head, trying to think of something smart and reassuring, but stilled as she leant over her dead husband's body and kissed me on the cheek. 'Everything is converging,' she said. 'If you won't leave, you must be ready.'

'Anwen, I saw something, at the bottom of the lake. Statues. What do they mean?'

Pausing, she ran her fingers over her dead husband's scalp, as innocuously as if she were stroking a cat. She said, 'I had an old friend . . . a pianist who'd been a student of Rachmaninoff. He told me that he was attracted only to music which he considered to be better than it could be performed. And that unless a piece of music presented a problem to him, a never-ending problem, it didn't interest him.'

'And? What has that to do with the statues?'

She regarded me with dismay. 'I don't know about any statues.'

Exasperated, I stood, returned to my seat beside Lewis. In his mouth was a cigarette. He asked me for a light, and I gave it to him, before realising the cigarette was rolled with liquorice paper.

Just then, footsteps from down the hall, and in the doorway, Clara. Her jaw was set, and she kept her eyes away from her mother. Rain clung to her auburn hair, dripped off the tip of her straight nose. Without speaking, she tore through the room and planted herself on a chair by the cabinet of Anwen's violins.

Clara had brought with her a man. He stood in the doorway, stony-faced and lean. His manner was slow, deliberate, and he walked to an armchair at the back of the room, with the same inevitability of the sea eroding the shore. His beard was dark, but streaked with white, and his skin was the colour of linseed oil. I felt like I had seen him about the estate, but could not quite place him, till I saw his hands. They were covered in dried earth, nails black with soil. This was Harris, the groundskeeper. He was tall and had developed an arched back from years of labour, but I suspected he was younger than the beard and bent back would suggest. He sat quietly, apparently unfazed by the corpse at the other end of the room.

Once everyone was settled, I spoke the thought that had been on my mind: 'Did we have to meet here, in this room?' Not only were we disturbing the scene, but it was also macabre. The bloodstains were not yet dry.

Everyone's eyes turned on me, as if to ask who I was. The only one who seemed vaguely sympathetic was Colm, who had sequestered himself into a corner. Until then I'd not noticed him.

Anwen answered, 'I will not let him lie alone.'

And that was all. Anwen would not leave him, and we needed to be with Anwen. The sitting room was where we would stay.

'So,' said Jim from his seat by the window, 'something terrible has happened—'

'Wait,' said Anwen.

'What?'

'Not everyone is here.'

Lewis laughed grimly beside me and took a long drag of the cigarette. I decided to follow his lead, and began to reach into my coat for my own, when there appeared another person at the door.

Her eyes were red-rimmed, her body rigid. She looked straight ahead, the way one is taught to do when speaking in public. Tilly.

Jim stood. 'You're bold to turn up like this, to stand in the same room as him.'

In response, she reached slowly into her cardigan pocket and produced a red lipstick. She applied it slowly and took her seat, as close to Anwen and the body as she could.

Jim pushed his way to the middle of the room. 'Get out,' he said to Tilly. 'I know what you did. I found the mess you made.' He pulled out her manuscript from his satchel. 'I know the conversation he had with you. He told you to destroy it. But you didn't like that, did you?'

'What is this?' said Clara.

Jim spoke with venom. 'Tilly wrote her own end to Malcolm's series. He rejected it. I call that a motive.'

Tilly, staring deliberately ahead, put away her lipstick into an inner pocket and took a deep breath. Still seated, she turned her head towards Jim, who stood incandescent beside her. She met his eye and said with a gentle voice, 'You hide your jealousy poorly.'

He inclined his head. 'Jealousy?'

Tilly smiled. 'I know things about Malcolm's world that you never will. That no one in this room ever will.' Her eyes flicked to mine, before returning to Jim. 'You have always coveted my position.'

'How dare—'

'Malcolm also knew you were jealous, and it's why he didn't destroy my manuscript after you told him to. He valued me.'

'Admit what you did,' Jim whispered.

The room watched as Tilly slowly rose, walked over to Malcolm's body. She crouched so that she was facing Anwen and, after nodding to her, she lowered her face to Malcolm's and kissed his cheek. Then, she returned to Jim, stood directly before him and said, 'I have always been loyal.'

He was speechless for a moment, then looked about the room, found his words: 'Can't you see what she's doing? Look at this, for God's sake!' He tapped the manuscript in his hand.

'He didn't destroy it. He told me he liked it. That was too much for you, wasn't it, Jim?'

'She's a lying parasite.'

Tilly finally broke composure and laughed with a manic energy. 'That makes two of us, then.'

'Where were you this afternoon?'

Anwen's voice cut through the room like a raven's wing. 'Sit down.'

'Am I the only one who wants to know?'

'I'd like to know,' said Clara.

Tilly met Clara's gaze, and sadness came to her eyes. 'I was in the glasshouse, with Colm . . . till he left.'

It was then that I cut in. 'And I saw him return from the glasshouse. It was after the gunshot. I told him to stay in his room till this was resolved.'

The room looked to Colm, who gave a nod of confirmation. He glanced at me afterwards, gratitude in his eyes.

'Everyone, sit.' The voice was Anwen's. It held such quiet ferocity that Jim faltered, cast about, then skulked back to his seat beside the window. He still clutched Tilly's manuscript in his large fist.

We all waited for Anwen to continue. She looked at every single person standing in the room, then set Malcolm's body down gently, stood to her full height, her silver hair pinned back, her pale complexion fierce in the light of the single chandelier. Her hands were steady, held at her sides. She spoke levelly. And as she spoke, I couldn't help but recall the way my sister used to reason with the monsters under her bed. 'My husband,' said Anwen, 'has been killed . . . by someone who was in this house.' She breathed in, exhaled with a shudder. 'I know each of you, here in this room. Malcolm and I cared for every one of you. But here we are . . .' She glanced down to her feet, where the dark shape of her husband's body lay. 'He was not a well man. I knew it the first time I met him: he had grown weary of normality, of things which bring most people joy. I always knew it would end like this. And . . . now it's happened.' She cast her gaze to me. 'As the telephone line is down, we will have to delay contacting the mainland. Until that time, we will deal with this ourselves.'

There was silence in the room. As far as I knew, this was everyone on the estate, and therefore the killer was here.

'Very well,' said Anwen. She gave an almost imperceptible smile. 'I want it to be known that I place my trust in Euan. Until we can contact the police, he is the authority.'

All were stunned, myself included.

With no further justification, Anwen lowered herself down to her husband's body again, rested her hand on his lifeless chest.

I cast about the room, saw everyone glaring at me.

'You're joking,' said Clara. 'He's only just arrived.'

Anwen was quiet, but glanced at me expectantly.

Taking her cue, I rolled up my sleeve and showed them Malcolm's brand. 'He trusted me,' I said. 'Enough to give me this.'

Lewis's eyes were wide, and the blood drained from his face. He pushed his chair away, threw his cigarette on the floor. 'This is absurd. Euan was alone in the house with Father when he died. He has the strongest motive of us all!'

'And what would that be?' I said, rising and facing him.

He stammered for a moment, before finding his fire and spitting, 'You are a failing writer who would do anything for a chance to finish my father's series. And now that he's dead, his books are yours. You have his legacy . . . more than his own children.'

'His books are not mine. In fact, Malcolm never shared his final manuscript with me. He entrusted me to finish his series, but—'

The corner of Lewis's lip curled. 'And now we have the reason: my father changed his mind, would not share his work with you. How galling, to have come all this way only to be rejected.'

'Actually . . .' The voice was Colm's. He had emerged from his corner and was standing, gripping an envelope so hard that his knuckles turned the colour of suet. 'I have in my hands a will.'

The room became deathly silent.

Colm seemed shocked at his sudden command of the proceedings, dabbed at his temples with his sleeve. 'It was left for me to find in my bedroom. It states . . .' He fumbled with the tongue of the envelope, pulling free the paper inside and almost ripping it in the process. '"On the condition that it first be inspected and confirmed to be genuine by Colm Hubert, whom I have requested specifically, due to his background as a counterfeiting solicitor, I bequeath my final manuscript, along with the entire ownership of my *Gravitation* series and its copyright, to Euan Irving."'

'Now hold on,' said Lewis. 'This is ludicrous.'

Then, Clara: 'How do we know this is genuine?'

Colm seemed, for the first time, to have a spine. He turned the will to the room, pointed to the bottom of the page. 'It is signed. And, as Malcolm states, I am well versed in distinguishing forgeries.' He glanced at me, then looked back to the will. 'The bulk of the Malcolm Furnivall estate, along with my assets, both liquid and material, are to be divided equally between my wife, Anwen Furnivall, and my daughter, Clara Furnivall. To my son, Lewis, I bequeath the Ford Prefect, of which he is so fond.'

I couldn't help but laugh, coughing to disguise the outburst.

Lewis shook his head, saying, 'It's a joke. There is no way of confirming whether this is real. Who's to say Euan didn't write it? Perhaps he and Colm are working together, sabotaging this family? Euan had the greatest motive, and the opportunity.'

Then, Clara: 'You were the only person in the house with him, Euan. You can't deny that.'

'No, he wasn't,' Anwen said softly. 'I was asleep in our bedroom. The gunshot woke me and . . .'

Clara spoke again. 'But Euan was the last person with him. We all know that.'

'I came and found you,' I said. 'And there was the pile of my burning books. You think I would do that? Set my own work alight? I saw someone running to the woods, and . . . and someone shot at me when I went looking for Malcolm's writing shed. No, someone has sent a message. They don't want me here.'

Tilly cleared her throat, then spoke with a sickly-sweet voice. 'These are all just words. We know for a fact you were the last person to be with him. And unless anyone can corroborate that you—'

'I can,' said a voice from the back of the room.

We all turned and saw Harris crack his neck and sigh. He grimaced, ran his dirty hands through his unkempt beard and said, while looking at the floor, 'I saw Euan through the window. He was by himself when the pistol fired.'

The knot of panic that had been tightening in my chest

began to loosen. But then I wondered why Harris would say such a thing, when I had looked out the window and seen nothing . . . only the girl in the white gown.

'Aye, he looked right at me,' said Harris. 'I was tidying the weeds under the window. I saw Malcolm leave the room, and Euan was alone. I swear it.'

Harris kept his gaze directed at the ground, and he had a habit of tapping his knee when he talked – a man more at home in the company of plants than people. Still, I caught his eye only briefly and saw something strong, something hidden. I wanted to speak with him, alone.

'You are certain?' said Jim, who had been quiet since his outburst at Tilly.

'My back may be bent, but my sight is keen. Euan was not with Malcolm.'

Lewis slumped into his chair, and Clara ran her finger along her jaw. I gave a small nod to Harris, which he didn't acknowledge.

When we were all again seated, thoughts of the girl in white swarmed me. Had I imagined her, or mistaken Harris's shape in the afternoon gloom? Lewis had denied any knowledge of a girl, and Malcolm had never mentioned one. I thought of the hobby horse in Malcolm's basement, and of Julia.

'Since this seems to be getting us nowhere,' said Jim, 'I volunteer to boat across and fetch the authorities in the morning.'

At that, Tilly let out a rapturous laugh.

'You've a problem?' Jim said.

'Awfully keen to leave, aren't you?' Tilly replied.

'I'm offering to help. The next ferry comes the day after

tomorrow. I have a boat and am more than willing—'

'Is there no one on this island with a working telephone?' I asked.

'No,' said Harris, after a long pause. 'This is an old place. The only other folks are up in the far hills, and they live simply. Malcolm and Jim had telephones, no one else.'

'Well then, someone will have to take a boat in the morning,' I said.

Jim regarded me, and I seemed to pass whichever test he'd performed in his mind. He cleared his throat and said, 'I am willing.'

'But we can't trust anyone at this point,' Clara said. 'And this would be the perfect opportunity to escape.' She inspected her nails, then met Jim's eye.

'We will vote on it,' said Anwen.

There was a murmur of acceptance, before Colm said, 'I will abstain. As solicitor, I think it is important that I remain impartial, so I might act as an arbiter to all parties.'

Anwen said, 'So be it.'

'May I suggest,' said Colm, 'that to keep things unbiased, we reveal our votes at the same time?'

There were nods of approval, and so Colm continued, 'If you agree Jim should leave, hold your thumb up. If you disagree, and think he should remain, hold your thumb down. Now, on the count of three . . .'

I noticed that Lewis was looking at his sister from the corner of his eye. Languidly, she scratched her knee, but I saw that her thumb was turned down. Lewis shifted, looked to the floor.

As Colm began the count, I turned slightly in my seat, so I could observe Harris in the reflection of the violin cabinet.

He knew something I did not, and I wanted to speak with him. So, I decided I would take his side. Did he trust Jim? He watched the old man with those keen eyes, tapping his finger on his knee. He seemed to come to a decision as the finger ceased tapping, and he sank back in his seat. A small smile came to his face. Then, he flicked his gaze to the cabinet and met my eye in the reflection.

I made my choice.

'Two . . . Three . . .'

We held out our thumbs.

Tilly's arm shot out – thumb cast downwards.

Clara and Lewis had voted together, both thumbs pointing down.

My thumb was pointing upwards. I believed I had read trust on Harris's face and, as I turned to see his vote, realised I'd been correct. He, too, had his thumb up.

Jim and Anwen also had their thumbs to the ceiling.

We all cast about, drawing invisible lines between ourselves; those who trusted Jim had won. He would leave for the mainland in the morning.

'You don't know what you've done,' said Tilly, throwing back her chair and storming across to Jim.

The old man was taken aback, and Tilly was quick enough to snatch her manuscript from his lap. He pulled back, and, after a brief struggle, pages flew across the room and Tilly slapped him across the face, before collecting the scattered pages and storming from the room.

Jim made to follow, but I stood and said, 'There's nowhere to go. For her, or anyone else. If just one person goes missing, naturally we'll assume their guilt.'

'But—'

'Let her have her manuscript, Jim,' I said. 'Nothing will come of it.'

Red in the face, Jim turned to Clara and Lewis and gave them the barb that was meant for Tilly. 'You both continue to bring shame on this family.' Then he left, cursing under his breath. In the doorway he said, 'I will be in my home, waiting for first light.'

Harris rose with a grunt. 'And I'll be heading back to my cottage.'

There were no objections. Anwen spoke, seemingly addressing everybody. 'It's decided. Now, leave us.'

We did as she said, bowing our heads as we passed her and Malcolm's body. In the time I took to collect my coat, put it on and pay my respects, Harris had slipped by me. I went to chase after him but stopped in the hallway, beside a cloudy window which looked out across the grounds. I'd had an idea. I stayed there, in the empty hallway, watching through the cloudy glass as Harris's figure disappeared across the grounds towards his cottage.

And then, like the path formed by first footsteps over wild land, a plan began to form. I made for Malcolm's study, and the cabinet of sculptures.

11

IN THE HEARTH, THE fire had sunk and left blistered knuckles of firewood poking from hot ash. I still felt its heat in my arm, throbbing under my shirt and coat. Moving into the study, I began to think of Malcolm's breath, lingering in the air. Like the fire, it would be gone soon, dispersed by the opening of a window, but for now, it was as if he were still here, made starker by proximity to darkness.

Hearing footsteps about the house, I closed the door to Malcolm's study and began to rummage through the deep drawers in his tables and secretaires, in the old dusty boxes which perched on bowed shelves. I did not let myself hope, but instead lost myself in the process of searching for the manuscript. Hope is inaction, I told myself.

When I was certain I'd scoured every part of the study, I moved to the cabinet of sculptures – the one I'd looked to when branding my arm. Each shelf held a world of fantastical creatures, objects and people. The sculptures were enchanting. I remembered how the girl in the gown had watched them . . . if it had been a girl at all.

Just then, I caught movement from outside the window, the same one I'd seen her through. I peered out into the swaying grass. Nothing. I had to entertain the possibility that my mind was playing tricks on me. It was common among men who had returned from war. Still, I would stick to my plan. Gradually, I tore my gaze away from the window and returned my focus to the cabinet.

There was a glass door. I ran my finger along its seam till I came to a little locked catch. I tugged on it once, and the sculptures in the cabinet shook. It was the most peculiar feeling, but I sensed their little eyes watching me, wary and disgruntled.

'It needs a key,' said Clara.

I turned to see her, standing in the doorway. My sense of being watched had been correct.

She remained there, leaning against the doorframe with a bemused look on her face, as if she'd just caught a child in the act of raiding a biscuit tin. 'Don't be embarrassed. You're quite right to be interested.'

'They're yours?'

Clara pushed the door nearly closed and strolled into the study, moving to my side and gazing into the glass. 'I think it was the first time Father ever sat down and played with me. He'd returned from a trip to Japan with a pouch of the things. *Netsuke*. He sat with me, lined them up, explained they had started as button fasteners and developed over time into ornate and delicate sculptures. I've collected them ever since.' She pointed to the top shelf of *netsuke*, at a cat, a frog and a dragon, all with a darker patina than the others. These were the oldest, and I could tell they held many memories. 'Making the mundane into art. Father liked that very much . . . and so do I.'

We shared a moment there in the quiet, the only noise being the rain against the window, and the dying fire.

'Why were you trying to open my collection?' she said.

I looked straight ahead. 'Curiosity.'

Each one of her teeth slowly emerged in a searching smile. 'You will have to do better than that,' she said.

'Well,' I said, thinking quickly, 'if you must know, I wanted a piece of this place.'

'Why?'

I finally risked looking at her. 'Because I have come all this way and it is seeming increasingly likely that I will leave empty-handed.'

Clara gave me a searching look, then appeared to come to some conclusion in her mind. She strode over to the window and perched herself on the ledge. 'You idolised my father.'

Though it wasn't a question, I said, 'Yes.'

'Why?'

'He was a great writer.'

Her lip curled.

'What?'

'You chose to say "writer", rather than "man".'

I hesitated.

Clara spoke while folding her arms. 'The words we choose, and those we omit, reveal a great deal.'

'I'm sorry.'

'Don't be. I happen to agree with your wording.' A darkness crossed her features as she looked to the faint glow of the fire.

'What was he like, as a father?' I asked.

She considered, then said, 'Too lost in his work to pay us any attention, as you would expect.'

I watched her and felt sympathy. I wondered then if she might have answered Malcolm's invitation out of some hope for catharsis – a moment of recognition, apology, comfort. Was it as simple as that? 'Go on,' I said.

She shrugged. 'The only time he would surface from his writing was when I won something. I never enjoyed swimming, you know. I only did it for him. Do you know what it's like to realise, too late, that you've lived your life for someone else?' She became very still and said, 'I am my own person now.'

I noted the conviction in her voice, the defiance and the relief. The word *now* stuck out to me. It was a cliff, jutting out into the chasm of the unsaid. *Now*... And in the silence that followed, the truth: I am my own person, *now he is dead*.

'My father was not content to know you. He possessed you, or discarded you. Often one following the other.'

I shifted on the spot and spoke while looking into the cabinet of *netsuke*. 'He writes regret very well.'

Clara considered, then looked down at her feet. 'I believe he had his share.'

'Yes . . . I think he did.'

She met my eye.

There was something about her look which made me speak candidly. 'I saw myself in his work. There are things I have done . . . or not done.' I faltered, taking a deep breath before continuing. 'I've thought myself useless for quite some time. So, when your father invited me here, I wanted to do my very best, and now he lies dead on the . . . I'm sorry.'

She took a long breath, waiting for me to go on.

'I've made many mistakes . . . When I received his first letter, I could hardly believe it. Surely there were better writers out there? But Malcolm Furnivall knew of me! Malcolm Furnivall, who'd won every literary award, made his name alongside the very best: Christie, Chesterton,

Forster, Woolf. I thought this would be my chance to change. We wrote back and forth for months . . . and I kept every letter.'

'You cared for him.'

'Yes. He, for whatever reason, saw something in me.'

'And what would that be?'

I gave a helpless laugh. 'I don't know. I am a coward, Clara. And . . . I have hurt people because of it.'

Her expression softened, and she said, 'No person is ever one thing.'

I blinked tears from my eyes.

She stayed there, watching me, tilting her head to one side. 'You said you went to my father's writing shed.' Her voice was gentle but sharp, like the blade of a feather. 'Was there anything strange there?'

'Yes, now you mention it. The hobby horse.' Memories of Julia crowded my mind, still – memories of her riding the hobby horse along the shore, her laughter playing over churning seafoam.

Clara raised her chin, said, 'What?'

I realised I'd spoken without thinking, revealed something I'd not intended. Clara had sensed softness and exploited it.

I collected myself and said, 'There were toys . . . in the basement.'

'Yes,' Clara said. 'Must be my old toys . . . I didn't know he'd kept them.'

I thought she looked unsteady, as if this revelation were casting her father in a new light.

'You don't remember the hobby horse?' I asked.

'Now you mention it, I do. It had slipped my mind, but

I think Lewis and I used to chase each other about on it. Was there anything else?'

'Nothing else.'

Seeming troubled, Clara rose from her place by the window and walked to the centre of the room, gazing up at the paintings of baffling perspective. 'Did you kill my father, Euan?'

I almost laughed from the suddenness of the question. 'No.'

'Seems you stood the most to gain.'

'*I* stood the most to gain? What about you? I know you and your brother were struggling for money. It's why you came here when he summoned you, isn't it? You hoped he would discuss his will—'

A look of satisfaction and pity crossed her face.

I realised I had, again, been goaded into revealing what I knew.

'Enough,' she said, with a smile. She narrowed her eyes at me, then walked over and took my hand in hers. She brought my hand up, opened each of my fingers slowly, then reached into her shirt and produced a necklace, on the end of which hung a small silver key. She placed the key into my palm. 'Go on,' she said, 'take one of the *netsuke*.'

Clara took after her father, in that a conversation with her felt like navigating a series of snares. I stood there for a moment, warily. 'You would give one away?'

'It's not free. You will give me something in return.'

When I didn't reply, she said, with a roll of her eyes, 'What we choose, and what we omit . . .'

' . . . reveals a great deal.' I hesitated for a moment, then slowly pushed the key into the cabinet lock and turned it.

As the door swung open, I imagined Clara sitting alone in this expansive house, surrounding herself with these ornate creatures while her mother practised her violin and her father locked himself away to write. They were vessels into which she'd poured her loneliness. She observed me while I let myself become lost in these miniature worlds, just as she once had.

There were bulls with horns like spears and furrowed brows, muscles bulging. There was a heron, balancing on a spindle of a leg, beak raised into the air. There was a reclining woman playing the flute, dress cascading out behind her. Each *netsuke* had its own personality. I took time to examine them all, before settling on the one I'd always intended to take.

I reached into the back of the cabinet, to the side which faced the window, and picked up the sculpture of two otters chasing each other. Compared to most, it was unremarkable: smaller and without any inlay of amber or jade. The ivory bodies were carved into a coil and had been smoothed over time by handling. I ran my thumb over their hides, tracing their circle, feeling the ghost touch of others who had done the same. It was like reading a second-hand book; it held traces of those who had come before. 'This one,' I said, running it over my fingers, feeling its satisfying weight in the palm of my hand.

Clara remained impassive. She held out her hand and I returned the key, which she slipped back into the lock after closing the door. A small click.

'So,' I said, 'what do you make of my choice?'

She faced me, dark green eyes boring into my own. 'That is for me to know, and for you to wonder about.'

'What's the story behind it? When did you—'

'I'm tired, Euan. I'm going to make some supper. Are you hungry?'

'You've grown tired of our game?'

'We were never playing a game.'

I watched her for a moment, cautious. 'No, I'm not hungry,' I said softly.

'Okay.' She turned, pocketed the key and walked to the door. However, just as she was about to leave, she stopped and said, with her back to me, 'I assume that it's started talking to you.'

'What?'

She turned her head, and I saw she was looking out the window, across the grounds. Rain was falling again, now in a thin mist which caught in the wind and danced like starlings. Clara spoke quietly. 'I always pretended I didn't hear it . . .' She caught my eye. 'You remind me of myself.'

I stood beside the cabinet, she at the door, and the space between us seemed to stretch out in the silence. A question formed on my lips: I wanted to ask about what Malcolm had written in his letter. He'd said time was different here; in conversation with itself. What did that mean? But I had already revealed too much to Clara.

As if sensing the question, she said, 'The shadows on the cave wall are comforting to those too scared to turn around and face daylight.'

I bowed my head, took a long breath, then said, 'Thank you, Clara.'

She smirked, glanced one last time to the *netsuke* in my hand, then left the room.

★ ★ ★

For how long I stood there, replaying our conversation, I cannot recall. Who, I wondered, had got the better of whom? Had there been anything I'd missed in the subtleties of Clara's movement, in the tone of her voice? I thought of what she had said, about living one's life for someone else, and wondered if she had been telling the truth. If so, I thought it was very sad. When I looked to the fireplace, I saw the last embers had died out.

I held my hand in my pocket, turning the *netsuke* in my palm. With every turn, I ran over the plan in my mind. It was an experiment to verify my sanity. If all went well, I would have an answer to the question I'd been considering ever since leaving for the war. Ever since I'd abandoned Julia. But this experiment could not be rushed. I would have to choose my moment carefully, or else it all would fall apart. I would keep the *netsuke* close and wait till morning.

Just as I was making to leave, two eyes, which would not have looked out of place on a crow, peered round the door. It was Mrs Gibson. She had remained out of sight for much of that day, but I saw, from her expression, that she knew every detail of the proceedings, having watched from doorways and corners.

I met her eye and beckoned her in.

'Sorry,' she said. 'I thought the room was empty.' She carried a duster, and a crisp white cloth hung from her apron. 'I'll come back—'

'No,' I said, pushing the *netsuke* deeper into my pocket, then gesturing for her to come in.

Keeping her gaze fixed on the floor, she walked a little closer to me, remaining near to the doorway. Her eyes were red, her head frizzy with broken hair, her lips white from being pressed together. She was about to speak, then seemed to consider the words unfit. She began to dust a cabinet, focusing on the same spot, which hadn't looked so dusty in the first place.

'You must hear a great deal, being a housekeeper in a place like this.'

She looked at me sideways, pulled at her ear, then moved about the edge of the room, dusting whatever surface she could manage. 'I was there when you gathered together. But no one thought to ask my opinion, and so I didn't share it.'

I watched her, admiring her well-practised movements, hoping, silently, to convey that I saw her now. We were, after all, cut from the same cloth. Though perhaps she didn't consider it that way. I spoke gently. 'Please, share it now.'

She circled around the edge of the room, stopping, only briefly, to say, 'Everyone here is guilty of something.'

'I'm sure.'

'Please' – she turned to me, and there was panic on her face – 'let me do my job.'

'You are adept at keeping out of sight, aren't you, Mrs Gibson?'

'It's something one learns over the years.'

'If only your servant girl had been as skilful.'

Mrs Gibson looked as if she'd had the wind punched from her. 'You . . . you will have to clarify—'

'The girl who followed Malcolm to his writing

shed . . . Tell me about her.'

She turned her eyes to the ceiling, took a long breath, and said, 'Her name was Daphne. She was a good worker . . . smart, inquisitive.'

I said nothing, waiting for her to continue.

She looked at me, and I could see she was expecting to be interrupted – not accustomed to having the full attention of another directed to her. 'She had worked here for three years, supporting her child and husband who live on the mainland.'

'Her husband?'

'He'd been involved in a factory accident . . . couldn't work. She found herself lost, and came to me looking for a job, so . . .' She was blinking hurriedly, then she turned her back to me and continued her dusting. 'Well, I asked Malcolm if she could work here, under my tutelage . . . He took to her quickly. She'd read his books, you see. She'd always been a reader, voracious—' She stopped herself, cleared her throat.

'She was your daughter.'

She said nothing, only moved about the edge of the room, dusting. 'When he caught her watching him work, he called us all together in the dining room, accused us of conspiring against him. He said he couldn't be certain as to who was guilty and who wasn't, so he fired everyone . . . everyone aside from me.'

'And why do you think that is?'

She hesitated, then tucked her duster under an arm and wiped down the desk with the cloth that had hung from her apron, folding it in half after every few strokes. 'Anwen and I are close,' she said. 'I think she spoke to him.'

She wiped the last section of the desk with a flourish, then made towards the door. She looked back at me.

'Mrs Gibson, where were you when Malcolm was murdered?'

There was an exhausted defiance in her expression, and she held my gaze. It was clear she didn't care what I, or anyone else, thought. She spoke in a muted voice. 'I was with Anwen. She likes me to watch over her when she rests.'

Then she pulled open the door and left, without making a noise.

12

I MOVED THROUGH THE house, turning the *netsuke* in my pocket. I knew that I would find no rest, so I decided to return to my room and change. My shirt and trousers were beginning to develop an offensive atmosphere, which, until then, I'd been too occupied to fix. I hurried back up the stairway, past the stag skull and the alcoves of chessboards. I stopped outside my room, hearing pounding from down the hall.

Deciding I would endure my own stench for a while longer, I waited and listened to the noise. It was a rhythmic thumping, growing in intensity. After the noise reached the peak of its violence, it calmed to a soft bump, like an unlatched window swaying in its frame. I listened, waiting for it to stop, but it didn't.

Keeping to the edge of the hallway, avoiding creaky boards, I moved towards the pounding. It grew even quieter as I neared, but did not stop. I stood very still. Then, a forceful slam, which, I realised, originated from a room just down the hall. I moved towards it, listening from outside. As I approached, a board beneath me gave a gasp. I waited for the pounding to continue, but there was only the faint whisper of wind against windows, of water through pipes, of wood warping in the cool of evening.

It was Colm's room. He'd mentioned he was only just down the hall from me. I knocked on the door, and, before I'd finished, it swung open to reveal Colm, standing in a set of silk Paisley pyjamas.

We regarded each other, waiting for the other to speak.

'You look comfortable,' I said.

He looked beyond me, then poked his head round the doorway and searched the hall. When he returned to my gaze, he smiled uneasily. 'We, as a race, owe much to the humble silkworm.'

I noticed there was a red mark on the side of his head. 'That looks sore.'

He put his hand to where I was looking, then turned slightly from me. 'Ah, it's nothing,' he said. 'I must have collected it when we had our little mêlée.' He made a meaty clack, which I assumed was laughter.

I was just about to ask about the banging, when he cut in: 'I think it's probably best if I wait all of this out in my room. I'm sure I've lost some popularity after reading Malcolm's will.'

'Thank you for that. You came to my rescue, Colm.'

He stretched his back, and his stomach swayed from beneath his elegant silk shirt. 'As you did for me.' He scratched his midriff. 'I am glad I shared my story with you on the boat. You remember what I said about honesty? I was right to put my trust in you.'

'A peculiar partnership,' I said.

'But a partnership, nonetheless.' He grinned widely and clapped me on the shoulder.

I rubbed the bridge of my nose, a wave of anxious exhaustion washing over me.

'I have a spare pair,' he said, pulling at his silk pyjamas. 'If rest is evading you—'

'It's all right, Colm.'

He watched me for a moment, before saying in a hushed voice, 'There were many people he left out of his will . . . What if someone knew they'd been excluded and . . . reacted, before he could formally—'

'They reacted too late.'

'Did they? If he'd read the will himself, it would have been unequivocal.'

'We have his signature.'

'And I pray that will be enough.'

'Surely it is. You're a solicitor, you must—'

'Yes,' Colm said. 'I will do all I can.' He softened, leaned into me. 'It seems you have found your fortune.'

'Found it, is precisely what I *haven't* done. I've no idea where he's hidden the manuscript, or if it exists at all.'

Colm's gaze intensified. 'When you find it – and you will find it – I will be right here. I will confirm it is genuine and, as the will's executor, record what has happened, to save any . . . confusion.'

I looked down the hall. Again, I had the feeling we were being watched, though I could see no one there. This unease persisted; we had drawn lines between us, and Colm and I had fallen together onto the same side. We would have to be careful now. More careful than before.

'Euan?' he said. 'Malcolm knew that, through the law, I could keep you safe. It is why he invited me, I understand now . . . You must bring it to me.'

'I will.'

'This door shall remain locked, and I will only open it to

you, or the police, when they arrive. We have targets on our backs.'

He was right. It was not long ago that I'd avoided being shot, and there was no telling who had done it. A part of me wanted to lock myself away, too, but then, I couldn't risk the manuscript falling into the hands of another. It was mine. I thought of the letter in my coat pocket, of Malcolm's challenge.

'Euan,' Colm said, 'is there anything else? Anything Malcolm might have said to you, anything you might have heard, or seen, that could help us?'

I looked to him. It would be useful to have another person know about the letter: someone impartial. Colm seemed a better choice than Anwen or Jim. Still, it would be a risk. True, we had become allies, though there was still much I didn't know about Colm. He was not a danger to me, but I didn't know yet if I could trust him. And Malcolm's offer had been to me, and me alone. Even in death, he held sway over me; I was inside his puzzle box, and if I were to deviate from the method, try to force it open, it would lock in a savage rictus, never to be opened. I said nothing of the letter.

'Very well,' Colm said. 'What will you do now?'

'The telephone,' I said.

Colm considered, then nodded. 'Well, remember, I will be here if you need me.' As I made to go, he said, 'Be careful.'

'Thank you, Colm.' I remained, for a moment, in the dark hallway, looking at him. I decided not to waste a moment on changing, after all. There was much to be done.

He reached out, began to close his door, paused when I

spoke. 'I would close that window.'

He looked at me through the crack.

'The thudding doesn't bother you?'

He cast his eyes behind me again, searching the hallway. 'I'll close it,' he said. 'Good night.'

I wanted to check the telephone because whoever had killed Malcolm had disabled any contact with the mainland, at both this house and Jim's. I thought they might have left a trace. I headed to the little room in the rear of the house which held the telephone, vaguely recalling the way from previous visits when I'd passed it on my way to the glasshouse. By now, darkness had swallowed the island, and the only light came from the weak wall lamps and the waning fires. It made navigating the house even more troublesome, and I briefly became entangled in the knotted corridors and stairways. I heard Clara and Lewis's voices echoing. And there was music, too – a record player turning. I imagined them together, bound by the tragedy and strangeness of the moment. And here I was, alone. Whoever shot at me out in the woods might still be following me. I became paranoid, seeing shapes in the corners of my vision. Fear roved freely through my body, and it was that, along with my curiosity, which pushed me towards the voices of the Furnivall children. I was seeking comfort in the presence of others, but I was also wanted answers, hoped that I might overhear something private, something that might paint a clearer picture of this family. The telephone room could wait.

The voices and the music drew me through to the study. I held close to the bannister as I approached from the first-floor gallery. Halfway down the stair, I heard Lewis excuse himself, saw him leave the room with an empty decanter. He walked across the hall, moving beneath the stairway and down along the ground-floor corridor.

I was quiet for a moment, listening to his footsteps fade away. Then, I crept down the last of the stairs and moved to the door to the study, pausing by the doorframe. I thought Clara was alone, but I heard another voice as I approached. There, in the room with her, was Anwen, speaking softly. '. . . were always inseparable. I think it's our fault for making you grow up here, so far from other children.'

Footsteps, and the sound of a glass being set down.

'Was it terribly lonely?' Anwen said.

'It was a long time ago,' Clara answered.

The record that had been playing stopped, and there was quiet.

'I thought I could be your friend. Perhaps that's where I went wrong; I was a friend first, a mother second.'

'You did your best.'

Anwen paused. 'Even now, you're so mature . . . My doing again, I expect. I never allowed you to be a child. I wanted a friend as well, you see. I was lonely, too.'

Clara scoffed.

'What?' said Anwen.

'It doesn't matter.'

'If you say so.'

Clara paused, then said quickly, 'You didn't have to follow him here. You could have . . .' Her voice lost conviction. 'You could have left.'

Then, Anwen's solemn voice. 'Impossible.'

'Were you afraid of him?'

'I loved him.'

'So did I.'

'But?'

Clara made a frustrated noise, and I heard her pace the room.

'It's been hard for you,' said Anwen.

The pacing grew louder, and I realised how close she was to the door.

Anwen spoke again. 'With everything that happened . . . I'm sorry the swimming career didn't quite pan out.'

Clara stopped. 'The swimming? You're sorry about the swimming?'

'No, I just—' Anwen's voice caught. 'It was all so unfortunate.'

'It was. But it's over now. It's done.'

I heard Clara sniff, then Anwen's light footsteps. I imagined her walking to her daughter, holding her. Their next words were muffled, and so I moved into the doorway, almost peering round the door.

'I don't blame you, Clara. I think, of everyone, you have suffered most.'

The silence that followed was choking. They were right by the door.

'What are you asking? You want me to forgive you, Mother?'

'No,' she said. 'I wouldn't ask that.'

'Well then, shall I apologise?'

'Please, Clara. I'm old. I just . . . There are things I wanted to say before my expiration date.'

Clara went on: 'I have hurt you, and you have hurt

me. Forget apologies. That's the contract you sign with someone you love.'

'That's just it,' said Anwen. 'The very thing I regret teaching you most.'

There was sniffing. A soft sigh of exhaustion. 'Let's not be silly,' said Clara.

A long quiet. I held my breath.

'The music stopped,' said Clara, and I heard her move across the room, change the record: Vera Lynn's voice, singing 'We'll Meet Again'.

'It's not too late for you to start afresh,' said Anwen. 'When this is all done, at least you have that.'

There was the sound of Lewis returning, moving quickly down the hall.

I wanted to remain there by the door, listening to what they might say in their last moments of privacy, but I tore myself away, moved across the hall, circling round the stairway so that I was hidden from Lewis, returning with a full decanter. I held there, nerves sparking, trying to understand fully what I'd heard: a private moment between mother and daughter. I realised how little I knew of the Furnivalls. I'd spoken with Malcolm about literature, science, art and music, but the topic of his family arose rarely. In Anwen and Clara's conversation, there was something vivid and painful. Something supressed, even now. The Furnivalls were a family of brilliance, capable of debating great theories over dinner, but incapable of discussing the intimate. These little potent matters were, to them, inconsequential. I felt that what I'd heard was two people bearing their plentiful little wounds to each other, understanding, towards the end, their import.

I left them there, moved away from the voices and music, and went towards the rear of the house, and the room where Malcolm kept his telephone.

13

WHEN I REACHED THE door to the little room, I saw it was ajar. It hung on its hinges like a loose tooth, popping and grinding as I pulled it open and stepped inside. Switching on the desk lamp, I waited for my eyes to adjust to the dim light. As I stood there, I began to ruminate on the peculiarity of this situation. Whoever had killed Malcolm was here, but no one had the authority to keep us together, nor to take charge of the situation. Anwen had given me control until the police arrived, but that meant nothing in the eyes of the others. Harris had returned to his cottage; Jim had gone back home to prepare for his morning departure. It was chaotic. But it was the game Malcolm had left me, and I was certain he'd have revelled in it.

Now the vague shapes in the room had gained form, and I saw immediately the black, rotary telephone. The paint around the receiver was worn, from where Malcolm rested it against his ear. The dial was flecked with spots of rust. I picked up the receiver, held it to my ear, heard nothing. The handset cord and the wire were intact, so whoever had disabled the phones must have cut the key telephone line to the mainland.

I lowered the receiver from my ear, filling the silence with aimless muttering as I tried to determine when this might have happened.

I found it hard to direct my thoughts, and instead became lost in my head: I was going about this all wrong; perhaps Jim had been right, and I was a target for torment. What if I was everything this family despised – another intrusive fan, obsessed with Malcolm's writing? What if they were all conspiring together, and they were there, in the far corner of the house, mocking me? Someone here had burned my books, after all. I had tried, in my work, to speak with my own voice, but it was undeniable; Malcolm's books had influenced my own a great deal. In many ways, I would always be an imitator. I felt foolish, standing there in that empty room, looking at the dead telephone. There I was, inhabiting this dead man's house, playing detective, like I had any idea what that entailed.

I noticed the walls were papered with scraps of pages. I could imagine Malcolm sitting here, speaking on his phone, leafing through old books, ripping out passages and plastering them to the wall. For a time, I looked at the pages, wondering why each one had piqued his interest. I thought they might perhaps have been inspirations for moments in his own novels, or perhaps for the cryptic crosswords he'd discuss with Jim. Names and phrases were written in sequence: Laplace, Leibniz, Sacrobosco and Lorenz. I skimmed over the scratchings until I noticed a particular passage, spoke it aloud: "'Time present and time past / Are both perhaps present in time future / And time future contained in time past.'" The words were T.S. Eliot's, a poet I admired greatly, and these were the opening lines of 'Burnt Norton'. I knew that Malcolm had counted Eliot as a friend, and had likely shared his thoughts on time and reality; the questions he interrogated in his own novels.

Seeing those words, there in that room, after what had happened, made me perceive them in an entirely new way. I was reminded of Malcolm's novel, *Man Follows Only Phantoms*, which takes place on an island that is a warren of mazes and passages. A man follows a passage and finds, at its end, the voice of the universe. The man bargains with the voice for the gift of infinite knowledge, unbounded by time and space. The universe grants his wish, frees him from the forward motion of time, connects him to every moment and possibility. But after seeing the web of infinite choice, he chooses to return to his home, sit in a dark room, speaking to a disconnected telephone. When they listen at his door, they hear him speak a particular name, over and over. It is the name, he insists, of his little brother. Though, he'd never had a little brother. Yet, when his mother comes and listens at the door, she reveals that long ago, she miscarried . . . and had intended to give the child that exact name.

In the faint light of the desk lamp, I pulled the leather chair away from the desk, lowered myself into it, and imagined Malcolm sitting in this very place, devising that story. I cast my eyes over the myriad of pages that had been stuck to the wall, and the pile of books which lay on the desk, pushed into a corner. Dust motes hung in the air, slowly descending, catching the tawny lamplight. I laid my hand across the warmth in my arm, where the new brand throbbed, and waited for an idea to come to me. Malcolm had chosen me. I had to remember that.

I heard the telephone click.

Breath catching in my throat, I looked down to the receiver, held my hand over it, ready to pick it up. I waited there, amid the falling dust motes, till I calmed. There was no way it could function. The noise must have been a board creaking somewhere in the house. Red-faced, I removed myself from Malcolm's chair and stood in the centre of the dingy room, eyes locked on the telephone. After hearing nothing for a minute, I realised I had been tapping my fingers together the way Julia had taught me.

I stormed from the telephone room, shutting the door behind me. My mind was playing tricks on me, exhaustion and paranoia causing me to hear things that were not there. They were not there. For every question there is an answer, and just because something is unknown, does not mean that it cannot be known. It only requires someone to face the darkness, open themselves to change. And there is no change without, first, destruction. I wonder, now, if I realised how far down the path of change I had already come; if I realised how much of myself I had destroyed in pursuit of greatness.

I stayed there, back pressed to the door, trying to focus my thoughts. I needed a cigarette to calm my nerves. I opened my coat, but just then saw a shape moving at the end of the corridor: a white shape.

The urge to call out after them was strong, but I held back, unsure of who I could trust to help. If others heard my voice, they could interfere. And worse, if there was no one there, and I was imagining the shape, I would be labelled insane, and they would surely use that as justification to destroy my claim on Malcolm's final manuscript.

Silently, I chased them down the corridor, then paused, imagining a person on the other side of the door, listening to me in the telephone room. Had they seen me sitting in Malcolm's chair, putting myself in his place? How small I must have looked . . .

I went on, glimpsing them only partly as they rounded turns and ascended stairways. We had entered the western side of the house, where long stained-glass windows cast bottle-green light over corridors lined with houseplants: *Monstera*, *Dracaena*, spider plants. We had come up through a back way, through the section of the house where the smaller quarters were tucked away, and, as I went on, chasing a figure which I was now certain I'd lost, I realised I was returning to my bedroom. Just a little way down the corridor, I could see my door hanging open, and there, beyond it, a person. They were making no attempt to get away. They were just standing there, staring at me as I approached them.

'Who's there?' I called out.

The figure stepped forward out of the murky green light, and I saw Tilly's face pulled into a sardonic scowl. Had she been the person at the door of the telephone room? She wasn't wearing white. But then, my eyes could have been mistaken, caused me to see what I wanted to see.

I moved down the hallway of stained glass and tumbling foliage, of jaunty paintings and creaking wooden floors. I stood at my open door, facing Tilly.

'I found it like that,' she said, gesturing to the room.

Whereas my chest was pounding, sweat running down my brow, she didn't seem out of breath at all, and there was no indication she'd just run through the house.

'You don't look well,' she said, with a faint smile.

I pushed past her and went into my room, saw my things strewn about the place. Clothes, valuables and the notebooks in which I was drafting various new projects. They had all been examined and tossed away.

'Seems someone thought you had the manuscript,' Tilly said from behind me.

I wheeled about. 'Was that someone you?'

'Oh, please. You think I would stay here and wait for you to turn up, after having ransacked your room? And in any case, I know you don't have Malcolm's manuscript because he did not intend for you to have it.'

'You heard, he left it to me in the will.'

She skewered me with a look.

'What?'

'That will was neither clever, nor bitter enough, to be Malcolm's.'

'You're saying it was forged?'

She laughed, like I'd been deliberately obtuse. 'I'll save you the bother of interrogating me, and tell you that I was coming to find you. I wanted to ask you a question.' She followed me inside my room and, with her foot, swung the door closed behind her.

'What question?' I said, standing in the mess of my personal effects. I couldn't conceal the tremble in my voice, and my eyes were twitching with fatigue. Everything that had happened that day coagulated somewhere in my throat. Voice thick, I said, 'What do you want?'

Tilly moved towards me as I backed up and sat on the bed, head bowed, hand in my pocket, gripping the *netsuke*. 'I understand,' said Tilly. 'You're an outsider here; no matter what you do, that's all you are. It was Malcolm who bound you to this place, and now that he's gone, you're nothing. This family will devour you, as is their habit.'

'Their habit?'

'Oh yes,' she said, reaching down, picking up one of my

notebooks, wrinkling her nose, as if she were holding a rancid fish. 'I thought you would have done your research . . . There have been people like you before. People that Malcolm has brought into his confidence: artists whose names you will never know. There is something about this place, about this family, which sent many of them into madness.' She held out my notebook, dropped it in my lap.

'And I suppose you're special.' I said, putting the notebook to one side.

She laughed. 'Of course.'

'It is quite something, to get that close to Malcolm. He must have told you many things.' I tried to play to her perception of herself, hoping she might drop her guard.

'He did,' said Tilly. She cocked her head. 'What?'

'Nothing,' I said. 'It's just . . .'

'Go on.'

'I'm curious about Harris.' And I was. He'd defended me in the meeting, and I still didn't know why.

She gave me a condescending look, then said, 'There's a reason Harris trusts Jim. They're working in concert. You see, Harris believes this to be his land.'

'Is it?'

She bristled. 'Whose house are you sitting in, right now? No, Harris may have lived here longer, but Malcolm made this place what it is. He brought in diesel generators, built better houses in the hills for the locals. Harris is from the oldest family on the island, and Malcolm allowed him to work on this estate out of kindness.'

'I see.'

'Do you?'

There was a pause as we regarded each other. She moved

slowly around me, taking a seat on the bed. She spoke with a saccharine voice, in my ear. 'What Malcolm and I felt for each other was genuine. I know you are searching for secrets here, but I will hold what he's given me till I die.'

'I don't doubt it.' Why did she remain there on the bed beside me? What was the question she intended to ask? 'Tilly,' I said, 'what did you think when he chose me over you?'

She sighed. 'If that was an attempt to goad me into something, then you will have to try harder.'

'I'd like your opinion.'

Tilly grimaced. 'Nothing is ever chosen. There is a universal script we all follow, and some can read it . . . Malcolm was one of those people. He wanted me to continue his legacy, I'm certain, but he's given me this test. A test of my faith. He did not intend for you to have it, not in the end.' She spoke with such conviction that it was hard not to be carried along.

'He did talk to me about you,' I lied.

She went quiet, and I saw something in her eyes harden.

'He said you were kind, smart, beautiful . . .'

Her vivid blue eyes traced their way down me, as if searching for a threat. She reached back and adjusted the tension of her bun, the skin of her forehead pulling taut.

'He said that if I were to give my loyalty to anyone, it should be to you.'

Tilly looked shocked for just a second, before her mask of nonchalance returned. 'Of course he did.' Then, after a little pause, she said, 'What else did he say?'

'He said you were the key.'

I looked down at my wrist, saw her fingers were toying

with the fabric of my sleeve. Slowly, she began to guide my coat off my shoulders. When it lay on the bed, I let her slowly unbutton my cuff and roll up my sleeve. There, on my arm was the red welt in the shape of the omphalos. She gazed at it.

I wondered if my flattery had got through to her, and if she would reveal something about Malcolm's death – perhaps a promise he'd made to her, a secret enemy, or even a hint at her own involvement.

She touched her fingertip to the tender skin near the burn. She whispered, 'Did it hurt?'

I watched her face, trying to discern the faint undercurrents of expression there. 'Yes.'

She cradled my arm and, without looking up from the mark, began to blow cool air across my skin.

Suddenly I wanted to melt away, to be comforted.

Between breaths, she spoke. 'His mark was obscured by another scar. A burn. Did he ever tell you how that happened?'

'No.'

'I asked him once, and he fell quiet. Then he said it was from someone he loved.'

I stayed still, closed my eyes as her cool breath soothed the burn. I felt her fingers weave in my hair, and I let her guide my head to her shoulder, let her pull me closer, lay her lips against the mark. After her kiss, she said, 'I came here to ask if you loved him.'

I pulled away briefly, stilled.

She was earnest, large watery eyes turned down to my arm.

I thought of the first letter I'd received from Malcolm, of

his kind words written in a spidery hand. I thought of my life as a boy, escaping into Malcolm's *Gravitation* books while Julia cried in the next room. Malcolm had always been with me. So, when Tilly asked if I loved him, all mental games fell away and I responded truthfully: 'I did.'

Her eyes met mine. 'I thought so.'

I winced, and she gripped my arm tightly, brushing her lips along the ridges of burnt skin.

So close now, I could smell her sweat, her faint perfume, and something else I couldn't quite place. A solvent smell. She moved her mouth to my ear. 'What if we left, you and I, joined Jim tomorrow morning? What you and I could create together . . . we could preserve a part of him. He chose us.'

I considered her offer. If I left now, I would be abandoning the manuscript, forsaking my promise to Malcolm. Still, he had already named me his successor. I wondered if that would be enough – if others would believe it without the physical evidence of his final manuscript. If so, I could allow it to be lost and, instead, make my own way, with Tilly's support. But in doing so, I would lose the chance to read his final written words. Haltingly I spoke. 'I have to stay.'

She sank back, ran her thumb along her lip to keep sharp the line of lipstick. 'He told me, the day before you came . . . he said it would all end. He said they would turn.'

'Who would turn?'

She held me, fast. Was it fear I heard in her voice? 'Leave with me.'

The prospect was tempting. There was still a way out. The Furnivall family was changing; I was not as welcome as I once was. Though it hurt to realise, Tilly was right. Our love of Malcolm had kept us safe, but now he was gone, and we were alone, anchored to a dead man. It was as if we were the lovers of a now dead king. Could his family turn on us? I realised I already knew the answer. Fervently, I spoke, to convince myself as well as Tilly. 'I must find the manuscript.'

She gazed at the omphalos, eyes still watery. 'Will you share it with me, if you do find it? We deserve it. Both of us.'

I pulled away, and there was something animal in her movements as she stood and pushed me back on the bed, kissing my branded arm over and over.

I yelped in pain as she threw off her cardigan, unbuttoned her dress.

She didn't seem to hear me, continuing to kiss up my arm, across my shoulder and then my neck, her eyes returning, always, to the mark. She pulled at my sweat-stained cotton dress shirt, ripping through to the undershirt beneath.

Something came over me. I held the back of her neck, felt the sinews in her body twine and stretch as she pressed her hips into mine. I pulled the shoulders of her dress down about her waist and kissed her chest, pressing my face against her. She, too, buried her face in my hair, wrapped her arms about me. We were finding comfort in each other's bodies, strangers mooring to each other in that tumult. I fumbled with the back of her girdle, till she, smiling, guided my hands to unfasten it.

She reached down to where our hips touched, undid my belt, felt me hardening and, in a swift motion, slipped herself about me. She grasped my arm, still cupping her neck, held it in place and watched the omphalos as she circled her hips.

I think, at the time, I knew what was happening, but

allowed it to happen, not just because of the visceral comfort of another body, but because a part of me wanted to be Malcolm. Looking again at that moment, Tilly and I occupied that fantasy together. A carnal act of worship.

When it was done, she unhooked her arms from about me, dismounted and sat there on the bed's edge, hunched over, face in her hands. 'There is some part of me,' she said, 'that expects him to appear through that door right now. He'd tell us how he bested death, and then laugh at how desperate we'd all become.'

'He may yet.' I spoke with the quiet helplessness of someone confronted with a problem too great to solve. The only thread through the labyrinth was the *netsuke* in my pocket. But even that seemed absurd now. I sat there, thinking.

The silence grew about us like a creeper, bearing a slow fruit of revelation.

Tilly spoke. 'My family were too poor to care for me, and the people who took me in were not good people. When I was old enough to hurt them, I did. I ran, hid in railway stations, clinging to the first *Gravitation* book. I realised the map of his fictional land corresponded with the map of ours. And his imagined city, with tiered and winding alleys, resembled Edinburgh. As soon as I arrived, I went to the National Library, and asked to speak to Malcolm Furnivall. Desperate logic . . .' She laughed. 'They took me to a back room, told me they would find my home, and, just as I thought it was all lost, and my past would be uncovered, Malcolm came through the door and took me away.'

I realised then the reason behind Tilly's love for Malcolm, her dogged defence of his work, and all he possessed. I collected myself, adjusting my clothes, rolling down my sleeve to cover the mark. 'Quite a coincidence,' I said.

She stared at me, grave and fervent. 'It was written that we would meet. He told me that. He said it was written.'

I bowed my head, feeling the lethargy in my bones. I wanted to wrap myself in my sheets and escape into sleep. There was the briefest impulse to ask Tilly to remain here, for the warmth of another being in my bed, but before I had made up my mind, she'd risen and moved to the end of the bed, gesturally tidying a few of my discarded things. Our shared fantasy was over. 'Find me tomorrow, if you change your mind about leaving,' she said. 'We could do so much together.'

When she was at the door, I said, 'Did you ever do that . . . with him?'

She pulled her bun tauter, sniffed, smoothed her dress. She opened her mouth to answer, then changed her mind and stalked over to me, leaning so that her mouth was to my ear. 'Try to get some sleep.'

She turned and, as she left, the fabric of her dress span, leaving behind the last traces of her scent. It hit me, then: the obscure smell which lingered beneath her sweat and perfume was petrol.

As the door clicked shut, I sat alone, imagining Tilly standing over my burning books, smoke rising about her.

14

I LAY BACK ON the bed and, in the phantom theatre of my mind, saw Tilly arguing with Malcolm, plunging a knife into his neck while he grappled with his pistol, firing and missing. I saw her running out the house, setting alight my books to send a message, then retreating into the trees. How quickly love transforms into hatred. We feel that those we love are a part of ourselves and, if they don't act as we expect, we refuse them with our entire being, like a rejected transplant.

What could I do? Tilly had left, and the only evidence I had was the smell of petrol. How could I present that to the family? Would they believe that Tilly could harm the person she'd loved most? I was not even certain I believed it. I left the bed and moved across the bedroom to the bathroom. My bones felt like glass, and I needed to straighten my thoughts before taking any action. I went to the shallow, claw-footed tub and began to draw a bath. The water came out in sputtering hot belches. I placed my hand into the rising water, felt pins and needles as the blood coursed back into my chilled fingers. It was only then that I realised how deeply the cold had wormed itself into my body. I closed my eyes. My head was pounding. I'd lost some hope of finding the manuscript, having searched the obvious places without success.

I needed to do something to escape these thoughts, so I returned to the bedroom, unzipped a pocket in my valise and took from it the first *Gravitation* novel: *The Limits of Your Longing*. I always travelled with it. Bringing it with me to the bathroom, I set it on the sink while I removed my clothes, toed the scalding water. Slowly, I stepped in, sat down, lifted the book from the sink and opened to the first page.

It is set on a city island, where cartography is a crime. The Czar tells his subjects that their island's edge is sacred and can never be found. The land is flat and vast, seemingly infinite, yet still, some believe the edge can be discovered. One day a young cartographer sets out from the centre of his district, with the intention of mapping the city, finding the island's edge. He walks and walks for many years, hiding from the law, mapping the towers and the gardens, the splendour and decay, till, eventually, he comes to a place: a wall, built of the same unique stone which is mined solely in his home district. And there, by the long-abandoned gate, waiting to meet him, is a cartographer from the other side, who has made the same journey. They compare maps, see that what they have drawn is exactly the same. They have come by the same way, discovered the same wall, made from the familiar stone mined in their district. The novel ends before they make the decision to continue, or turn back.

Sinking deeper into the hot water, I kept my branded arm on the cool edge of the tub, and flicked through the book. Though I could hardly focus enough to read, to skim through the familiar words was a comfort. They brought me back into the world, gave me respite from my thoughts.

Towelling off, changing into my nightclothes, hanging

up my coat on the door. I checked the pocket to make sure the *netsuke* was still there after my encounter with Tilly. I felt its shape and sighed with relief. Then, I reached into the inner pocket for one cigarette before bed. I pulled out my cigarette case, flicked it open, lit a cigarette and began to smoke. I closed the case, slipped it back into the inner pocket, then paused as I was about to walk away.

I began to laugh. Sucking on the cigarette, I returned to my coat, drove my hand deep into the inner pocket, and realised the feeling I'd had was correct. Malcolm's letter was missing.

I stood there, smoking. Then, when I had sucked it down to the filter, I went to my bed, collected my notebooks and, in a rage, slung them at the opposite wall, one after another. I remembered Tilly's hands, pulling at my clothes, feeling their way over my body. How could I have been so stupid?

There was no way I could retrieve it this evening; exhaustion overwhelmed me. I didn't even want to consider the kind of damage Tilly could wreak with Malcolm's letter. Would she share it, or keep it to herself? I imagined the latter, and this gave me a modicum of respite. I sank into my bed, switched off the bedside lamp and pulled the blankets up about my neck, utterly defeated. Sleep. I needed sleep. As I drifted off, I tried to recall the words Malcolm had written, always returning to the postscript and those peculiar words: *To arrive at being all, desire to be nothing.*

Sleep was stunted and harassed by dreams. The kind of sleep which drains more energy than it returns. I was a boy again, following my father about his tailoring shop, watching him pin, pinch and preen the fabrics, passing silent judgement on the garments. He leant down to me, so that I could see the red pores in his nose, count the white whiskers above his lip. 'Your mother used to make the displays,' he said. 'She had the eye for it . . . Something neither you nor I possess. People like her are rare – with an ability to impress their own beauty onto the world about them. Your mother had it, before she passed. And now your sister has it. You and I, Euan, we are draughtsmen; they are artists.'

The tailoring studio broke into a kaleidoscope of images, and in each was Julia's face the first time she found me and asked for help. 'He makes me wear mother's dress.'

A moment of waking, turning, sweaty sheets glued to me.

Malcolm's voice, calling to me from across a great distance. Imploring me. There was something of vital importance, just out of sight. He was begging me to face it, to recognise the truth in its snarled and grim totality. If only I could make out his words, trammelled by distance. The words of a drowning man.

Then, water. I was suspended in the lake, breathing the cold and dark. Eyes of quartz blinked away a rime of lichen. The stone men beneath the water circled me. Their bodies were unscarred, no pockmarks or fractures. The water was vivid with the light of the full moon, and, as I pushed to the surface, I saw men and women gathered about the lake. The sky was filled with stars I didn't recognise, from a lost time. A throat was slit, a body given to the water. The quartz eyes glowed, and the moon turned its face to this place.

I awoke in a cold sweat. As the dreams burrowed back down into the murk of my subconscious, I grasped for their luminous tails, trying to catch one and keep it with me. I wanted to dissect it, peel back its flesh and examine the miasma of thought which had given it form.

I pushed the sweaty blankets away and sat with my head in my hands on the side of the bed. Picking my wristwatch up from the bedside table, I saw it was just past four in the morning. There would be no more sleep for me that night. Standing, I dressed, and decided to leave my room. Walking the house in the dark was like seeing the structure's nervous system, marred here and there with the glow of wood rot. The thick green leaves of the houseplants gave off a dim vegetable gleam, which, like little waypoints, guided me along the corridors. I felt like a child again, weaving past monsters in the dark, seeking comfort.

When, in my life, had I determined that the monsters were not real? That dreams were illusions, that spells could not be cast, and that this earth was wrought of solely solid things? It had happened at a young age. I saw every event as a logical sequence. Action unfurled to consequence, so on and so forth. To see the world in that way makes one strong, makes one capable of witnessing horror, of participating in it, without fear. Action. Consequence. Nothing more. Horror is necessary, I have found, for the world to function.

But there, creeping down the stairway of Malcolm's house, I felt what I had been feeling ever since arriving at the estate: a sense of gathering. It was like the demonstration of relativity, when a bowling ball is set in the centre of a tensioned sheet, it draws the surrounding marbles to it. As darkness pressed in around me, and I felt my way down to the sitting room, I touched my fingers together and spoke the word 'safe', letter by letter.

I was at the door to the sitting room, peering through the crack. There, on a wide chair, beside the swaddled corpse of her husband, was Anwen. Her mouth was moving, as if intoning a silent prayer. Her eyes were closed. To me, she looked like a priestess guiding an ancient king to his place in the afterlife.

I walked into the sitting room and stood before her.

Her eyelids fluttered open.

I stood there, fists tight, gaze averted. The room was cold from the breeze that floated through the broken window. The heavy velvet curtains were pulled to, but they could not keep out the chill.

Anwen watched me with an impassive face, and then, as if determining the true reason for my interruption, she smiled and went back to whispering to Malcolm.

I stood there, still. There was a weakness in me, which, in that moment, was threatening to consume everything that I was. My past was returning. I couldn't be alone.

Head bowed, I walked over to Anwen and slowly lowered myself to the floor, sitting in the space between her and Malcolm.

Anwen made no comment, accepting me there as if it was right where I belonged. I was sitting between my parents, seeking comfort from troubled dreams. Anwen reached down and smoothed my hair. She said gently, 'Rest with us.'

I laid my head on her knee. I think she saw, in that moment, the conflict within me, between reason and strangeness. She saw the will of the island, the pull of Malcolm's world, the tumult of the day past. She saw why I had come to her, even if I did not at the time.

'Thank you,' I said.

She stayed silent.

I glimpsed again the glistening body of my dream.

I saw the tailor's shop, smelt the pungent perfume my father would spray, felt my sister's hand clutching mine. The words came to me unbidden: 'There was someone I cared about. Who relied on me. But I abandoned her, because that . . . that was easier than the choice I had to make to save her. And when I came back, it was too late . . .'

Anwen's body tensed slightly, and her hand stilled in my hair.

'But I'm seeing her again.' Head still on Anwen's leg, I gazed across the room into the cabinet of violins. 'A long time ago, I closed a part of myself. A part of myself, which, whether I like it or not, has begun to open.'

'What part was that?'

I tried to formulate the right term but couldn't. Instead, I said, 'Recently everything is charged with meaning. I feel the world wants to tell me something, send messages through patterns and signals. But at the same time, I can't translate these signals into words.'

Then, Anwen's voice tender and searching: 'It is for that very reason they are crucial.'

I gazed at the violins, considering each of her words, turning them like little ornate stones in my palm.

She went on: 'I think of Heloise and Abelard. Two of the great medieval minds find each other and fall in love. And, for all their brilliance of thought, what we best remember is their love story. A story they wrote together. You know it?'

'Yes, I do. Brought to a violent end by Heloise's cruel uncle.'

'And you know Abelard's final words?'

I knew them well; they had stayed with me ever since I'd first encountered the story during the few terms I'd spent at Oxford, before being called to war. I spoke them with quiet reverence. "'I don't know.'"

'Yes. A man who had dedicated his life to the pursuit of knowledge, and his final words: "I don't know."' She smiled. 'The last step of reason: realising the infinite number of things beyond it. There's a deeper language . . . It links our internal lives with the general way of all things. It's a language spoken by the world. Perhaps you closed yourself to it because you didn't like what it told you.'

Her meaning washed over me until, suddenly, it crashed against a wall and fell into stillness. To surrender myself to these ideas of symbols and magic would help no one. I was here to solve a problem, and every problem has a concrete solution. I raised my head from Anwen's thigh and tried to calm the discord of my thoughts.

'What do you say to him?' I asked quietly.

There came a little laugh from behind me, and she said, 'I tell him that when we meet again, he's in a great deal of trouble.'

'You think you will see him, in another life?'

'Yes, I do.'

'What makes you so certain?'

I felt Anwen moving behind me, reaching out to touch her husband's body. 'I didn't believe in an afterlife till I met him. And in a certain way, I still don't. What I do believe in is the knotting of souls. I was meant to meet Malcolm because something that lives within us, beyond choice, made it so. There is no heaven or hell for me; what I see is two souls, reaching. We will meet again, with different faces perhaps. But we'll know who we are, in that space within us, beyond choice.'

I was silent, until she asked, 'Do you feel the same?'

And, again, I felt the thread of my certainty being pulled, unravelling into myth and story. A part of me wanted to agree with Anwen, to reassure her that Malcolm and she would meet again, somehow. A part of me believed her. But I could not give in to those thoughts. That way, I felt, led to madness. The way I thought I would survive, the way I would solve the problem of Malcolm's death, would be through the adherence to reason. I could not abandon that, for the sake of comforting an old woman. 'No,' I said. 'There is only this life.'

In reply, she stroked my head and made the gentle, sympathetic sound a mother makes when her child is injured.

Breaking from a stupor, I pushed myself away from the wide chair in which Anwen and Malcolm sat. I stood in the centre of the blood-stained room. 'I feel I should tell you, Tilly visited me.'

Anwen faced me benignly.

'She's given me cause to believe—'

'Before you go any further, let me say that Tilly MacArthur has been a great help to this family. Unless you have real evidence, I would stop where you are.'

'Anwen,' I said, 'sometimes our feelings can blind us to the truth. If it wasn't her . . .'

A smile appeared on Anwen's face like a crack in porcelain. 'Go on.'

I remained there, facing the pitiful sight of an elderly

woman holding her murdered husband. 'Please, Anwen. Help me understand.'

'Go back to bed, Euan,' she said. 'You look tired.'

My breath had quickened, and a slow rage had settled in my chest. I felt as if I were staring at a sentence of jumbled words, trying to pare some sense from it, achieving nothing. Then, the last spark against wet tinder: 'Let me ask you, Anwen. What do these words mean to you?'

She turned her face to Malcolm, almost like he might reply.

'"To arrive at being all, desire to be nothing."'

Her eyes closed, and she rested her forehead against his shoulder. 'Nonsense,' she said. 'Pretty-sounding nonsense.'

★ ★ ★

I left them there in the cold sitting room and walked back through the house. By now, the watery pre-dawn light had begun to filter through the fissures between curtains, bisecting the darkness. I moved between the patches, the way a fox darts through allotments, looking over my shoulder.

I came to the intersection of hallways, where the stag skull leered. I saw then that beneath the skull, in the alcoves containing chessboards, something had changed: the stools were pulled out, as if players had just risen from their game.

I looked over my shoulder, saw only an empty hallway in the latticed dark. My palms were damp with sweat. I wondered, for a moment, if I were the subject of some sadistic joke.

Walking over to the alcoves, I saw what I'd already known: again, the pieces had moved. They were in mid-game configurations. It was something that might have gone unrecognised by another, but to me, these games held the same significance as surface mould – the face of something which plunges deeper.

I reached into the alcove, picked up the Black queen, felt the heat of fingertips lingering on the wooden piece. I could very well have imagined it, but in that moment, I felt certain I'd only just missed the phantom player. Who were they? I thought of what Anwen had told me about Malcolm's desire to overcome death. Was he reaching out from an afterlife, leaving impressions for me to find? It was impossible. I knew that. But I also knew that, throughout time, across cultures, it has always been in the space between night and day that boundaries fall away, and even the most logical man can be made to suppose.

I set Black's queen back in her position, then waited. The cold air of the stone alcove clutched at the hems of my clothes, making me shiver. I breathed in the old dust and smelt, at the same time, something warm, earthy. The smell of a body. I moved White's knight to an outpost, between two of Black's pawns. Then, I stood and held my breath.

A breeze blew down the hall, more light slipped through the drawn curtains, the leaves of the potted plants turned their broad faces upward. The pieces on the board remained in place.

I backed away. Of course, the pieces remained in place. Of course they did. I was pleased; this had provided me assurance that I was not losing my mind; that there were still laws which governed the world that could not be subverted, corrupted, ignored completely. I turned from the pieces, not looking back, for fear that I might see something which upset my newfound assurance.

Instead of returning to my bedroom, I thought I might venture through the northern passage, towards where the family's bedrooms were situated. With the alcoves to my back I went on, wondering what secrets Anwen and her family were keeping from me. Did they all, in fact, know where the manuscript was hidden? Was it, as Jim had said, an elaborate way to torment me? Though I did not believe it, these thoughts festered in me. Who was I to take over Malcolm's legacy? After what I had done, how could I deserve it? I had never spoken to Malcolm of Julia, never told him of my shame. But I'm sure he saw it. Malcolm saw everything.

I was so lost in these thoughts that I almost knocked down Jim in the darkness. He was standing silently in the corridor, outside someone's room. When he saw me, he pretended to be walking away, but I'd seen him waiting.

'I s'pose you're lost,' I said.

He pushed his chin at me. 'Be quiet, you'll wake her.'

'Her?'

His eyes widened and the hollows around them deepened. In the gloom, his face was pocked and grey. 'Clara,' he said dejectedly.

'Thought you went back to your house,' I said.

In a cold whisper, he said, 'I came back.'

'You understand how this looks? I find you alone outside a sleeping woman's door.'

'You came here as well,' he replied. 'What was your reason?'

'I got lost.'

Like two scoundrels meeting in an alley, we sized each other up.

Jim's teeth leered out of the darkness. He spoke quietly, 'I feel bad about what I said to her at the meeting. I wanted to apologise.'

'At this time?'

Jim rolled his fingers across the knurled head of his cane. He couldn't meet my eye. 'I've known Clara since she was a girl. Look, I need her, as much as she needs me now.'

'What do you mean by that?'

'I was never blessed with children,' he said. 'Just as Malcolm welcomed me here as his brother, his children welcomed me, too. Now, I will be the best father I can to them. Before I leave for the mainland tomorrow, I wanted to . . . to let them know I am here. And I will be for as long as I live.'

'And that couldn't wait till a reasonable hour?'

'Damn it,' he said through gritted teeth. 'A man grows tired of being alone. I came here because . . . because . . .' And there were tears in his eyes.

I thought of where I had just been, and what I had done this night. Fear acts as a magnet, pulling together disparate bodies that might never have touched. Jim, though he was too proud to admit it, seemed scared.

'I just wanted to offer my condolences,' he said. 'I see that was stupid now.'

'It was,' I said. 'Come on, let her sleep. We'll have a coffee.'

And as we walked back to the western wing, passing the corridor of chessboards, the great stag skull, I noticed Jim looking back over his shoulder.

15

AFTER MY SUGGESTION, JIM agreed to take me along to his house, which was a short walk to the south. It was a small stony dwelling of two stories, with wind-pocked walls and a roof that drooped in the middle, as if some great bird had chosen it as its perch. In the morning twilight, the dew on the shingles glowed.

The inside of Jim's house smelt heady and sweet, which I soon learned was from his greenhouse at the back, where he proudly told me that he grew the most potent Indian hemp in the United Kingdom. 'An old man's pastime,' he said, rolling some of it in a large paper as he leant over the kitchen table. 'During the war, I was stationed out in Bombay, working for Naval Intelligence. Easy decryption work, which afforded me plenty of recreation time . . . I managed to smuggle back a seedling, and now here we are. I have always had a talent for recognising opportunity.' He put his own rolled hemp cigarette in his mouth, then handed one to me, along with a strong dark coffee.

He smoked and sipped his coffee, saying, 'They go together very well, I must say.' He struck a match for me, held it out.

A moment there, as we teetered in the semi-dark. I was wary of the man, but wanted to gain his trust. 'You are full of surprises, Jim.' I lit up and inhaled. A warmth bloomed

THE MAN ON THE ENDLESS STAIR

in my throat, then began to radiate through me. My head became light and I forgot, for a moment, the panic of the day before.

Jim smiled. 'When you are my age, new avenues of thought are hard to come by. I find this helps.'

Placing a hand on my shoulder, Jim cleared his throat and pulled me on, guiding me around the cluttered rooms of his dwelling. The tables were piled high with puzzle boxes and cryptic mechanical devices which came in the shapes of pyramids, cubes, locks and rings. The walls were papered with crosswords, with sections circled in red pen, clues scratched onto yellowed paper. When we reached the living room, Jim gestured for me to take a seat on the sofa, beside a low coffee table, upon which were scattered intricate origami patterns. I smoked and sipped my coffee, examining the patterns and watching Jim from the corner of my eye. He moved in a jagged way, hobbling from one corner to another, searching for something.

The room became hazy, taking on an air of unreality. Suddenly Jim spoke, with his back to me. 'Malcolm never spoke about his past. In all the years I knew him, he never told me anything . . . Why do you think that is?'

'A mystery can be more exciting than the truth. Perhaps it wasn't so interesting.'

Jim tapped his cane on the floor, considered, then said, 'No. Malcolm was ashamed of his past, didn't like to remember it. That is why he saw something in people like us. I was wretched when I met Malcolm . . . Perhaps I still am.' He turned to look at me from the corner, and the lines on his face were deep and shadowed.

'People like us?'

He took a long drag, exhaled a thick plume of heady smoke, then looked at me with bloodshot eyes. 'I know about you.'

Just as I was about to rise, Jim turned his back on me again and began to search through books stacked in a cupboard. He spoke in a relaxed manner. 'I researched you, when Malcolm told me he'd chosen a successor. I obviously knew about your books, but upon digging deeper, I found the articles in the papers. Read about your father.'

'What about my father?' I felt tension in the back of my neck.

'You must know.'

'I want you to say it.'

Jim shrugged and said, 'The papers said he drove the family business into the ground, then met a tragic and . . . inglorious end, when your sister went missing.'

I was quiet. Pain and guilt made me clumsy, and I did not want to speak, to fumble my words and give away how deeply he'd hurt me. He'd spoken so casually, as if my history and I were disconnected. Slowly, I gathered myself. 'It's not my duty to atone for my father's sins.'

'You're right. But nevertheless, that is what you have done. I see it in you, that need for greatness. You are ashamed.'

'I am not him.'

'*I* know that.' The space beyond his words echoed. Did he really think he knew me better than I knew myself?

I stubbed out the hemp cigarette in an ashtray on the coffee table and glared at Jim. I lifted my coffee cup and drained it.

Jim sighed and said, 'I am simply suggesting that Malcolm himself had a mired past, and chose misfits like us out of a

THE MAN ON THE ENDLESS STAIR

sense of empathy . . . Perhaps he recognised your situation.'

'And what was your situation?'

Jim stilled, seemed to find what he'd been looking for in the cupboard, then turned and said matter-of-factly, 'I am attracted to those I shouldn't be.'

I regarded him quietly.

'Are you revulsed?' Jim said, with a chuckle.

I pushed my back into the sofa, straightened. Jim met my eye, and though he'd laughed, there was an earnestness to his face.

'No,' I replied. 'I have known men of that persuasion. Good men.'

'Good,' he said, clearing his throat and moving on quickly. He produced a flat, rectangular puzzle box from the cupboard. 'The only clue to Malcolm's history is this. When he gave it to me, he said this was the key to his past. If I understood this, I would understand him entirely. It is a enigmaphile's dream . . . or nightmare.' He came over and sat beside me, puffing sweet smoke while setting the box down on the coffee table. After sipping his black coffee, he slid a series of inlaid panels on the puzzle box, and then lifted its lid. Inside was an old book, bound in plum-coloured leather. Its edges were deckled, and the corners dog-eared, and when Jim picked it up from the box and set it upon the coffee table, he did it with great care. He looked at the book the way one admires an old friend.

When I straightened and looked across at him, he said, 'I'm sorry to say this is not the manuscript for which you're searching. But look . . .'

In the centre of the cover lay a wooden panel with a disc in the centre, upon which was a young girl, intricately carved.

Her finger was outstretched to the edge of the disc, and on her little heart-shaped face was an expression of peace.

Again, it felt as if the world were drawing together around this idea; that my sister was somehow here, emerging from the void. I blinked, trying to collect myself.

Jim laid his fingers lightly on the girl and turned the disc so that her finger was pointing to a lunar diagram – one of many ringed about the outer edge of the disc.

'It is a lunary,' said Jim, without looking up. 'Once, we believed that the motions of celestial objects had an acute effect on our lives . . . that our fates were at the mercy of the moon. The lunary tracks the sidereal month, allows the reader an insight into the mysteries of the cosmos. You ask the book a question, and it will tell you when it is best to act.'

'It's nonsense, then. A relic from a time before modern science.'

Jim glanced across at me with gimlet eyes. 'Malcolm made this.'

'What?'

'There is an element of truth to all fiction. Malcolm believed this with his entire being, became fascinated with lunaries. In the end, I think he forgot it was fiction at all. When he gave me this book, he said it was the key to his past, but I have examined it, read it cover to cover, and learnt only that Malcolm was a better puzzler than I ever was.' He paused, and I pulled the book closer.

I placed my fingertips against the wooden disc and the carven image of the girl.

'That is the disc which tracks the movement of the moon through the lunar mansions. There are twenty-eight segments around its edge, each with its own prognostications. Inside the book are tables that help the reader determine on which page they will find their answer. So, for instance, if my question were pertaining to the topic of war, the table might direct me to a page where I would read the advice that a bone should be burnt, and a scar to be made, on the seventh day of the sidereal month. When the moon is in the mansion of Al Han'ah.'

I opened the book, caressed the inner leaf, felt the careful marks of the tables written in Malcolm's hand.

'Perhaps you would like to ask him a question and see for yourself?' Jim said.

'*Him?*'

Jim's face reddened, and he laid the finished hemp cigarette down on the table.

I understood then. Jim wanted to speak with his old friend, wanted to reach out into death and say goodbye. This book was the closest thing he had. A book of pre-answered questions. A conversation already finished. I spoke tenderly. 'Then we will ask him a question.'

Jim nodded, rubbed his eye.

I read out the subjects as I ran my finger along the table: 'Intellect, art, travelling, friendship, pain, betrayal, passion, music, strategy, time . . .'

I stilled, finger pressed against the paper. Time. An obsession of Malcolm's, and a subject which had been on my mind ever since reading his letter and seeing who I thought was my sister at the window. Jim had also said that this lunary was the key to Malcolm's past . . . and so, I chose the subject of time.

Jim looked at me from the corner of his eye.

I turned to the page it suggested, found the passage.

The swollen womb of the spring tide births a changeling, stolen by time.

Hear the changeling sing, in the crashing of waves upon cliffs, in the silent stillness of the pools.

When the buds rise from the earth, blood will reveal the passage.

'This entry is unlike any other,' said Jim. 'And I have returned to it often. The first line is a reference to the full moon in April, or *bolg reothairt*. Gaelic, for "swollen womb of the spring tide". The rest, I struggle with.'

'A changeling. That is a child, stolen by the fae,' I said.

'Indeed,' said Jim. 'A particularly nasty piece of folklore. Which, in my opinion, was used to hide an even nastier reality.'

'How so?'

'The changeling myth was long used to justify the disposal of unwanted children. Children who could not work, children who brought shame to families of the pre-industrial era.'

I grimaced, read the passage again. 'There is an element of truth in all fiction,' I said, echoing his earlier words.

Jim thumbed the grizzled nub of his chin. 'And it's often far worse.'

'The girl carved on the front cover, who is she?'

Jim chewed his lip, said, 'I asked Malcolm once. He said, "The girl with the moon in her eyes."'

The changeling and the figure of the girl, how could I not associate these with Julia? Hers was the story of the stolen child, the changeling. While I was fighting in France, she had disappeared from this world, leaving no trace whatsoever. There had been an investigation, a search party, days of restless hunting, but to no avail. No one had seen her leave. No one had noticed anything amiss. In my mind I had blamed my father, for I knew his temper, knew how he'd looked at my sister. I had cut him from my life, blaming him for what had happened. Then, he had taken his own life. But what if I had made a mistake? What if he was not to blame?

I became convinced then that there was an answer to the terrible riddle of her disappearance, hidden somewhere on this island. If I could only uncover the secret of these words, perhaps I could have my answer. Perhaps I could find the truth.

'"Blood will reveal the passage,"' I said.

'Does that mean something to you?'

'No.'

Jim grumbled. 'I'd hoped you would shed some light on this, but it seems you're as clueless as I am.'

'Passage to where?'

'The changeling, possibly. But I think you have focused on the wrong part of that clause. What concerns me more is the blood.'

We fell off into silence, staring at the words on the page like novices peering at the grimoire of a master.

'Have you heard of Laplace's demon?' Jim asked.

The name was familiar to me. It struck me that I had seen it written on a page, plastered to the wall of Malcolm's telephone room.

'A theory, proposed by Pierre-Simon Laplace, of an entity who could understand everything all at once. Who held the knowledge of all particles, their positions, velocities and forces. An intellect for whom everything was certain: Laplace's demon.'

'What relevance does that have?'

Jim thumbed the corner of the lunary and said, 'If anyone could have bargained with a demon, it would have been Malcolm.'

'Now that is pure nonsense.'

Jim fell silent, looking bereft. He said, 'I often wonder why that entity was described as a "demon". After all, isn't God omniscient, too?'

The answer came to me, as natural and dreadful as sudden illness: 'To bear that knowledge, the terrible weight of all things . . . how could one not become wretched?'

Jim regarded me, then said quietly, 'Quite right.'

I closed the book, looked at the disc on the cover and the little girl's finger which Jim had moved earlier. It was pointing to a lunar diagram of a waxing gibbous moon. The diagram beside it was of the full moon.

'Is this the right date?' I asked.

Jim nodded. '*Bolg reothairt* is tonight.'

'Then we have till tonight to make sense of this thing?'

'If there is sense to be made of it,' Jim said. He looked worn, as if he had just woken from a harried sleep. He coughed, rubbed his eyes, picked up the book and set it back in the puzzle box.

'I must confess,' said Jim, 'I did not share this out of the goodness of my heart. Like you, I want to be remembered. Not for my disgrace, but for the good I have done. Will you write me into your stories? Will you make sure my name doesn't fade?'

Lowering my gaze, I saw that he was wringing his hands together. I saw in him, then, the same compulsion that had driven me all these years, and had also driven Malcolm – a desire to be remembered, to be loved, to escape the story that had been written for us, and to forge one of our own. 'I promise,' I said.

He bowed his head, and his hands stilled. Slowly, he reached out, began to reseal the box.

I watched the sequence in which he slid the panels, heard the soft click as the puzzle box returned to its locked position. Jim laid his hand upon the box, muttered under his breath. I could not make out the words he spoke, but in his eyes, there was the pain of parting with an old friend.

He stood, picked up the box and walked over to the cupboard in which he'd found it, buried it inside beneath a pile of dusty books.

He faced me from across the room, stared as if seeing something approaching, something inevitable and consuming. Knuckles white about the tip of his cane, his eyes widened. It was unmistakable, he had realised something. 'The key to his past,' he said under his breath. He began to laugh.

'What is it, Jim?'

He looked scared. 'He plays with us, even now.' Then, there was ecstasy written on his face, the look of one in the presence of the divine. He wailed with laughter.

'Jim?'

He lurched across the room to me, dropped his cane and set both his weathered hands on either side of my face. He peered into my eyes. 'Beautiful . . .'

I pushed him off me, backed out of the room. I turned,

moved through his house, out onto the lawn. He made no move to follow me, and, as I left, I heard nothing: only shameful silence. Above, the stars still shone in the morning, like oracle bones cast over a silver hide.

16

SHAKEN, I STRODE BACK towards the Furnivalls'
house in the distance. The weeds mulched under my feet
and I felt, not for the first time, like a creature – brushed
by morning dew, wild and wary – as I approached the
mansion. Heavy clouds pulled the world in tight. I
waded through the quicksilver morning, praying that
the sun would soon rise and burn away the smothering
atmosphere and, with it, the madness.

I stopped halfway. On the lawn was a figure, tall and
dark. I watched it from my place among the weeds,
crouching so that my head peered over the tufted
hair grass. The figure walked further out, stretched its
back and cast a wide, strong shadow across the waving
grass. It touched its toes, and then reached up to the sky,
till a spear of silver light grazed its face and illuminated
its profile. Clara. She remained there, in front of the
mansion, no longer stretching. She looked out to the
bordering trees, curling a strand of hair about her long
finger.

I began to rise, and, as soon as I did so, she snapped
to face me. I hailed her as I approached, and she waved,
saying as I neared, 'Mrs Gibson has just laid out breakfast.
Would you like to join us?'

I pulled my foot from a well of wet heather. 'Of course.'

She raised her chin, looked down her nose at me. 'Last night, I heard noises in the house.'

'Apologies if I woke—'

'It was you?'

'I was restless and . . .'

She spoke, distantly. 'I couldn't sleep, either.'

Our eyes met and we recognised something shared. Then, I told her that I'd found Jim outside her bedroom door: 'He said he wanted to offer his condolences.'

Her face was as hard as marble. She spoke softly. 'We all feel lost.'

We stood for a minute, the low wind picking at our clothes. Watching her stern features, I recalled what I'd overheard Anwen tell her: *I think, of everyone, you have suffered most.* I imagined Clara then, a little girl all alone; her mother away performing, her father sequestered in his shed. She was the younger sibling, but had taken on the role of mother for Lewis; she had, from a young age, been burdened with responsibility.

'Clara,' I said, 'forgive me saying so, but I think I understand.'

'Understand what, exactly?'

'Why you came back here. You didn't have to.'

She fixed me with a searching look.

'I don't know how much you've been told of my family, but . . . my father, when alive, was not a kind man. Still, I would have returned to him if he'd asked. Call it duty, call it weakness. But I would want to know . . . would want to hear him admit how wrong he'd been.'

'Family is complicated,' was her guarded reply.

I thought, again, of what I'd overheard between she and

her mother. 'Yes,' I said. 'And the answers we receive are rarely the ones we want.'

She pulled down her sleeves and folded her arms. 'What about your mother?'

I took a moment to reply, meeting her eye, seeing her focus intensify. 'She died giving birth to my sister.'

Clara's face softened, in a way that was more powerful than any apology she could have offered.

'We make do,' I said.

She pursed her lips, nodded in recognition of our shared duties. 'We make do.'

We said nothing more, only walked together, quietly, back towards the house.

In the dining room, Lewis had placed himself at the head of the table, in Malcolm's seat. He had not waited for our arrival to begin eating. He piled bacon, eggs, toast, tomato, sausage high on his plate, and he looked up at us, mouth full, as we took our places.

Mrs Gibson flitted between us, filling cups with coffee, setting more bacon, spooning portions of fluffy eggs onto our plates, until Clara caught her by the shoulder, whispered something into her ear, and she nodded sombrely before leaving the room.

When Lewis raised an eyebrow at his sister, she said softly, 'We are perfectly able to serve ourselves. If anyone needs Mrs Gibson, it's Mother.'

Lewis lowered his gaze, returned to his mountain of food. It was shocking to see such an abundance, what with rationing still in effect. Between mouthfuls, he glanced across at me, said, 'It hardly feels real. Here we are, eating breakfast, while in the next room ...' He sucked up a string of bacon fat, swallowed and sighed. He raised his fork and pointed it at me. 'Your friend, Colm – he didn't want breakfast?'

'I don't know. And I wouldn't call him a friend.'

Lewis snorted, looked to his sister. Then, he returned to his plate, said, 'You seem to look out for each other.'

I watched him while smiling thinly. I had grown tired of Lewis. 'Plenty of food there,' I said, gesturing to his plate.

'Yes,' he said, smiling back at me. 'Father had certain arrangements. If he wanted something, he usually found a way of procuring it, or, better yet, getting others to. But you know that.'

Just as I was about to reply, Clara interrupted. 'Tell us a story about our father, Euan.'

I looked at her, wondering if she was joking.

'I'm sure you have plenty,' she said. 'He adored you, after all. I think you have known a side of him that very few others have.'

I considered while watching the siblings, who were quietly eating their breakfast. Whether the question was asked in good faith or not, I didn't care. I smiled as a memory returned to me, decided I would tell it: 'On one of my visits, he instructed me to bring binoculars because we were going birdwatching. I'd never been before. I wanted to impress him, so I purchased the best pair I could afford, spent months learning the different kinds of birds. When I arrived, he made sure that I had brought my gear, nodded approvingly when I showed him the binoculars. And so, we woke early next morning, headed out to the cliffs. When we got there, I took out my binoculars and noticed Malcolm start to grin. He reached into his bag and, rather than producing a pair of binoculars, he took out a bottle of whisky and two glasses. Apparently, Anwen had told him to cut back on the drinking, and the whole birdwatching story was just a way to get some privacy. When I told him how much I'd spent on the binoculars, he laughed until he lost his voice.'

The room was quiet. Both Clara and Lewis looked down at their plates. Then, suddenly, Lewis started to chuckle. He caught my eye, and then I was laughing too, looking across to see Clara, head in her hands, laughing with us. She pointed at her brother and said, through teary laughter, 'Remember the tennis court?'

Lewis wiped his eyes and said, 'There was a court, just behind the glasshouse. He would take us out there and play us when we were children, maybe once or twice a year. He would play the both of us and beat us every time, no matter how hard we practised. Then, one year, when we were – what, fourteen and sixteen? – we managed to tire him out and won. The next week, we went outside and saw the court was completely missing. He'd ferried workmen to the island to take it down.' He wiped his eyes, barely managing to get through the story without laughing.

In truth, he could have said anything; we were, all of us, so desperate for laughter, for a chance to forget what had happened. No matter what we thought of each other, what suspicions we might have had, we were, in that moment, released. We coasted into comfortable silence, finishing our breakfast – Lewis eating what was left on the serving plates, while Clara took measured bites of her marmalade toast. I took a roll slathered with butter, filled it with bacon, and ate while Lewis rubbed his stomach and said, 'I made a promise to myself during the war that I would never leave a plate unfinished again.' He burped and held up a hand in apology.

Softened by our shared stories, I nodded in agreement.

Lewis then gestured to his sister. 'Clara would have been the better soldier, in all fairness. And she actually wanted to join, unlike me.' He sniffed, looked away.

I glanced across at Clara, saw her shaking her head. 'I did what I could.'

'Land lassie,' Lewis said. He pointed to Clara. 'You're in the presence of a supervisor in the Women's Land Army. Can you imagine her, tilling fields? I expect she still did more at home than I did in Normandy.'

'Enough, Lewis,' Clara said. 'I doubt Euan wants to talk about this.'

'You were in Normandy?' I asked.

He nodded, and it was as if a layer of him had been stripped away. He met my eye, all joy gone from him.

I said, 'Me too,' and left it at that.

Lewis cleared his throat, drummed his fingers on the table and said, 'Let's go for a walk.'

I thought of the *netsuke* in my coat pocket, and what I had planned to accomplish today. I was keen to leave, but Lewis had risen and moved to the door, gesturing for me to follow. I looked to Clara, who leant back in her chair and motioned for me to go with him. 'You two have fun,' she said.

'Sorry, Lewis, but I've only just returned from a walk. I visited Jim for coffee.'

'We will walk the house, then. The library! We'll take a visit to the library. You ought to be comfortable there.'

'Really, I—'

'None of us should be alone.'

They both watched me, and I felt everything slow. 'Right,' I said, rising.

'You can pick me out a book to read,' Lewis said.

'I'm not sure there's a children's section.'

He glanced at his sister, then let out a mighty laugh, slapped me on the back and left the room with me in tow, saying, 'That's the spirit.'

Together we walked, out to the main hall, up the stairway and along the first-floor gallery. Lewis talked as we went, pointing out a dent in the wall from where Clara had once thrown a tantrum and swung a croquet mallet into the plaster. He said I had been lucky to not yet experience one of her rages. After I nodded, he smiled warmly and then turned down the eastern corridor and through a series of small stairways, going till we reached the tall turret lined with books that was Malcolm's library. Dawn light swept in through lancet windows, catching the gilt-edged books, the dog-eared volumes left half-read, the piles of musty yellow paper which emitted plumes of dust if brushed. The room held the warmth of a place well loved, holding in it the smell of moth-eaten cushions, spilt whisky, soft leather. It was a place that allowed one to drift off into another world; there were no open spaces, no harsh light, nothing cold.

I stood in the doorway while Lewis walked the circumference of the lower floor, picking up books, thumbing them, setting them back. I waited for him to speak, certain that he had taken me to a private place for a reason. When he gestured for me to look around, I kept an eye on him as I moved between the bookshelves, beneath the groin-vaulted ceiling. The distant pointed arches were supported by columns, between which the heavy oak shelves were positioned. Along one wall ran a slender staircase which led to an upper gallery, where long lancet windows stained the light with rich hues: gold, emerald, ruby. The light lay in satin lengths across the floorboards. I remembered how Malcolm had looked, silhouetted as he sat in an upper-gallery niche with one of my books in his hand. I walked up the staircase, began to search through the shelves, looking for something Malcolm may have left for me to find. I came to where he had shelved my novels, stopped. The shelf was empty, aside from the furrows of dust which had lain between the books. I remembered the worn dustjackets of the hardcovers, the cracked spines of the softcovers, the translated editions with their well-thumbed pages. These, more than anything, had been evidence of Malcolm's love. All were gone. Whoever had taken my work from this library had succeeded in tearing me out at the root, making me feel like an outsider in a place where, once, I had felt most at home.

'A shame Colm didn't join us at breakfast,' Lewis said from behind me. He stood at the top of the staircase, casually leafing through a collection of Chekhov's work.

I continued to survey the shelves, though my attention was keenly fixed on Lewis. 'He must be a late riser,' I said.

Lewis made a grunt of agreement. 'How well do you know him?'

'Enough.'

'Enough to trust him?'

I turned from the shelf. 'Why do you ask?'

He turned his attention back to his Chekhov, licked his top teeth. 'I only wish you'd realise who your real allies are.'

I spoke very slowly. 'You'll have to be clearer.'

Lewis sighed and said, 'We both know he was on some

colonial posting, drinking port while we . . .' He looked up at me. 'He is not like us.'

'Yes,' I said. 'I know that.'

Now there was veracity in his expression. 'The will Colm read out; it was false. That must be clear to you.'

I grimaced, but didn't cut him off.

'It was too obvious, almost a parody of my father. And' – Lewis smirked – 'he once said that without me, he would be nothing. I think he was drunk when he said it, but he meant it. I could tell. He said that after he passed, he would leave *me* this house, and all that it contains.'

'What are you telling me, Lewis?'

He closed his book, walked towards me and said, 'If you were to find something of value in your friend's house, you would, no doubt, return it to your friend.' He reached out for my wrist, took it before I could flinch back. 'We are friends, aren't we?'

I snatched my hand away, stood before him, fists clenched at my sides. 'Be careful,' I said.

He looked calm, as if he were enacting a scene he'd planned.

I waited for him to press the subject, to mention the manuscript.

He walked past me, took a seat in a niche, folding his legs and speaking with a faint smile. 'This was always my favourite place. I found it so peaceful.'

Leaning on the balustrade, I looked down from the upper gallery to the concentric circle of shelves below. I wanted to know more about Lewis, about his childhood here with Clara. He had given me an opening, so I took it. 'Was it not lonely?'

He held the Chekhov collection and ran his fingers along the cover. 'I never knew anything different. When I wanted a friend, I would go to Clara. And . . . and I have always been an inward person. Perhaps it doesn't seem so now, but I would always choose quiet contemplation over a party.'

'I wouldn't have thought that.'

'I know how to entertain. I treat it as a performance.' He shrugged, as if to say he didn't mind if I agreed with him or not.

I considered. Perhaps he was right. If one is the centre of attention, one is in control. Lewis's affability was a way to manoeuvre the conversation's eye away from himself. I remembered how he had looked after Malcolm had hit him; how he'd fumbled with the hem of his shirt like a lost boy.

He went on: 'If I weren't an actor, I would have liked to live as a monk.' He sniffed. 'I've always felt . . . formless. Always desired structure and silence.'

I perched on the balustrade, laughed. 'The image of you as a monk is certainly interesting.'

Lewis grinned, raised his hand in the sign of benediction.

We chuckled together until he said, 'Escaping into roles comes easily to me. It is vaguely religious; it requires total faith, the adoption of a fully formed self, a code to embody. I have always dedicated myself to others . . . and now I have made a career of it.'

'Do you ever lose sight of yourself?'

He looked out of the lancet window; face half-dashed with red light. 'You want to know the truth?'

'Please.'

'There is no one to lose sight of. I have never felt like my own person. It is how I survived on the battlefield . . . I'm a follower. And I pretend to be nothing else.'

'You must have dreams, things you want that drive you on.'

'I do,' he said, 'but they were always secondary to Clara's. Father loved her . . . very much. He and Mother pushed her, paid for her to live and train on the mainland for months at a time. She was on the 1940 Olympic team, but you won't hear her talk about it. It's a raw wound; when the games were cancelled, she lost her chance to compete. From what I hear, she could have won . . . She is truly brilliant, my sister.'

I took in his words, sensing a note of self-pity.

'Don't mistake me, I'm not trying to martyr myself here. I'm telling you that I'm content. People like you and Clara live hard lives.'

At the comparison, I laughed and walked away from the balustrade, moving towards the stairs but stopping when Lewis held up Chekhov's works and spoke again: 'In *The Seagull*, Konstantin loves Nina. He calls her his seagull. She is his dream, but she is in love with another man. And at the end of the play, what does he do? He shoots a seagull and gives it to her as a gift. When she still doesn't reciprocate his love, he finally kills himself. So, what does the seagull symbolise? A seagull is a wild thing. As it flies, you can chase it, follow it, but if you want to touch it, you must kill it. To have your dream, you must destroy it.' He looked at me with sadness. 'I pity you, Euan.'

I inclined my head at the man, who rose slowly from the niche.

'He promised the manuscript to me, Lewis. Whether

the will is real or fake, you were there at lunch. You heard Malcolm say it.'

I stood still at the top of the staircase.

Lewis smiled, walked towards me, arm outstretched.

I went to step back, felt my foot hover in the air.

There was a change in Lewis's face.

A voice from right behind me said, 'I've been looking for you.' It was Mrs Gibson. She had appeared from nowhere and now stood a few steps beneath me.

Lewis's hand was still outstretched, in the gesture of a handshake.

I took his hand in mine, shook.

'Euan, you need to come with me,' Mrs Gibson said. Her eyes darted over to Lewis, who held on to my hand after I'd released.

'Room for one more?' Lewis asked.

Mrs Gibson looked at me. Her hair was in disarray, her face wan, and I thought she, more than anyone in the Furnivall household, embodied the spirit of this house. She'd slowly been broken down by this family, but still, she served them. 'You'd be more than welcome, of course,' said Mrs Gibson. 'But I have left your mother alone . . . Clara said you might comfort her.'

Lewis pressed his other hand to the back of mine, gave me a wide handsome smile and stepped back, with his arms wide. 'Go in peace, my child.'

I followed Mrs Gibson as we descended the staircase and wound through the library, watching Lewis all the while. He returned to his niche, picked up his Chekhov. He put his nose to the book, inhaled deeply and then caught my eye. He painted the sign of the cross in the air and laughed.

17

WHEN WE HAD MOVED from the library, back through the eastern corridor and along a series of shadowy passages, Mrs Gibson turned to me. From the weight in her limbs, I knew something was wrong. I had learnt, from a young age, to anticipate danger in the smallest details, as had Julia. I'd wished, throughout my life, for that unease to fade. I wanted to move with the grace of my fellow lecturers, to enter parties with the convivial ease they did, to strike up a relationship without the expectation of collapse. But, at the same time, it was this learned response that had kept me alive. My father had trained me for the war, better than any officer.

'Hurry,' said Mrs Gibson. She beckoned that I should come close. We had been walking in silence. I'd thought of asking what the matter was, but something about her manner made me wait. As I moved closer, I saw the look of panic on her face.

'What is it?' I asked, glancing behind me. There was the plan I had yet to enact and I didn't want to delay any longer; too much of the morning had already passed.

She caught me by the shirt. The whites of her eyes were jaundiced, and fatigue had made her eyelids heavy. Still, the look she gave me was fearsome. She spoke through gritted teeth. 'It's your friend.'

My stomach sank. I thought of Colm, hidden away in his room, wondered how anything could have happened to him. He'd recognised his vulnerability, taken precautions. For someone to have harmed him, they would have had to break down his door . . . or he'd left his room.

'Come.' She pulled me by my shirt, till I was striding beside her, along the passages which led to the western wing and Colm's door. As we approached, I began to hear a dull beat, like the house's waning pulse – unable to sustain the weight of its own frame. Mrs Gibson paused outside Colm's door, stared at the floor. 'Listen,' she said.

The thumping came again. I recognised it. 'You brought me here for this?' I said. 'He's only left his window open. It's banging against the—'

'No,' said Mrs Gibson. 'That window has been sealed permanently.' She watched me, peering from under heavy lids. Her voice was grim. 'He won't answer me.'

I stepped so that I was facing the door. I placed my hand against its frame. Apprehension clipped my words, made my tongue thick. 'Colm, it's me. Let's talk.'

The thumping went on in a steady pattern, some beats louder, some lighter.

I knocked on the door.

The thumping continued.

I turned, saw Mrs Gibson looking at me with a sour expression, as if she'd smelt something going bad. 'Can't you open the door?' I asked.

'No.'

I turned back to the door, knocked again. 'Colm, open up!'

It went on, soft thuds knotting the string of silence.

'I'll kick it down.'

Mrs Gibson rose to her full height. 'You will not.'

'But—'

She moved close to me, and the shadows in the pits of her wan face deepened. 'You won't harm the house.'

Shaking my head in disbelief, I called out again to Colm in desperation: 'I have it,' I said. 'What we spoke about, I've brought it to you.'

The thumping ceased. I cast my gaze to Mrs Gibson, saw that she was staring at me. Turning back to the door, I felt her eyes boring into the back of my skull.

Floorboards creaked from inside Colm's room, and I realised that he was now standing on just the other side. Then, his voice: 'Euan?'

'It's me. Please, open the door.'

There was a dreamy quality to his voice: 'I'm not quite—'

'Let me in, Colm.'

A gentle click. The door opened slightly, just enough for me to see Colm's solemn eye. 'You have it?' he said.

'Let me in.'

He paused, and I thought for a second that my ears were playing tricks on me, until, he opened the door further and I saw that he was laughing. 'Well, pass it here,' he said.

I froze.

'What is it?' he asked.

I turned towards Mrs Gibson, but she was gone. Only her shadow remained, flickering at the far end of the hall before vanishing altogether.

I stood, facing Colm. His temple was a swollen mess of bruises, and his left eye had folded itself shut. A narrow trail of blood ran from his forehead, down along his nose and across his jowl.

He pulled me inside his room, slammed the door shut behind us. We stood there, cooling in the silence. I could not take my eye from his temple.

His eyes were wild, flitting every so often to the far corner of his room. I followed his gaze and saw, there, on the wall, a dull smear of brown blood.

I tried to imagine what else could have caused the thudding, searched for an open window, or anything else that may have made the noise. The single window on the near wall was closed. I went to it, tried to push it open, but found it was painted shut: sealed, just as Mrs Gibson had said. I already knew what the cause had been. I felt another barrier fall away between myself and Colm; here was the reality of his state. It was plain: he'd been beating his head against the wall.

He spoke with a thin voice at the back of his throat. 'He's here.'

'Who? Who's here?'

He rubbed his eyes with the heels of his palms, turned his face to the ceiling.

I cast about his room, searching for another figure, but saw no one – only Colm's clothes and books scattered about the gloomy room, illuminated by a desk light, wreathed in a moss-green shade.

'Who's here, Colm?' I thought of the chess pieces, of the presence I'd felt. Perhaps some might have looked at Colm then and thought him deranged. But what I saw in him was very real. I gathered him by the arm and guided him down to sit on the bed, moving a white silk shirt out of the way. I placed a hand on his back and waited for his breathing to slow, for the film over his eyes to melt away.

'No one,' he said eventually. He took my hand in his. 'This place is quite terrible. But . . . but you have the manuscript, at least? We should aim to leave—'

'I don't have it. I only said that so you would open the door.'

His mouth hung open, and a tremor passed through him.

'Let go of my hand,' I said.

He looked down, saw my hand crushed between his. Apologising, he released and stood, moving to the other side of the room, leaning against a bookcase.

I rose slowly, standing by the bed, watching him.

'You should leave me,' Colm said. His wide back was wet with perspiration, and his shirt was slick, clinging to his skin. 'I know how I look . . .'

'Colm, I have seen things as well . . . things from my past.'

His face darkened, and he wrapped an arm about himself. He looked at me with a vulnerability I'd not yet seen in him. 'How do you go on?'

I felt my resolve give way, before catching myself and speaking firmly. 'There is a natural order which determines all processes. Every happening has a rational explanation, even the most unknown and mysterious. Listen, Colm, I am already closer to finding Malcolm's killer. I'm certain it was Tilly who burnt my books, and she had both motive and opportunity. But before I can reach any conclusion, I intend to confirm that this place is like any other. I have a plan. A way to test our sanity. To explain why we've been seeing these phantoms.'

I stopped speaking when I noticed Colm smiling. 'Does it matter?' he said.

'What do you mean?' I stayed where I was, yet the space

between us seemed to expand.

He spoke again, looking down at my feet. 'Whether they are real or not, we see them. That is our punishment.'

'Punishment?'

His eyes widened, and he seemed to return to himself. 'I'm sorry,' he said. 'I didn't mean . . .'

I thought of Julia, of all the things I could have done to save her. Punishment. He might have been right. I turned my eyes to the smear of dried blood on the wall, imagined Colm in this room alone, pounding his head against the plaster. Then another thought occurred to me: what had Colm done to deserve punishment? Seeing him there, curled into the space between the bookcase and the wall, I did not ask him. I was afraid of what I'd learn, but I had also found a friend here and did not want to ruin that by prying into the past. After all, there were things I had done which haunted me. Things I wished buried. That is friendship; learning that which is to be ignored and accepting what is presented – the alloy of truth and lies which form our current selves.

'Colm, will you promise me something?'

He unfurled slowly, waiting for me to go on.

'Promise me you will rest, that you will ignore whatever it is you've been seeing, until I return with the manuscript. If not for your own sake, then for mine. We will need each other before this is over. If it gets out that Malcolm's solicitor was not sound of mind, then who knows whether Malcolm's final wishes will be honoured? The validity of the will can be called into question. You understand?'

He was standing at his full height now, white-faced. He nodded. 'I'm sorry. I . . . I will do better.'

'Good.'

I watched Colm melt into a plum-coloured chaise-longue, its velvet worn away in places to reveal the muslin beneath. Its arms were furred with dust that rose in a dim cloud as Colm lowered his bulk into the cushions. 'How does one prove one's sanity?' he asked. 'You have a plan, you say?'

'I do.' Instinctively, I touched my hand to the pocket which held the *netsuke*.

Colm watched me expectantly. When I didn't elaborate, he said quietly, 'Can I help?'

I reached down behind me to the bed, took the white silk shirt I'd moved earlier. 'Can I have this?' I said.

'Of course. I offered it to you earlier. But . . . can I help with your plan?'

I took the white shirt, held it up in the mossy light.

He gave me a quizzical look.

'Thank you, Colm.' I said, rising and making for the door. 'And please, look after yourself. I won't be long.'

I stopped briefly in the doorway and looked back at him. He had closed his eyes and, with his smooth plump fingers, he pressed into the bruised flesh of his forehead.

18

WHEN THE SONGBIRDS FLITTED between the sedges, which had turned green-gold in the late-morning sun, I held the *netsuke* up in the light. It was time. Like a lucky coin, I pressed it to my lips and closed my eyes. The heavy clouds were burning away like old parchment held over candleflame, and I felt solid, reassured that I had a plan to follow. I ran over it: the events of last night had led me to believe that I was not in my right mind. How could I reach any form of conclusion if my instrument for reasoning were damaged? And so, I would conduct an examination on myself, to see whether the phantoms that had plagued not only me, but also Colm, were imagined. As the clouds receded, my chest swelled and I breathed easier; it was a bright morning and conveyed to me that reason would always triumph over mysticism. With Colm's white silk shirt bundled up and tucked under my arm, I set out across the wild field, following the trammelled way out towards the forest.

I had to speak with Harris. Everything else would have to wait. I left Malcolm's house behind me, watched it blaze in the light: a mass of stone elbows, eaves and furrowed shingles. I walked round to the east of the lake, into the thick trees. Smelling the fresh morning pine, I thought of Harris, how he'd defended me in the sitting room yesterday.

He'd known something the others did not. Who was this man? Tilly had told me he was from the oldest family on the island. Perhaps he'd been privy to secrets even Malcolm's family did not know? A flake of last night's dream glistened somewhere in my brain, but it dulled before I could examine it.

I pushed on through the pines and, when I heard the dim tumble of water, went further east, where the ground swept downwards, and the badger setts and fox holes attacked my ankles. There was a faint path through the deepening forest, to which I held. Eventually, I came to where the slope levelled, and there, sitting in the centre of a swathe of flat rocky ground, was Harris's cottage. It looked like a stone mausoleum, encrusted with creeping ivy. It brought to mind holy places: a kirk, but in a world where Christianity had never been known. A hallowed building for a strange god. There were white flowers stippling the path towards the house: wood anemone and primrose. The roof of the old cottage was high and crooked. The door had been painted yellow, but the paint was peeling and brown at the bottom. Worn and rusted gardening tools stood beneath the windows. The curtains were drawn, but I saw smoke coming from the little brick chimney. He was inside.

Still covered, I edged around the bordering trees until I could see the side of the cottage and its little window. I bent and arranged the flowing white shirt on a low branch, jutting from a briar. I stepped away, squinted my eyes. It would do.

Moving back round to the front of the cottage, I approached the door, with my hand in the pocket of my coat, touching the *netsuke* of the two otters. My fingertip contoured to the grooves in the little ivory piece, slipping over their tails, the raised heads, the pattern of the current in the carved water. I knew that for my plan to work, timing would be everything. I would have one chance.

I knocked on the door. No noise from inside, only the slow rolling of the wind through trees, the lark song, my heart in my head. I knocked again, louder. This time, there was the sound of feet over flagstone, and then a brief stillness. It was the stillness which scared me: what was Harris doing on the other side of the door? I stepped out of the doorway and waited just to the side.

The door swung open, and Harris stood in the threshold with a tin cup of coffee in his hand. He looked sidelong at me, as I tipped my imaginary hat to him. He looked beyond me, into the trees, and out across the rocky ground. Seeing only thistles and flowers, he tucked a weather-beaten hand under his armpit and looked down his nose, finding me at the end of it.

'Morning,' I said.

He sipped his coffee, said, 'You're trouble.'

'So is brushing your teeth, but both will do you good.'

His leather skin wrinkled an expression between a smile and a frown. 'A sharp tongue can cut your own throat.' He attended to his coffee, leant against the doorway as if to convey he could do this all morning.

I let the sounds of morning fill the silence before saying, 'Can I come in?'

He smiled at me, and there was an intelligence in his eyes. He was strong-featured. Possibly handsome, beneath a layer of sweat and dirt. 'Of course,' he said.

The cottage was sparsely decorated: candles with dripping

wax frozen to their stems; deep and comfortable chairs; tables stained with wine, worn down by many elbows. As I cast about, I noticed a rifle leaning against the wall beside the doorframe.

'For hunting,' said Harris. 'Deer.'

My expression hardened. Could Harris have been the one to shoot at me in the trees? 'Deer?' I said.

'Deer,' he answered, turning his back to me, walking through the large open room to the stove, where the coffee pot sat. He poured me a cup without asking, thrust it at me and perched on his table.

Now with a cup of coffee in hand, I said, 'You take care of the land?'

'I do.'

'And what does that involve?'

'Early mornings. A lot of walking.'

'You've lived on the island all your life?'

'Aye.'

Looking into the swirling dark coffee, I said carefully, 'You must have seen things.'

I could tell his eyes were firmly set on me. Speaking with Harris was like conversing with a grim stone. 'I don't know where he kept it,' he said finally.

'Kept what?'

'His manuscript. I don't have it.'

I drank from the coffee, then set it down on the table. 'He never spoke to you about it?'

He rolled his head and his neck cracked. The space about him seemed to darken, the cold rough granite walls drinking the candlelight. 'He would visit some evenings. I could see he was troubled. He'd ask questions.'

'What kind of questions?'

Harris grunted. 'The kind a man asks at the end of his life.'

'Go on.'

'He asked about fate. I told him I didn't believe in it. He seemed to think that was funny. Then, he said he could write a spell to determine fate. But Malcolm often spoke in that way, making grand claims, drinking too much.'

'The spell. You think he was talking about the manuscript?'

Harris sniffed. 'Could've been.'

I thought over that, remembering what Malcolm had told me in the study yesterday. He told me he'd written of something beyond conception. Was this what he'd meant?

'Harris,' I said, 'I'm going to be frank with you. I think you know more about this place than anyone in that house. I've come to you for help.'

'What are you talking about?'

'Well, first of all, you vouched for me yesterday. You said you saw me in the study when Malcolm was killed. Why did you say that?'

'I had my reasons.'

I weighed the moment, watched the redness that flowered across his neck, watched him tap his fingernails against his tin cup of coffee. This was the time.

I drew back a curtain and gestured out the window to the briar where I'd hung the white silk shirt. It moved with the cadence of the wind and, from this distance, could have been a young girl, playing. 'Is that the reason?' I said.

I watched Harris's face as he turned his eyes to the window, praying that his expression would give me the answer to the question that had been threatening my thoughts since yesterday. I saw him search for a moment, and then darkness crossed his face like ink spilled over cloth. He threw his cup of coffee down and barged past me without a word, moving out the door and on towards the billowing shirt.

I didn't have long. I had to push every doubt I had aside and focus on what I'd planned. Now there was no altering the course. I called out, 'I'm a friend.'

I waited. No response. I began to question myself; had I really imagined the girl? If so, was I fit to take on Malcolm's legacy?

Then, the creaking of a floorboard from upstairs. I walked softly to the bottom of the staircase, leant against the bannister. I took the *netsuke* from my pocket. 'I brought it with me. The one you were looking at.'

Quiet. How long would it take for Harris to discover my trick? Surely it would be soon. I felt my face growing hot, the thickness gathering in my throat. Had I imagined it all? In my panic, I spoke her name under my breath. 'Julia.'

A face, peering around the wall, looking down the stairs, meeting my eye. Her face.

All doubt dissipated and perhaps I should have been relieved: the girl I had been seeing was, in fact, real. I was not mad. However, a part of me realised then that the simple explanation of madness would have put to rest the issue. Now, instead, the ghost in my mind had hardened into someone real. Someone I was certain I'd known. Someone I loved. Now, there were more questions than before.

'Is . . . is it you?' I asked.

There was fear in her expression, and, as I moved up the stairs, she backed away, moved down the hallway. I stopped at the top stair, sat down with my hand out, offering the *netsuke*.

Shivering, she remained in the middle of the hallway, crouched, hands wrapped about her knees.

'Go on,' I said. 'Take it.'

She moved towards me like a wary cat, reaching out a thin white arm, plucking the *netsuke* from my palm. We met eyes, and I gave her a small nod.

She pressed her lips together in a tentative smile. Then, she spoke. 'Who's Julia?'

I couldn't take my eyes from her face. She looked just the same as when I had left her, all those years ago. But that was impossible. 'Do . . . do you recognise me?' I asked.

'Yes,' she said.

My heart pounded faster, and it was all I could do to stop myself from reaching out, pulling her into a great hug and telling her I was sorry. So sorry for leaving her with him. For allowing him to hurt her. I should have been stronger.

'You are the man in the window,' she said.

I closed my eyes, bowed my head. 'Yes. I am.'

'I saw you. You were alone and then the big bang . . .'

'And did you tell Harris what you saw? You told him I didn't hurt Malcolm?'

She looked at me with the openness of a happy soul. 'I saw you,' she said. 'You were kind.' She looked down at the *netsuke* she held and smiled, making the same circle with her fingertip around the bodies of the otters. 'Have you brought me a new dress?'

Confused, I shook my head.

She nodded, then returned her attention to the *netsuke*.

I dared to reach out and touch her lightly on the arm. She flinched away, but I stayed there, still, hands held in the air. She was real. She was flesh and blood.

Relief welled up inside me as I realised I'd not imagined her. She had told Harris that I was innocent. That was the reason he'd vouched for me. I owed her everything.

Realising that Harris would soon be back, I shuffled forward, fighting the urge to reach out, touch her face, confirm she was my lost sister. 'Do you remember anything else about me?' I said.

She frowned, backed away so that her little spine was pressed against the corridor wall. She rested the *netsuke* on her knees and pressed at it gently, the way a young deer touches the earth. She made no answer.

'What's your name?' I said.

There was noise from outside, a voice hollering and tramping steps. The girl's body stiffened and she wrapped her hands about her knees again, cast her head downwards.

'Please,' I said, desperation creeping into my voice. 'Just your name.'

'I shouldn't say.'

'You can tell me,' I said. 'I only want to help. Are . . . are you safe?'

'I'm not meant to be seen. I have a hiding place.'

The door opened. I turned back, looked down the stairway.

'Do you need to hide?' she asked. 'I can show you my hiding place.'

'Get away from her.' The voice was Harris's and it thundered through the cottage.

I made a calming gesture to the girl and rose, walking

softly down the stairs. I saw Harris standing there, gripping his rifle, aiming loosely at my stomach. The white shirt lay in a crumpled pile at his feet. His movements were sharp with rage, but in his face I also saw fear. The barrel of the rifle wavered in his heavy hands.

There was the scatter of little footsteps from behind me, and I knew the girl was gone. 'Tell me what's happening,' I said, unable to hide the tremble in my voice.

Harris raised the corner of his lip and said, 'None of your fucking business.'

'She saw me yesterday, when Malcolm was killed. That's why you defended me, isn't it? She told you.'

'I'm starting to regret that choice.'

I moved further down the stairs, then said, 'Who is she?'

Harris circled me as I came to the bottom of the stairs, guided me with the rifle so that I ended up standing near the door. 'I don't need to tell you anything.' His face was wolfish as he spat the words at me.

All cunning had left me. I pleaded with him.

The barrel of his gun sunk down to my knees.

'Who is she?' I asked again. 'Please.'

His expression softened as he glanced behind me to the top of the stairs. She was listening to us, we both knew it; wherever she was hiding, she listened.

'She's my daughter,' Harris said.

I reached out, slowly, steadying myself on the wall. Breathless, I tried to take in his words. She was his daughter. She only resembled Julia. Could I believe that? I stared at him, asked, 'Why the secrecy?'

Harris's eyes flicked to the corners of his cottage, as if the shadows were listening.

'I only want to help,' I said.

'They would take her,' he said.

'What do you mean, take her?'

'Because of who she is. She has a good life with me. She shouldn't have been at the mansion. I tell her, but she doesn't listen. She slips away and then—' He caught himself, then said with tight lips, 'Do you know who I am?'

'Tilly told me you're from the island's oldest family.'

He seemed to broaden in that moment. 'I know the hills and the glens, the burns and the creatures. It is a good and peaceful life. I would have Connie live this life, not the one they'd force on her, worshiping baubles, marrying a forelock-tugging dolt. I keep her out of sight to save her.' The rifle was hanging at his side now.

'Connie,' I said. 'Is that her name?'

He faltered, then gave a small nod.

I reached out slowly towards the table, picked up my tin cup of coffee, which was now lukewarm, and tried to soften the atmosphere by sipping from it.

Harris stayed still, watching me with hard eyes. 'Her mother left us,' he said.

'I'm sorry.'

He clicked his teeth, ran his hand along the barrel of the rifle. 'What drove you to come here today?'

'I wanted to be certain.'

'Certain of what?'

'That I wasn't imagining things.'

Harris raised the black plumes that were his eyebrows and said, 'And now you're certain?'

I sighed, held up my hands and said, 'I've learnt a great deal.'

'Listen to me,' said Harris. 'This family sees more than you think. They will know you came to visit me here today. You must not tell them about Connie. Understand?' He kicked the white shirt into a dark corner of the room.

'Why?'

'They're watching. The only reason you are still here is because they think you're a fool. Why did Anwen put you in charge of the investigation? You seriously believe it's because they thought you capable? You're a writer, for God's sake. They've done something terrible, and they want time to cover their tracks.'

'You think it was someone from the family?'

He toed a flagstone and said under his breath, 'Just . . . keep your wits about you.'

I considered my words carefully. 'They say keep your friends close, and your enemies closer . . . What does that mean to you?'

'Nothing.'

'I am only trying to understand why you would want to serve Malcolm.'

Harris looked up the stairs briefly, to where Connie had peered at me. He said, 'When Malcolm first arrived, we hated him. We came down from our hills and burnt his buildings. But then he came to us, alone. We found that he understood this place . . . Soon our elders began to call him Corvus, after the Raven Stars. Folk once believed that souls became birds after death. They thought those stars were the soul of an old king, flown away into the sky. They said Malcolm was the king returned.'

'What did he do to prove himself?'

Harris's brow was furrowed and dark, and a sinew

shimmered in his neck. 'He knew things no man could know.'

A clatter from upstairs. The sound broke both of us from our conversation. We turned to the noise, and Harris began to back away, to move up the stairs and away from me. 'For her safety,' he said, 'you keep this to yourself.'

'And for *my* safety?' I asked.

He grimaced, gestured to the door, then turned and went up the stairs.

Leaving the house, shutting the yellow front door behind me, I stood in the midday chill and considered what I now knew. I had not imagined the girl. But from meeting her, more questions had arisen. I felt as if I were slowly excavating the bones of three separate skeletons. Walking back towards the trees, I began to think of Clara, of how she had reacted when I'd chosen the *netsuke* of the otters. There had been a blankness to her face. It was clear Clara had learned to master her feelings, but I have learned that blankness implies expression, just as darkness implies light. There was something there. Harris had not told me who the mother was. He'd only said that she'd left. What if she had left, but not gone far?

Still, I could not shake the idea, or perhaps the dream, that Connie was in fact my sister, lost in time.

19

THE MOON STILL LINGERED in the midday sky as I left the clearing and Harris's cottage. I felt as if I were in one of Malcolm's books, swarmed with conflicting stories, carried by an endless sweeping gyre on towards a destination I would only recognise at the very last moment.

As I walked through the pines, I smelt wild garlic and realised the path veered close to Malcolm's writing shed. I drifted from the path and moved towards the building, which emerged like a mole, surfacing. The scent of garlic was pungent and cloying, and the shed's walls were dappled with cool light that settled over the hardwood like fine dust. I saw, through the trees, a swaying fern. It moved differently to its neighbors, as if it had been brushed aside. Then, there was flickering in the window: a body, moving hurriedly.

I thought that perhaps someone was searching for the manuscript and, keeping my gaze on the window, I saw one more shadow pass across the glass before everything stilled. Walking closer, pulse quickening, I once again felt that sense of gathering. I trod quietly through the garlic and knapweed, veered about the burgeoning nettles which bit at my ankles like mangy strays. I thought about the last time I was here, when the bullet had torn through the air and burst the tree trunk beside me. Where was the shooter now?

I edged around the shed, towards the front door, readying

myself for whoever was inside to come out. But nothing. Not even a noise from inside. Keeping away from the window, I put my hand on the wood of the front door, barnacled with crottle and crusted ivy root. I waited a little longer, in the spring air, laden with pollen, which, in the pillars of light, formed ghost shapes. There were voices, speaking in the trees, laughing and calling out. It was as if I were existing across all time, hearing the voices of everyone that had occupied this place at once. They were discordant, rising and falling in time with the morphing pollen. I heard Malcolm, his words forming like sediment forming stone: 'Desire to be nothing.'

I pushed open the writing-shed door. As I stepped inside, I nearly tripped over something long and heavy. It was a slow, dawning realisation, as my eyes adjusted to the dim light: the object was Jim's cane. It was slick with a liquid, almost black in this light. I cast my eyes along the trail of glimmering fluid, finding a grim shape protruding from the floor in the centre of the room.

Sickness bubbled in me as the mineral taste of gore filled my mouth. His face was a jumble of bone and flesh, shards of white cartilage protruding from a bloody pulp, like rocks in a hellish sea. His gullet was still pulsing. It was Jim, crumpled there, on the floor of the writing shed. Wisps of his gossamer hair curled up from the bloody bolus.

I retched, fell backwards out of the doorway and into the garlic and nettles. I wanted to run back to the house, to do everything in my power to escape that place. There was evil here. Something nameless and old. It had seeped into the people, and I could feel it then, seeping into me. But something made me stand, walk back into the shed, shut the door behind me. There was a reason Malcolm had given me his brand. I had a strength that few possessed. The ability to endure. I stood there in the dark shed, fighting back bile, trying to imagine what had happened. I'd seen Jim just hours ago, and he was supposed to have left this morning for the mainland. Why, then, had he come here? Perhaps to search one last time for the manuscript? And he'd been found, by someone who didn't want him to leave. That was my conclusion.

Looking about at the scattered books, the desk bashed from its position by the window, it was clear there had been a struggle. But whoever had done this had won. They'd disarmed Jim, used his own cane to bludgeon him. I stared down at him, muscle and sinew vivid and raw. His face had lost all recognisable human features and now, as the spittle and blood leaked from him, seemed more akin to some repugnant vegetable. It was a terrible way to die.

Hands going numb, vision narrowing, I tried to keep moving. Careful not to leave any trace of me being there, I searched the room for evidence of other people. I had, after all, seen shapes in the window. Where had they gone? I'd not seen them escape through the front door. And there was no way they could have climbed out the basement ceiling I'd fallen through the day before. So, it slowly dawned on me that whoever had killed Jim must be in the room below, listening, waiting.

If I'd had a gun, I might have drawn it. But I didn't and, if I am honest with myself, I don't believe I had the stomach for any more violence. So, instead, I worked my way around the edge of the room, careful to not make any boards creak. I moved to the doorway to the basement, laid both my bare hands on the door, and pushed it quietly open.

There was the empty stairway, the smell of mildew and earth. As I stepped down, darkness pressed against me like wet felt. The slope of the stairway meant I had to crouch, feel my way along the brick walls until I came to the final step. My eyes began to adjust to the gloom, with the help of the pool of jagged light that spilled down through the hole in the ceiling I'd made the day before. The floor was wet with rain that had dripped in through the hole. I stayed there, on the bottom step, still concealed in the stairway. I waited there in the semi-dark. The shapes in that basement began to take on forms of hunched people. It seemed they were waiting for me to take that last step, to move out into the basement and meet my end. But, the longer I looked at the shapes, the more they came into focus, morphing into desks, playhouses, piles of dresses. This is how it always is, I reminded myself. There are no phantoms waiting in the dark, only rot in the imagination, to be expunged. If there was someone there, they would be scared, just as scared as I was. I crept down off the last step and spoke into the gloom. 'You can come out.'

Only the whisper of trees from above, and the faint drip of water from sodden ceiling boards.

'I'm unarmed. I want to talk.'

I cast about for movement, saw nothing.

'If you have the manuscript, we can forget about this. That's all I'm here for.'

Still no movement. I began to walk around the edge of the basement, clambering over the piles of clothes and toys, conscious that at any moment, someone could come bursting from the dark.

CHRIS BARKLEY

When I'd walked the perimeter of the room, I stilled. There was no one here. But I was certain I'd seen movement in the window . . . I gazed up at the ceiling hole, which would be nearly impossible to climb through. Whoever was here couldn't have climbed out. So, where were they?

Crouching in the dark, I stared down at the floor. Across the wooden floorboards, between the toys and clothes, was a scattering of dirt which had come through the ruined ceiling. In that dirt I saw the back end of a shoeprint. I moved to the print, which was half-formed and messy, placed my own foot just over it. The shoe had been smaller than mine, and it was pointing in the direction of the hobby horse.

It was as my eyes settled on that familiar object that a realisation came to me: I remembered how Clara hadn't seemed to know about the toys in this basement. She'd not remembered the hobby horse. Clara told me these toys had been hers. Jim said the same thing. But what if they were lying?

Another memory came: Connie had asked me if I'd brought her another dress. I gazed at the pile of neatly folded dresses, now covered in rainwater and fallen dirt. What if Malcolm had collected these for Connie? I was certain of it now: Malcolm had known Connie. So why hadn't he mentioned her to me? My thoughts returned to what he had written about time, how it behaved differently on this island. I thought, again, of Julia.

As these ideas snaked about my mind, I smelt a familiar chemical sharpness. Petrol. It was faint, but cloying. Then, there was smoke. Like frayed rope it unravelled through the threshold, coming down into the basement, spreading.

Cursing under my breath, I bounded back up the stairs

and into the writing room, saw the floor writhing with fire, flames licking the walls. Books on the shelves erupted into lines of white fire, and Malcolm's miscellaneous papers, left upon his desk, were already ashy leaves. I rushed over to the door and pushed against it, but found that it was locked from the outside. I peered through the window glass, trying to see who was out there, but the smoke was stinging my eyes, and my lungs burnt. Striking my elbow against the window, trying to break the glass, I inhaled more of the thick smoke, felt myself sinking to the floor. I would pass out before I could break it. On my knees, I looked across and saw Jim's body. I determined that I would not be found with him. Not here, and not like this.

I crawled back to the basement door, rolling down the stairs and landing, smouldering, in the empty room. I lay there coughing, before lifting myself up, patting myself down, gulping in the air that I could. The hole in the ceiling taunted me from above, but there was no way I could reach it.

I'd landed beside the half-obscured shoeprint. Standing, I followed the direction in which it pointed, came to the wall beside the hobby horse. I felt along the wall, scrabbling for a way out. There were framed pictures hanging from hooks driven into the brick. Just to my left, about five paces from the stairway, was a small square frame. I lifted it from the nail, felt across the wall behind it. There was no variation in the brick, no indicator that there might be a hidden passage. I pulled on the hook, beat at the wall, tore my fingertips scratching at the cement.

Realising it was useless, I stopped and examined the picture. It was illuminated by the fire from the doorway and the grey mottled light through the broken ceiling, and I became lost in its shrouded beauty. There were stairways, beams, pillars, cornices, arches, façades. It was a recursive network of architecture, painted in the same style as those pictures in Malcolm's study. Gazing at the painting, I glimpsed something hidden inside: a circle of ancient pillars. They sang with the silent eloquence of geometry. A message meant only for me. Paring meaning from the patterns held within the angles, I glimpsed their truth. The way was strange, recursive, cold. But it was also beautiful. I just had to step back, surrender and observe. The stone pillars were speaking, just like the stone men beneath the lake. Secrets are like wary deer; stay still, watch, and they will come.

Above, a bookcase collapsed and broke me from my reverie. Flaming books tumbled down the stairs and I backed away from them, the picture still in my hands. Head heavy, eyes stinging, I unhooked the back of the frame, pulled it free and saw, pasted to the back of the painting, a note.

My beloved,
On the night of the full moon, we'll meet and we'll part.
May you always find the path through our little labyrinth.

Follow anew Abelard's dear love
Betwixt the arches curved above.

By now, the smoke was thick in the air, making me cough, and it scattered the light, formed gurning faces in the pockets of the room. The flames had caught the dresses now, and dragged them into its glittering, writhing mass.

I turned my face to the ceiling, ready to pray. It is curious how our instinct, when the end arrives, is to return to a story we were told as children. I'd lost my faith years before, but still, I turned my eyes upwards. There is comfort in stories. But 'comfort' is not the right word. Perhaps finding the right word is impossible, and that is precisely the purpose of stories. To describe that impossible word.

I peered again at the note, nerves sparking: the final two lines formed a cryptic crossword clue, I realised. I'd not seen one in some time, and had only attempted to solve one when I first visited Malcolm. Choking laughter pitched up in my chest; I imagined him watching me, applauding. I recalled what Jim had told me, about Malcolm's other identity: the great cryptic puzzler, Sestina.

Quickly reading the whole note again, I believed the first lines confirmed what I'd suspected: that the clue's answer would somehow reveal a path. In the haze and the dark I cast around and saw nothing. I could only read those words, repeat them until I either understood their meaning and escaped, or died in the dark. Then, I grasped it: 'Abelard's dear love' was Heloise.

So, I was to follow Heloise. But I did not understand how. I tried to speak the name, to understand if the sounds might be broken down, remoulded, but the smoke was too thick in my chest for even that. I slumped back down to the floor . . .

The final line instructed me to follow her between the arches. Though, the only arches I could make out were those in the painting. It made no sense. Once more, I read the cryptic clue and realised that the word 'anew' had been used. This, to an experienced puzzler, indicates that a phrase is to be unscrambled. I remembered Malcolm telling me all the hidden codes one evening, incanting them like a litany as he'd sat with his paper before the fireplace.

But I could find no hidden phrase within 'Heloise', and so I returned to those last two lines, focusing on any word that seemed out of place. I settled on the archaic 'betwixt'. The word 'between' would have been the obvious choice, surely?

Desperate and clumsy, I covered the rest of the passage with my fingers, focused on that single word. Then, I closed my eyes, holding the letters in my mind, joining them with those of 'Heloise'.

BETWIXT
HELOISE

Ecstatic light struck my heart, refracted, sent shimmers through me. Unscrambled, the words revealed: THE EXIT IS BELOW.

Choking, I raked at the floor immediately below me and found a space between the floorboards. I pressed into the space, hooked my fingers under the floorboard and found that it retracted, along with three others, sliding back into a space under the wall. With the last of my strength, I threw myself into the hollow, without a thought of how deep it was, or what might be beneath.

I fell down a narrow stairway, landing upside down at the bottom, coughing and wheezing, but at least able to breathe the damp air. It was dark and cool, and I lay there, just drinking in the air, before I turned onto my knees, rose gingerly and crept along the passage. Whoever had been in Malcolm's writing shed must have escaped this way.

I realised that this tunnel resembled those in *Man Follows Only Phantoms* – squarely cut through rough granite. Malcolm must have constructed it with his novel in mind. His main character had encountered the voice of the universe at the end of his path, so what would I find at the end of mine?

As I walked along, feeling my way through the semi-dark, I began to wonder who had written the note in the back of the frame. Perhaps Anwen had gifted Malcolm the picture, and he had framed it there, with her note in the back. I wondered if he had added the cryptic clue himself. There was a sense of satisfaction growing in me. It was clear that Malcolm had laid those artefacts together in that way as a kind of test. The painting, the note and the passage. I had solved the problem, in the direst of circumstances. I wondered, as I walked, if Malcolm had intended for me to find that passage someday, and had left that problem there just for me, the same way he'd left those chess compositions in the hallway of his house, the same way he'd left me his letter. I touched my fingertips to the mark on my arm and continued through the tunnel.

Eyes adjusting slowly, I began to make out shapes chiselled into the granite walls. There were shapes I recognised from his books – each of his fictional islands had been assigned an emblem – and, as I walked, I placed my hand against them. They were carved throughout the passage, and I found that the final shape was a new symbol. One for a book I had yet to read. It was the omphalos. It was clear to me then that this was the symbol of the final book: the manuscript I had yet to uncover. I went on.

The underground passage was longer than I expected and

sloped steeply downwards before gradually rising again. I must have been pressing uphill through the dark for twenty minutes before, eventually, I came to a sliver of light. There, up ahead, was a spiral staircase. The rusted metal caught what meagre light had accumulated over the years. I walked up the stairway, pulled open the mahogany door, found that I was looking through glass into Malcolm's sitting room. His body had been moved, and Anwen was no longer there. I cast about and saw that I had emerged through a false back in the glass-fronted violin cabinet. I closed the mahogany door, pushed the glass door open and stepped out into the sitting room.

Whoever had been in that writing shed had escaped this way. And now, they were in the house with me. But who had set the fire? It struck me then that there must have been two people. Before I'd arrived, one had left, gathering supplies to burn the shed – that would explain the swaying fern I'd seen on my approach. The other had escaped through this passage. I was outnumbered, ensnared.

Head pounding, I staggered over to the wide chair in which Anwen had cradled Malcolm, and collapsed into it. I found, tucked down the side of the cushion seat, one of Malcolm's books. Digging it out, I saw the title: *Man Follows Only Phantoms*. Anwen must have read it here with him. I held the book to my stomach, drew my knees up, rested my head against them, and laughed.

20

BREATHLESS, I STARED AT my bunched knees. I could not escape the memory of Jim's cane lying in the gore, the wisp of his hair crowning the pile. My mouth hung open. The cold air which seeped through the broken window dried my tongue. Balling myself tighter, I felt Malcolm's book pressing into my stomach: a physical sensation to distract myself. His work had always been a comfort to me. When I read Malcolm's words I vanished. How lovely it is to vanish. That is the strangeness in writers; we desire both immortality and invisibility. I looked down at the pages, some folded, others furrowed with water damage, and spoke to him. 'Please,' I said. 'Let me see.' I felt like the character in his book, bargaining with the universe. I was tired of being trapped, like the faceless characters occupying Malcolm's paintings, lost in their prisons of perspective. Of course, there was no answer. I lowered my knees and the book fell on the floor, cover down. I stared at it: the work of a great man.

I knew I couldn't linger, couldn't let whoever I had chased from the writing shed escape. I stood, picked up Malcolm's fallen book, set it back on the chair. For a moment I felt my sight pulled in the direction of Malcolm's stain on the carpet. It felt disrespectful to look. I turned away, steeled myself and went on.

I stalked through the corridors, looking for figures flitting out of sight, for smears of blood on the walls, smelling the air for traces of smoke and petrol. I was seeing Tilly's face in every painting, around every corner, so certain was I that she had burnt the writing shed, just as she had burnt my books. But who had helped her? Who was I chasing? I suddenly remembered what Harris had said about this family working together. If I found someone, what would the family do? Would they help me? I thought of Colm, sitting alone in his room, beating his head against the wall. That man was my only friend in this place. If I found the killer, I would take them straight to him. Then, together, we would escort them from the island. I could trust no one else.

I moved through the ground-floor rooms, the dining room, the study, the drawing room, the billiard room, all empty, aside from the scent of dry rot and woodworm. I returned to the central hall, vaulted up the staircase and walked around the upper gallery, gazing down at the floor from above. Every so often, I would turn over my shoulder, sensing someone there, only to see faces leering from the corner mouldings. They were faces of green men, leaves of oak, ash and birch obscuring bulbous features.

As I pushed out to the further reaches of the mansion, I began to feel a sense of helpless panic, as if the house were pushing me through its system, to its outer edges where discs of fungus crept through old timbers and vegetation sprouted from gutters and burst through chimneys. How long had it taken for the edges of the house to fall into disrepair? It seemed to me that it had happened supernaturally fast, that the land had gone out of its way to meld with the mansion, recompose it into something verdant. Perhaps it had been the force of Malcolm's spirit keeping the walls steady, and, now that he was gone, the binding circle had been broken, and the earth was eating this palace of recursion.

But thoughts such as these should be put out of mind. Again, I saw Colm, pounding his head against the wall. That was a man powerless to his thoughts, unable to pare the real from the fictional. Had Malcolm also suffered the same fate, towards the end? Anwen had mentioned his inability to separate reality from his created worlds. Could it be that no one had murdered Malcolm, and that, instead, he had grown weary of his madness, chosen to end his life? No, he couldn't have. I said that to myself, 'No, not Malcolm.'

At the mention of his name, I felt the corridor through which I moved constrict, and an invisible force took hold of my throat, pulled the breath from me. And then I saw him, standing in the dark end of the corridor, body caulked in murky light – the greenish kind that lurks in pockets in the depths of the sea. His eyes were misted over. His frame was hunched, arms knurled in to his torso, but his head peering up, face bleached and turned to me like a dead spotlight. He leered back and forth, as if his feet were sunk in thick mud, and his body pulled by a subtle current.

I closed my eyes, told myself that it was not possible. I had proven my sanity. Malcolm was not alive, and the figure before me was not him. How could it be? I had seen his corpse, held him as his arterial blood congealed on the floor. I opened my eyes again. The figure remained there, at the end of the corridor, but now his hand was extended upward, his fingers curled, reaching up to something I could not see. He looked in incredible pain.

'What do you want from me?' I was speaking before I

could stop myself. The words had come from a place beyond thought, beyond rationality – a place that existed in me, no matter how much I ignored it. I did not understand, until then, how vulnerable I felt, how lost and alone, how scared. Was this how Julia had felt? I knew then that this was a cruel symmetry; it was something I deserved. 'What do I do?' I asked Malcolm.

When he did not reply, I screamed, holding my head in my hands, feeling the shell I'd formed to safeguard my sanity melt away, leaving behind a quivering jelly. I was pathetic, had lost almost everything. And now, I was being tormented. I wanted it to end. More than anything, in that moment, I wanted it to end. I charged down the corridor, crashing into the walls, breaking light fixtures, hearing the glass shards shatter and dance on the floorboards behind me. I had closed my eyes, wincing, expecting to crash into him, but nothing was there. Eyes still shut, I slowed and stopped, reassuring myself that the corridor was empty. I had run at him face on, encountered nothing. Slowly, I began to reopen my eyes.

His face was before mine, pulpy flesh drooping from his skull, broken pegs poking from his gums, mouth hanging open as his eyes peered upward. Still, his hand groped for something above us.

I couldn't move. I remained face to face with him, unable to breathe, unable to look away. The fine hairs of his scalp caressed each other, writhing in a feathery mass as if suspended in water. He looked lost. I realised, for the first time, that it was not me that had been trapped by Malcolm; he, too, had been choked by his legacy. I felt then that he was reaching out, from wherever he now was, begging me to make amends for the mistakes with which he'd drowned himself.

His eyes sank down to me, and, as they moved, the slick algae which had furred his eyeballs floated away, revealing black pupils. His bloated, sodden skin sloughed away, leaving behind only an impression in the darkness, and dead lips, recalling in the memory of muscle, a final thought, held in the body. They shaped the words 'Save her'. Then he was gone.

In the darkened corridor, I fumbled with my cigarette case, hoping to find comfort in the familiar motions; taking out the cigarette, lighting it, breathing deep. *Save her.* I cursed as my trembling hand lost the cigarette, and it scuttered across the boards, tossing embers as it rolled. I sank to my knees, fumbling for the cigarette, giving up, holding my head in my hands. I wept – the kind of weeping where pressure builds behind the eyes, in the throat, but no tears come. I realised that Malcolm was like me. In the end, he'd had no answers, only a decaying body and a string of regrets. He was no god. Of course he wasn't. He was a man, just as trapped as the rest of us. I had known this. All along, of course I had known it, but still there was a part of me that believed Malcolm to possess some supernatural power, some ability to transcend. Rising to my feet, disillusioned, cold, I understood that nothing had changed. Not really. Yes, Malcolm was different to the man I'd held in my mind, but I was still his friend, and he had promised me his legacy. While doubt and phantoms swirled about me, I held fast to the line I'd been pulling all this time. I would find the manuscript. I would find Jim's killer. I would know the truth of Malcolm's death.

Colm. I had to find Colm, to tell him what had happened at the writing shed and, truthfully, to find comfort in his company. I would tell him about Malcolm's letter, how it had been stolen from me. I would reveal to him everything. I could not do this alone. Not anymore. And so I hurried along the corridor, making my way along the edges of the mansion, where the cold mustered and the dust was thick, hoping to somehow find the western wing.

I went along the hallway in a daze, running my hand along the wall, as if I were navigating a labyrinth, clinging to one side. It anchored me to the physical world. I moved past statues wrought of marble. The hewn figures were chimerical – marble skin melding with tufted fur, or long blade-like feathers. A statue of a faun looked down on me as I turned past it, moving hurriedly on. Had I seen these statues before? In one of Malcolm's novels, a character had become lost in a house of statues; this was why they were familiar. But I had not seen them in this place before, and I was certain I'd walked this hallway. I went on, trying to ignore the eyes of the statues on my back, turning again, dragging my hand along the wall, until it slipped into a recess.

I was at the corridor of alcoves, where the lonely chess sets waited. I pulled my hand back. The alcoves were dark, hidden from the light which slipped through the high window, but I saw their configurations had, again, been changed. Just as I was wondering who might be changing them, a white hand stretched from the nearest alcove.

I stopped, watched the hand linger in the gloom, descend upon a bishop and slide it slowly to the centre of the board.

With Malcolm's image still fixed in my mind's eye, I

approached the alcove, seeing the figure gradually come into focus.

The hand belonged to Colm. He sat, hunched like a gargoyle, unblinking. His suit was crumpled, his skin slick with sweat, and his mouth hung open, gasping.

Trying to keep my voice steady, I spoke to the trembling mass of pale flesh. 'You're the one who's been moving the pieces.'

He said nothing, only staring across the board, to the empty space opposite him. 'He wins every time,' Colm whispered.

'Who? There's no one there, Colm.' I peered into the space opposite him, where there was only the stone seat wreathed in shadow.

'I didn't mean to hurt him.' He caught my eye. 'You know that?'

It was quiet as we regarded each other, wondering what the other might do. Who had he hurt? I held up my palms, made to sit opposite him in the alcove.

He let out a cry of pain, shouted, 'Not there, he won't like it!'

I stood back up, waited outside the alcove, watching the empty seat. I could hear Colm's breathing – wet and pained. 'I can see you're upset, Colm. Why don't you come away? We can talk.'

'Colm can't talk,' he said, hysteria creeping into his voice. He moved another piece across the board, then wiped a heavy bead of sweat from the tip of his bulbous nose. 'He wouldn't give it to me,' he said. 'He wouldn't give it, so I took it.'

'What did you take?'

His eyes bulged from their dark hollows and he wiped furiously at his face. Then, a stillness came over him. He looked at the invisible player opposite him and smiled.

'Colm,' I whispered.

He burst from the alcove, knocking me over.

Scrambling to my feet, I saw the little rectangular pocketbook had slipped from his jacket and was lying open on the floor of the alcove.

He was off, down the corridor. I didn't chase him. Instead, I reached into the alcove, picked up the pocketbook. When I saw what was inside, I shut it, whirled about. But Colm was gone. The photograph in the pocketbook was of another man. He was slim, tall and had thick black hair. He had his arm wrapped languidly about a slim, jaggedly beautiful woman, and between them was a young boy, who resembled them both. He had a sharp nose and a snaggletooth smile and was unmistakably their son. I saw the photograph had been scratched around the woman's face, perhaps with a fingernail. And there, on the first page of the pocketbook, a phrase, repeatedly scrawled: *Forgive me, Colm.*

The story this material told chimed dissonant with the story I'd believed. Looking again at the slim man gazing out of the photograph, I felt certain that this was Colm Hubert.

So, who was the man I had met on the ferry, the man I had come to trust? Until now, I'd believed him to be something like a friend. I was even going to tell him of Malcolm's letter. But he had lied to me. If he was not Colm Hubert, who was he? Had he aided Tilly? Perhaps it was him that I'd chased from the writing shed? Could he have killed Malcolm? I had a sinking feeling, knowing now that all along, he had been playing games with me. I began to think back on what

I had shared with him, hating myself for defending him, for thinking that he was on my side. I slipped the pocketbook into my coat. Then it was rage that stirred me, drove me on after him. I would catch him. I would hurt him.

As I ran down the corridor, past the great stag skull, whose shadow split the floor into a branching pattern, I saw his wide back slip down a passage which led out to the upper gallery. He moved quickly, with a grace that I lacked as I stumbled over the corners of rugs, bashed into the walls. How long had he wandered these upper halls? I called to him, screamed for him to stop. There was no reply, only the muffled padding of feet and a low, throaty laugh.

A crash. Out on the upper gallery, there was the heavy slap of a body against the floor. I followed, making the last turning and seeing him there, halfway through the broken railing. His head peered down at the ground-floor hall, and his lower body was pinned by none other than Mrs Gibson. She'd tackled him and now sat atop him, sombre-faced. I wanted to hug her.

'Thank you,' I said as I approached, catching my breath.

Beneath her, the man who I'd come to know as Colm was still laughing that low, throaty laugh, wheezing heavily.

'I was following,' Mrs Gibson said, brushing herself down, readjusting her hair. She took the hand I offered and rose, standing with me, looking over the pitiful man.

'How long have you been following me?' I asked her.

Mrs Gibson was quiet.

'It seems you were my guardian,' I said. Relief washed over me. I was right; someone had been following me all this time, but in the end, she was my protector, not my tormentor.

She tugged at her earlobe, then faintly smiled as she glanced at me sideways.

The man I'd come to know as Colm groaned and rolled up to face us, spittle running from the corner of his mouth. His face was a nest of bruises, and he looked almost nothing like the man I had first encountered on the ferry. His eyes flitted about, tracking something that was not there.

'Who are you?' I asked, crouching before him.

He met my eye, still wheezing.

I pulled out the pocketbook, showed him the picture. I pointed at the man. 'This is Colm Hubert, isn't it? So, who are you?'

Slowly his heavy lips pulled back to reveal blood-browned teeth. He said, 'Did you find it yet?'

'That's what you wanted, isn't it? You wanted me to find the manuscript and bring it to you . . . Then what would you have done to me?' I snapped him towards me, pulling him by the shirt.

He was silent for a moment, then made a noise between a moan and a laugh and said, 'The same thing I did to Colm.'

I released him, let him fall back. He sat looking at me.

'You forged the will,' I said. 'Of course you did. You didn't want to verify the manuscript; you're no counterfeiting specialist.'

'Wrong.'

Mrs Gibson and I waited, seething.

'That is precisely what I am. A rare goods dealer must be skilled in determining forgeries . . .' He looked over my shoulder again, and his words died in his mouth.

'Rare goods dealer,' I said.

He brought his attention to me again, nodding slowly. 'It was at university that my friend Colm introduced me to the *Gravitation* series. Over those novels he and I bonded, became . . . close. When we finished our degrees, he went on to work for the firm who represented Malcolm, and I turned my passion for collecting into a career, trading in rare goods, first editions, artefacts. Colm helped me, even when my business was dying. He gave me legal counsel, and he would purchase things from me which I knew interested him little, perhaps out of guilt . . . He'd married, insisting that it was the conventional thing for a solicitor to do.' Colm's voice broke, and he made an anguished whine, before hardening again, taking a shivering breath, continuing. 'Being a married man made him more trustworthy. But even his support could not save my business . . . so, when he told me of Malcolm's new work, I decided I would take it and sell it. And that was Colm's last gift to me.'

Backing away from him, I looked to Mrs Gibson, whose face was dark with fury.

'At our last meeting, I told him I loved him, that he had saved me . . . He has always watched over me. And . . . and he does still.' His gaze flicked over my shoulder, and he began to quiver uncontrollably, muttering under his breath.

'Did you kill Malcolm?' said Mrs Gibson.

The man held himself. 'No, not Malcolm.'

'Jim?' I said.

Mrs Gibson turned to me, and I nodded sombrely.

The man's eyes were wide, and he was blubbering now, but through the heaving sobs, he said, 'No.'

'Why should we believe you?' I asked.

He snivelled, covered his face, beat his forehead, then looked at us, vacant. 'I have nothing to lose. Everything is gone, and this place . . . I see them all.'

'What is your name?' I asked.

He considered, then cast about. He was sitting with his back to the broken railing, and below him was the drop to the darkened hall. 'I'm no one,' he said.

I struck him just as he went to throw himself backwards, knocking him cold, sending him sprawling sideways. He lay there, unconscious, while I and Mrs Gibson stood, reeling.

About us, the house creaked and moaned, the faces of the green men watched us from the corners, and the warmth of decay sucked at our skin.

'Mrs Gibson,' I said slowly, 'there's something I should admit . . . I saw Colm in the house just after Malcolm was killed. I did not see him return from the glasshouse, like I said in the meeting. The alibi was false. What's more, after lunch, he was with Tilly. They could have plotted this whole thing then. Will you watch over him while I look for her?'

She grimaced, then turned to me, laid a hand on my shoulder. Her touch was light, and in her face I saw that it was not Colm, but she, who had been my ally all along. 'You have my word,' she said.

'Please, if there is anything you know that you have held back from me, say it now.'

'I've held nothing back,' she said. 'But I heard someone race through the house, not long before you returned,' she said.

'Who was it?'

'I didn't see. But they went out through the back, to the glasshouse.'

I was already moving by the time she'd finished speaking, but she caught my hand, spoke with desperation. 'I told you of Daphne, of our family's situation . . . When this is done,' she said, 'will you help me and my daughter?'

I stopped, caught by the candour of her words. 'Yes,' I said. 'You have my promise.'

The tension in her face dropped, and she squeezed my hand warmly.

I bowed my head, then went on, racing down from the gallery to the hall, through the winding ground-floor corridors and on towards the glasshouse.

2 1

WHEN I OPENED THE door to the glasshouse, warmth swallowed me. The air was heavy with the mucousy sweetness of orchids. Roots and vines mustered on the path. I stepped over them, pushing through the dense, low canopy, sensing the quiet presence of another being nearby. As I moved, I somehow became certain that whoever was in this garden knew I was here. We were both aware of each other, but neither would run. There was an inevitability to our meeting. I walked about the edge of the glasshouse, reaching out to touch the warm condensation on the glass, feeling it drip from my fingers. The path then pushed inward, between the probing arms of overgrown shrubs. I walked on, in towards the central pond, which filled the garden with its mist, made the skin clammy.

I found her huddled over the central pond. Her head was bowed and her forearms were laid over the wet slate of the pond's perimeter. She was soaking her hands in the water. I walked slowly, stalking towards her. The leaves of the giant water lilies floated on the pond's surface, collecting moisture, like sweat on the back of a wrist. Clustered about the edge of the pond were tree ferns, and from their bark hung the delicate stems of the orchids. They were curtained about her and almost seemed to part when she looked up at me. Then, her eyes darted to the pond, before returning to the floor.

I stopped where I was, rooted to the spot. 'Clara,' I said. Her broad shoulders were hunched, her auburn hair matted with reddish crust.

I went across to the pond, looked into the water, saw it was rusty from where she'd cleaned her hands of blood. Flecks of it were dashed across her forearms like freckles. She stared into the water as it lapped at her wrists, pruned her white fingers.

'Why, Clara?' I said.

'It's not what you think.'

'Tell me what I think.'

She glared at me. Her eyes were wet and dark. 'You think I killed Jim to prevent him leaving . . . You think I killed my father.'

Lowering myself slowly onto the edge of the pond, I faced her. 'And I suppose you have a smart alibi?'

She scowled at me, flashing sharp teeth. 'You, my father, Jim. You're the same. Weak little creatures clinging to riddles to make yourselves feel smarter than everyone else. And evil forms purest in weak men.'

There was truth in what she said. I had seen it myself – the pain weakness can inflict upon others. I bowed my head. 'I may be weak. In fact, I know I am . . . but what you did today, that is evil.'

She made a small contemptuous laugh, then spoke with a detached voice. 'When my father invited Jim to come live here, we welcomed him. A part of me believes my father invited Jim to raise us on his behalf – to act as his surrogate while he wrote his books. Jim had no children of his own, no wife. We all grew to trust him and welcomed him to the family. But soon, I came to understand why the man had never dared have his own children. He was afraid of what he might do to them.'

Her gaze faltered, and she looked down into her hands, wringing them together.

'I was fourteen, and when I came to my father to tell him what had happened, he didn't believe it. And then, when I fell pregnant, he did nothing. He allowed Jim to remain here, told me this was the way it had to be.' She took a long pause, and her hands stilled, fell into her lap. 'Weak men,' she said again.

Moments accordioned out in my memory: how Clara had voted against Jim; how I had found him at her door this morning, the look of guilt on his face. Then, at Jim's house, when he told me he was attracted to those he shouldn't be . . . All seemed to add up to this conclusion. The ground beneath me became unsteady as the revelation washed over me in a dreadful wave. I understood then that it was the pregnancy that had ended Clara's swimming career, that the war had been a convenient cover. Searching her face, I saw the pain there and believed her.

'Connie,' I said. 'She's your daughter.'

Her head fell, and her breathing became ragged.

'You lied about the toys in the basement. They weren't yours. Malcolm collected them for Connie. He . . . he cared for her. And when I chose the otter *netsuke* . . . you knew it was her favourite.'

She buried her eyes into the butts of her palms, racked with deep heaving sobs.

I was on my feet, unsure where to go, but unable to sit. I ran my hands down the sides of my face, understanding now why Connie had been kept apart from the family, why

Harris had been so secretive. I thought of Malcolm's letter, and of the buried obscenities.

'I did not kill my father,' Clara said. She looked up at me, fire burning through her wet eyes. 'But I killed Jim . . . and would again.'

An acid quiet. I held her eye, absorbed what she'd told me. Carefully, I spoke. 'Tell me exactly what happened.'

'I . . . I went to the writing shed to collect memories of my father, and I found Jim waiting for me. He said he knew I'd come there, that he wanted me, one last time before he left . . . We struggled, and then . . . I don't know, it happened so quickly. When it was over, I found the passage in the basement. My father had shown it to me when I was little.'

'And you had help,' I said.

Her eyes widened.

'Someone burnt down the shed after you left.'

She stilled.

I watched her, trying to make sense of the shifting story. Colm had denied having any part in Jim's death . . . and I realised that I believed him. I'd not witnessed he and Clara speak at any point and, in fact, I suspected Clara disliked him. So, who had Clara partnered with?

Clara's voice, softly: 'She pitied me. She only did what I asked.'

'She?'

Clara said nothing more. She didn't need to.

'Tilly,' I said.

She lowered her head, acquiescing.

It made sense in my mind: Tilly had also hated Jim. Perhaps she'd known about his obscene habits and had helped Clara. She made more sense than Colm. The picture was painted in my mind; they were broad strokes, but I had the outline plain: Tilly had killed Malcolm after he'd rejected her manuscript, and she had helped Clara kill Jim. At that moment I had no interest in punishing, or even in reporting. In fact, I pitied Clara, and after the revelation that Malcolm had defended Jim, I also pitied Tilly.

All I wanted was to find the last manuscript. Let fate examine the scales of morality, I thought. I had a single intention.

Clara straightened her spine, displaying her wide shoulders, her long neck. She looked around the glasshouse, peering through the thick humid air, drinking in the cloying scent of orchids. The light was greenish and unreal, and seemed to almost be vegetable itself: an organism, slowly absorbing us.

'My mother didn't want the child in this house, but wouldn't let Jim take her. So we gave her to Harris . . . He has taken good care of her.' She was silent for a while, before saying, 'I remember after it happened, my father spoke to me. He said that I should view the child as a gift. He said . . . he said she was special.' She laughed, reached out and plucked a nasty thick leaf from a nearby plant. Fingering it, she said, 'I wanted it all to be over . . . A parent should love their child, but I have never loved her. In fact, I think my father cared for her more than I ever did.'

'Why didn't you go to the police, tell them what happened?' She let the leaf drop by her foot. 'My father exerted his will. It was to stay a secret. Perhaps he thought it might upset his legacy? Perhaps he was ashamed.'

We remained there together, in the humid air, droplets

of sweat rolling down our faces. There was a feeling shared. An understanding. I reached out to place a hand on her shoulder, but she flinched away. I let my hand fall by my side.

'Things are clearer now,' I said.

She looked beyond me, into the spiny lacing of leaves, the canopy of branches. I wondered what it was she saw there, in this sickly greenish womb. Her eyes glinted, and, when I turned, I saw her brother.

By then my head was light from the overpowering odour of the plants, and the smoke still in my lungs. But I saw him approach, like a spectre through the damp air.

'What's happened?' he said, reading our expressions.

Clara burst past me, running along the path to where Lewis stood. She wrapped her long arms about his shoulders and buried her face in his neck. They stayed there in that way for a minute. Clara spoke with him, and, as I neared, heard her say, 'He's dead. He's dead.'

Then, they broke slowly apart, and Lewis watched me with a careful eye.

'She told me everything,' I said. 'About Connie. About Jim.'

Lewis's mouth twitched.

'I don't blame you . . . for lying to me about the little girl. You were protecting your sister. Or, at least, you thought you were.'

Lewis stepped towards me, a slim man, but with the jagged energy of his father. The kind which hints at a supernatural endurance. I'd seen men like him, fought them. He spoke, a force contained behind his wry smile. 'There is no black and white. I'm sure you understand . . . I'm sure all men like us understand. To have fought and returned alive, one is either lucky, or insensate. Are you lucky, Euan?'

'No,' I said.

He nodded, a look of pain, but also sympathy, on his face. 'What will you do, after what you've seen?'

After considering, I said gently, 'Nothing.'

He grinned, then said through his teeth, 'Help me believe you.'

I took a moment, let my gaze float between the two of them. They were standing between me and the doorway, bodies charged with a wary energy, like beasts encountering each other in the wild.

'We were marching to an outpost,' I said, watching their faces as I prepared to speak the story I'd supressed for so long. 'A farmhouse outside of Caen. We'd been in a skirmish and our lieutenant had been killed. I was the commanding officer. After three days hiking, hauling mortars through woodland, we came across a building in the trees.' I paused, saw Clara and Lewis listening carefully. 'We were tired, low on food. I became convinced that the soldiers who'd caught us in the skirmish had fallen back to the building. We could have left it, circled around them . . . but what if they had artillery? What if by leaving them, I was sentencing other men to die? I thought I could catch them unawares. So, I formed up my men, prepared the mortars and waited for night to fall, keeping an eye on the windows. It was quiet for some time – so quiet that we began to suspect they had moved on. But then, I saw it, the flickering of a candle flame. I gave the command. We shelled the building till it was a black mess . . . When it was done, we marched on, over the wreckage, without a word. But my men all knew, as did I, that the blackened bodies inside were not those of soldiers. We were trampling over a family's home. Mother, father . . . children.' I paused, tried to compose myself, but my voice caught, and tears ran down my cheeks. 'I've let fear rule my life for so long, and I have done awful things. Worse than what I have seen here.' I looked at Clara, then at Lewis. 'We are, all of us, sinners. Who am I to judge you?'

They both regarded me quietly, before Lewis turned to Clara. A look was passed between them. As if to confirm that I was now trusted to keep this family secret, Clara walked to me, placed a tender hand on my shoulder and then drifted away, moving to a corner of the glasshouse, where the orchids grew in a thick troop. She remained there, like a seer passing from one realm to another, facing the glass wall, staring outward at the weary afternoon clouds.

Lewis watched her for a time, before saying under his breath, 'I see why my father welcomed you. You're as ruined as the rest of us. Tell me, did you want him to forgive you?'

'What do you mean?'

'You don't strike me as a man of faith.'

'No.'

'But still, it's natural to want forgiveness.'

I looked at him with grim concentration, sweat forming on my temples.

Lewis laughed. 'He would have relished that power. Believe me. I learnt long ago that secrets are like strands of nerves. If you gave one to my father, he would tug at it and wield you like a marionette. Even with the most benign information, he could do awful, and tremendous, things. So, I learnt from a young age to conceal what I wanted.'

I stepped backwards, glanced over my shoulder to Clara, who was still gazing through the glass.

He spoke again. 'My advice to you would be not to worry about what you are. The main purpose in life is to become something that you were not in the beginning.'

I couldn't look at him. He was wrong. No matter how much I had tried, how far I had ascended, I could not erase my origin. It was as Malcolm had written: *The place we start from guides us to our end.*

'We cannot change our nature,' I said.

'We can. And I can already see the change in you.'

It had come to the point where every word Lewis spoke felt like a thorn pressing against my flesh. The longer the conversation went on, the deeper they pressed. 'There is nothing constant about this life,' he said. 'If a thing does not interact with what surrounds it, it may as well not exist. Change is what makes us a part of this world. I believe my father knew this. He believed it so deeply that he thought he could even change time.'

The sound of condensation dripping into the still pond. The thrumming of slow vegetable life. The atmosphere was womb-thick and mossy. Overwhelmed, I said, 'Time. You believe he could change time?'

He raised his chin, the smirk remaining on his face. 'Imagine being able to go back and act differently. To be able to alter the course of things.'

'Impossible.'

'My father loathed the word.'

I felt dizziness returning and, putting a hand to my forehead, wiped away the sweat, tried to concentrate. Malcolm had once asked my opinion of H.G. Wells, and we had spent the night debating the merit of an early short story, 'The Chronic Argonauts', in which an inventor travels back in time. Malcolm told me he'd preferred it to Wells' more widely known later work. Recalling our discussion then, I saw, again, the frenzied look in Malcolm's eye.

'Are you playing with me, Lewis?'

'No. I am telling you what I believe. I lived with the man for years, followed him, watched him when he didn't know it. I saw him change as he delved into forbidden knowledge, saw it possess him. He would stare for hours at old manuscripts, books of prediction. One time he told me he would write down my future and hide it . . . then he left, laughing.'

'Why are you telling me?'

'Because,' he said, 'I hope that when the time comes, you will remember who your real friends are.'

I thought, then, of Colm. He had been a friend; one I'd thought to be real. Looking at Lewis, I wondered what else I'd got wrong. 'You mean, when I find the manuscript? You believe he's written down his theory . . . about changing time?'

'If he has, I trust you will share it with me, just as I have shared this with you.'

I rubbed my temples, sucking in the air. I nodded curtly, then said, 'I need to go. Tilly, where is she?'

He gave me a long, hard look.

I said nothing, only held his gaze.

'Around this time, she walks the grounds,' he said.

I went to leave, but he put a hand on my chest. 'You think it was Tilly?'

Taking his hand, I removed it from my chest, held it a moment in the narrow space between our bodies. 'I'll know soon enough.'

He pulled away. I saw his face darken, the hollows under his eyes sag, the lines around his mouth tighten. 'Tilly has always been good to us. She loves this family . . . loved my father.'

I stayed quiet, acknowledging his words. My silence was enough. He read my thoughts.

'And he did not love her.' His eyes moved back and forth as he ran over the theory in his mind.

'Stay with Clara,' I said.

He looked to his sister, breathed air through his teeth. 'It's linked, isn't it? The manuscript, my father's death . . .'

'I don't know.'

Shaking his head, he moved away from me, on towards Clara. 'We expect it all to make sense in the end, but it never does.'

'If only reality were as soothing as fiction.'

As he left, I heard his voice pulsing in the thick air. 'No mystery is stranger than that we live ourselves.'

22

THE STONY HILLS ROSE on either side of Malcolm's estate like the spines of circling dogs. From the deep glen they surrounded, the tips of the hills were indigo in the low sun. Their presence was both comforting and ominous – ancient formations upon which the locals had built their homes. Living on this estate, one felt permanently watched. I felt this distinctly as I made my way out across the grounds, towards Tilly.

She was sitting on a great flat stone, reading. Her eyes were moving over the page, but in a distracted, distant way. She was coiled. Her attention was on me, but she didn't want to show it.

I moved through the long grass, seed pods sticking to my trousers, skylarks hovering overhead. Before I'd left the house, I'd taken an apple and a slice of toast for a late lunch and felt them now sitting heavily in my stomach. Filling my lungs with the cool evening air, I readied myself. In the distance, a slender ribbon of black smoke rose from where the writing shed was.

Finally, she looked up from her book, which was, to my surprise, one of mine. She closed it and set it down beside her. I saw the cover, recognised it as the last book I'd written, *Ex Libris*.

'You have good taste,' I said, stopping a little way from her.

'There's no truth here, only artifice,' she said, tapping the cover. 'I can see the strings . . . like a puppet theatre.'

'Then, why read it?'

'I want to understand why he chose you.'

'I wish I knew myself. Perhaps he saw potential.'

She gave me an anaemic smile. 'Forgive me. I don't see it.'

'Is that why you burnt my books?'

She stiffened, then slid off the flat stone and stood opposite me, grass sighing around her. She pulled her bun tighter and looked at me with scorn. 'What evidence do you have?'

'When you came to my room, I smelt petrol on you.'

'Whoever burnt your books did the world a favour,' she said, straightening her cardigan and dress. 'You're a second-rate pulp novelist, and we all know it.'

'Why shouldn't I find Anwen right now, tell her what you did?'

'What I did?'

'You were jealous. Malcolm chose me to finish his series, and so you killed him, burned my books on the lawn. As he bled out, he found a gun and shot at you. Have I got that right?'

Her mouth hung open, and her eyes watered with quiet fury.

'Was it you I chased into the trees?'

'Whatever you think happened, believe me when I tell you there is nothing straightforward about this. Even if I did do what you say, you'll have a hard time convincing anyone.'

'I know about Jim, what he did to Clara. I know Malcolm kept it a secret. Is that also why you killed him? Is that why you helped Clara murder Jim?' I pointed to the black smoke coming from the woods. 'I suppose that was your doing? While Clara escaped, you burnt the shed, and Jim's body with it.'

She followed my finger, saw the smoke, glowered. 'You've hammered together a fantasy.'

'I understand why you did it,' I said. 'You'd protected Malcolm for so long. You'd concealed terrible things, helped him bury his secrets, and then when the time came for your reward, he rejected you. I know you stole the letter he wrote me. You must have seen what he offered me . . . what he promised me.'

Tilly shook her head, a look of bewilderment on her face. 'I don't know of any letter.'

'The letter in my coat pocket. It was missing after you left.'

'Stop,' she said, a desperate rasp to her voice.

'You killed Malcolm, and you helped Clara kill Jim.'

She looked at me with a mixture of pity and disgust.

I stepped towards her, hand outstretched. 'Come with me,' I said.

She roared, then said with grim conviction, 'I burnt your books on the lawn. But as I set the fire, Malcolm shot through the window to scare me off. That was the gunshot you heard. So, it *was* me you chased into the trees. But that is where the truth of your story ends. I had nothing to do with his death. There was another person in the room with him when he fired his shot at me, but I ran before I could see them fully.'

I was quiet, watching the minute changes in her face, trying to discern any traces of untruth.

'Jim,' she said, eyes narrowed, 'he's dead?'

Uncertain what to make of her, I said, 'If you weren't with Clara, who was? Who burnt down the shed?'

She stayed quiet, looking at me like I was a fool.

And she was right. I looked at her blankly, until she said, 'They care for no one but each other. Since childhood it has been that way. He would do anything for her.'

Like a map unfurling, it suddenly became plain. I saw the paths we had all passed along, how they interwove and fractured. I remembered how Lewis had burst into the glasshouse, the concern on his face, how Clara had whispered in his ear, telling him the lies she'd spun. They had worked together.

'And . . . and the letter?' I said.

'I told you, Euan, I have no letter.'

And then I recalled the gathering we'd had the day before, how I had sat beside Lewis, taken off my coat. I remembered that he'd smoked the same liquorice cigarettes as me. He must have rummaged in my pocket, taken the letter as well as one of my cigarettes. He'd been flaunting it, daring me to notice him. And then there was the sentence he'd uttered as I left him . . . 'No mystery is stranger than that we live ourselves.' It had sounded familiar when he'd said it, but now I recalled it was from the letter. Like his father, he was revelling in his trickery. The difference was that while Malcolm was a genius, his son was a crude imitation. I felt a mass of rage forming in my chest, draining blood from my face, the extremities of my limbs.

A grin formed on Tilly's face. 'I will never forget that look,' she said coldly. 'The moment you grasped how wrong you were. What have you realised, Euan?'

'Lewis,' I said. 'He took the letter from my pocket during our meeting. And . . . he burnt down the writing shed while I was inside. He was there, with Clara, when Jim was killed.'

Her composure was faltering. 'I suppose they put the blame on me?'

I was broken from my reverie by the look on her face, a slow curdling. It was the look of someone who has had their worst fears confirmed, who has been betrayed wholly.

She spoke distantly. 'He said they would turn . . .'

There was a gruesome abandon to her movements as she swept through the grass, over to me. She gave a scathing laugh. 'I want you to ask yourself something,' she said. There was a tremble to her mouth, her eyes were wet. 'Who are you doing this for? Is it for Malcolm . . . for Anwen? Are you doing it out of some kind of love? Some imagined devotion? I know you, Euan. I know you because I, too, was a lonely child who found meaning in Malcolm's words. He was my friend when no one else was. He was my guide. But, what I did . . . what I did was build an effigy of the man in my mind. Through his words, I built a person, a hero, a good man. He was who I needed him to be. And that is how I have always seen Malcolm . . . how I have always seen his family. I constructed an idea of them in my head and never saw them as anything other than that. I allowed them to take everything from me. But what have I been given in return? What love have I been shown? Where . . . where do I go now?' She gripped the lapel of my coat with a strong hand. 'He promised me so much . . . said I was part of the legacy.' She laughed again, a wild and sad laugh. 'We are told great men live in the minds of others for generations. But the truth is just the opposite. Men obsessed with legacy dilute themselves, with every mind they occupy. Great men devote themselves to few. They live quietly, gently, and fade to nothing. It is beautiful to be forgotten.'

I took her hand from my lapel, held it gently. 'You're wrong,' I said. 'There's nothing purer than devoting your life to a craft and being remembered for it.'

Her face fell. 'That is what you want for yourself?'

'It's why I came here. I know what it's like to be nothing. There's no beauty there.'

'It's selfish.'

'No,' I said. 'It's the opposite. There are people I have lost . . . but who would live on in my work.'

'Will it bring them back?'

I went quiet. Lewis's words rang in my mind, about Malcolm's knowledge of time, about the secrets he'd written. Perhaps one could bring back those that are lost. Perhaps he had found a way.

Before I could reply, Tilly said finally, 'After a life devoted to his craft, was Malcolm happy?'

I let her hand slip from my grasp and stood there, holding her gaze, as the wind picked up about us, blowing my coat against my knees, toying with the flyaway hairs escaping Tilly's bun. 'Happy is just a moment,' I said. 'It's fascination that lasts.'

She gave me a knowing look, laced with pity. 'It's a slight difference, between being fascinated and being consumed. Sometimes I wonder if there even is a difference.'

'I don't think that matters,' I said.

She spoke quietly. 'We could still leave. Come with me to the ferry.'

I weighed her offer, seeing that choice play out like a puppet show, where the marionettes break loose, wobble free for a moment, then collapse, lifeless. I met her eye, saw her desperation, her hope. 'I will,' I said. 'But there are things I need to do.'

There was something inside Tilly then that fell and broke. 'No,' she said. 'There aren't.'

I gave no reply.

She watched me as if I were an alien creature. Then, she pushed me away lightly and said, 'Go on, then. Be consumed. I hope you have better fortune than me.'

The wind ceased. Stillness crept across the grass like a tide from the trees. And then, like a song playing through the threshold to another world, Anwen's violin sounded from the house, made its way to our ears. I recognised the melody: Mendelssohn's *Violin Concerto in E minor*. Looking up, I saw Anwen standing in the arched window of a room on the upper floor, looking out over the grounds, violin resting on her shoulder, her long slender arm threading the bow in and out. She wore a long dress the colour of sage and, in the arch of the window, she looked like an actor on a proscenium stage, with the estate, and everything beyond it, as her audience. In fact, she did seem to be looking beyond, out towards the northeast, where the trees burgeoned about Harris's cottage, where the deep glen sloped down to meet the sea.

The music brought back the memory of the girl in the window. This was the piece that had been playing on the turntable when Connie peered into the study and the cabinet of *netsuke*. I remembered her little rain-scoured face, and how peaceful she'd seemed standing there all alone. Why had she come there, to Malcolm's study? What had she expected to find? I knew that Malcolm had given her dresses . . . Clara had told me that he'd cared for her.

'What is it?' Tilly asked, as I backed away.

All the moisture had left my mouth. My thoughts raced. As Anwen's music pierced the gauze between past and present, I felt the nerves between moments fuse, and suddenly it was clear.

Tilly looked from me to Anwen in the window, then back to me.

I began to move, not towards the house, but out towards the trees.

'Lewis and Clara are inside the house,' said Tilly.

'I know . . . There's just something I have to do.'

I saw Tilly come forward, almost as if she might follow me. But then, she stopped. The desperation left her face, and the expression that replaced it was one of sheer exhaustion. It looked as if whatever had once possessed her had been exorcised, and what was left behind was a vague thing. Something jettisoned. I wasn't certain if it was a peaceful look, or something worse than before.

I left her there, by the house, with Anwen's violin ringing about her, and I moved away, back out towards Harris's cottage.

23

IN HIS LETTER, MALCOLM had written of buried obscenities and treasure. He'd written that there was not so much difference between them. It had taken me some time to understand the phrase, and, as was to be expected with Malcolm, it felt various in its interpretations. I thought, as I made my way through the thick pines, that I had just grasped another meaning, and it was, like Ariadne's thread, guiding me out of the labyrinth.

But I didn't dare consider it for long. It felt as if the sheer act of observing the theory would alter it and render it useless. I recalled Malcolm's novel *Under the Last Dust*, wherein a woman lives on a small island, dense with high towers from which she looks out into the cosmos and observes the future. Though she has the ability to see what will happen, the moment she takes any action towards achieving that future, it crumbles away. So, instead, I allowed the thought to move within me, holding it in my body rather than my mind.

When I reached Harris's cottage, I paused at the border of the trees, observing the little building in the middle of the glade. A meagre trail of white smoke rose from the chimney. I also saw the gardening tools which had been leant against the wall weren't there. Harris must have left.

I followed the path I'd taken earlier, down the sloping

dell and out towards the yellow cottage door. Though Clara
had revealed the perverse story of Connie's birth, I still felt
there was something I didn't know, could not shake the idea
that she was somehow Julia, borne forwards on a current
of time, to this moment. I raised my hand to knock on the
door, but stopped myself. I'd heard something. Closing my
eyes, setting my ear against the peeling paint of the door, I
waited. Again, it came: the sound of a little voice, humming.
And I was sure I'd heard that same voice before, humming
that same tune.

I couldn't help myself. 'Julia,' I said. 'Come open the door,
it's me.' I was at the window now and looked through into
the cottage, saw the shape of her, there on the top stair.

She stilled, and the humming ceased.

I was breathing from the top of my lungs, and it was
all I could do to stop myself from breaking down the
door. I saw, through the glass, her heart-shaped face
tilt in confusion. There was something in her hand, and
I recognised it was the *netsuke* I had given her. Forcing
myself to smile, I gestured towards the door.

She remained still. Then, she tucked the *netsuke* into the
pocket of her dress, and cast about.

'He's gone,' I said. 'Don't worry. You remember me, don't
you? Euan. I'm Euan.' I had to pause, collect myself. This
was insanity. There was a dam inside me, holding back a
fantasy, and cracks were deepening. Ever since I'd arrived
here, they'd been forming. It seemed that everyone here
could see something I could not, like my eyes were turned
to the walls of the cave and theirs were turned towards
the opening. But these were the thoughts of a fool. I had
come here for a reason. I had a theory, and I would prove it.

Suppositions, fantasies and strangeness would do nothing for me. I told myself that again and again . . . but there is a difference between knowing and feeling.

'Julia,' I said again. 'You remember that name, don't you?'

Her body shrank into itself in a way that made me understand this was a girl who had spent her life hiding.

'It's okay,' I said, pointing, again, towards the door.

She looked over her shoulder and then crept down the stairs, over the cold stone floor, towards the front door. The latch clicked, and the heavy wooden door opened just a crack, and there, in the thin dark sliver, were the eyes of my sister. I held my breath, tried to push away the impossible.

'Connie,' she said. 'My name's Connie.'

'I know,' I said. 'I'm sorry.'

'What do you want?'

'Can I come in?'

She regarded me warily. Then, she stepped away from the heavy door, let me push it open and come inside. When I entered, she ran around behind the sofa, which faced the dwindling fire. She knelt on the cushion and looked over the back of the sofa. 'Who is Julia?' she asked.

My eyes were watering now, and I tried to hold my composure as I said, 'She's no one, my love. I just thought . . . It doesn't matter.'

'Did you bring another toy?'

I padded round to the sofa, took a seat on the arm, watched her as she curled her body into the cushions and observed me. 'I came because there's something important I think you can help me with.'

She furrowed her brow, clearly upset that I hadn't brought her something.

'The old man who used to come here and give you dresses, do you remember him?'

She fiddled with the tassel of a pillow and looked behind me, towards the door.

'It's okay,' I said. 'I'm a friend.'

'I'm not supposed to—'

'Julia . . .' I reached out to her, and she leapt back, running away.

'My name's not Julia!'

She stood at the bottom of the stairs, and I approached her slowly. 'I know. The old man was kind to you, wasn't he?'

She was panting, and her thin arms were wrapped about herself.

I lowered my posture and held my hands out. 'I was a friend of Malcolm's. I know how much he cared for you.'

Her stance softened, and she chewed her lip, put her hand into her pocket.

I looked at her hard, thinking of Malcolm's phrase about obscenities and treasure. 'I think he gave you something, didn't he? Something very important.' I approached her again, lowered myself onto the bottom stair.

She lingered for a moment, then joined me, sitting with her knees bunched and her hand still in her pocket, toying with the *netsuke*.

'I can't imagine what you've gone through,' I said. 'The things that have been taken from you, without you even knowing.' Looking in her eyes, I saw silver crescents. They were formed of little flecks, floating in her deep brown irises. It was as if she had stared at the moon for a whole night, and its reflection had remained, the way light clings to photographic paper. Did Julia have those crescents? I couldn't remember.

'Don't cry,' she said, reaching out with a little hand and offering me the otter *netsuke*.

I smiled, closed her fingers about the toy, and said, 'Don't worry about me.'

We sat there together on the bottom stair, while the lattice of light through the window shutters became taut as the sun dimmed. Then, Connie said, 'I can show you my hiding place.'

'Yes,' I said with a choked-up voice, 'I'd like that very much.' I swallowed, wiped my face.

'Your voice sounds funny,' she said. 'Like Grandpa when he last came.'

'Malcolm?'

She nodded, with wide curious eyes.

'What did he say, when he sounded like that?'

She perked up, then beamed at me. 'He said I was his favourite.'

'He did?' I said with a smile. 'I can see why.'

'He knew about my hiding place and wanted me to keep it there.'

I felt weightless. It took all my will to supress the giddy anticipation building in me, to speak calmly. 'Will you take me there now?'

She made an overly serious face, holding her fingers in a circle about her eye, as if they were a magnifying glass. When I passed her inspection, she lowered her fingers and whispered, 'Follow me.'

I trailed her as she scampered up the stairs, turned down the hallway, moved into a small room, hardly bigger than a cupboard and with a small bed crammed into the corner. The plaster beside the bed was chipped from where little fingers had picked at it. The floor was covered in little notebooks. I picked one up and saw it was filled with handwritten stories, illustrated in broad, spiky pencil strokes. It took only the briefest moment to realise the illustrations were of people here on the estate. Flicking to the last page, I saw a picture of me. This was Connie's life; sequestered away, she would observe the lives of others, write stories about them that the world would never see.

'Grandpa liked them,' she said, crouching in a corner of the room. 'He said I could be a writer just like him, but I would have to work on my spelling. He said it's okay, though, because even he struggles with some words still. Like onomatope—'

'—poeia,' I said.

She stuck her tongue out at me, then turned and slid open a hatch in the wall. It led to where the chimney should have been, and, when I peered inside, I figured that half of the chimney must have been bricked up to make space for the hatch. It led down to a very dark and narrow space – a room between the top and bottom floor, crammed between the floorboards. Julia slid inside and looked back at me.

'I don't think I can follow you,' I said.

'Come on!'

I pushed my head and shoulders down through the hatch and into the narrow space. As my eyes adjusted to the darkness, I saw ornate toys arranged with obvious care. Years' worth of Malcolm's gifts. Connie weaved through the between-space, slats of light coming through the boards, passing over her agile body. She was comfortable here. She began to pick up different toys, blowing dust from them, arranging them into patterns.

Horizontal, I pushed my head further into the space, searching for the manuscript. It was just as I was beginning to feel stupid that Connie turned to me and said, 'I kept it safe, just like he asked me.'

'What a good girl you are,' I said.

She raised her fingers into the magnifying glass shape again, gave me a final examination, before turning, slipping into the shadows in the furthest corner of the space, pushing her hand into a pile of neatly stacked dresses.

I didn't dare say anything, for fear it would somehow alter her decision. Instead, I watched, dry-mouthed, heart racing.

Slowly, she re-emerged from the shadows, her body shelled about a loosely bound sheaf of yellowed papers. Beneath a furrowed brow she peered at me. The manuscript, to her, was another toy, more valuable, and more peculiar, than the others. She cradled it, stopping just out of arm's reach.

I saw then, illuminated by a seam of light through the boards, a title, clearly typed upon the page: *The Man on the Endless Stair*. Upon reading those words, I felt a sense of slow movement, inevitability, transformation. I had no doubt that this was the title of Malcolm's last work. If I could, I would have launched myself through into the space, snatched the manuscript away, but I couldn't move from where I was. All I could do was reach out, try to hide the desperation in my voice. 'Can I read it, Connie?'

She looked up at me, smiling; then, upon seeing the look on my face, stopped smiling. 'What is it?' she said.

This little girl had in her hands what I saw as the key to greatness. The reason I had come here. Connie held my future. I tried to soften my expression, speak in a calm, steady voice. 'Remember, I was a friend of your grandpa. He wanted me to see it.'

She inched closer to me, and I considered reaching out, grabbing her and snatching away the manuscript. But I didn't . . . for fear of ripping the manuscript, or hurting the girl, I still don't know. Instead, I said again, 'Come here, sweetheart. You can play with your toys while I read. I promise it'll be safe, and you can keep your eye on me, too.' I gave her a conspiratorial wink.

Finally, she inched closer to me, extending the manuscript. I took it from her.

We shared a moment there, looking at each other, she below and me above. I extended a hand and helped her out of the space, back up through the hatch. Then, we sat together on the bed in the little room, she with her otter *netsuke*, me reading the title of Malcolm's manuscript again and again. I looked across at her.

As I watched her toying with her *netsuke*, I knew what Malcolm had meant when he wrote of obscenities and treasure.

24

I OPENED THE MANUSCRIPT to the first page. Upon reading the first paragraph, I felt a heat building in my face, a tremor entering my hands. I read it again. 'Impossible.' When I came to the bottom of the first page, my entire body was shaking. The novel was written from my perspective, detailing things only I could have known. Forcing myself to read on, I saw that Malcolm had written my innermost thoughts, as if he'd been inside my head. It was a recording of my reality. There was no fiction to it. The novel opened with my meeting of Colm on the ferry and continued from there. It described the past two days in vivid detail. I felt nauseous, invaded, and, as I read on, these feelings only intensified. I soon began to flick through, to this very moment. I found these sentences, describing my present. And then, I read Malcolm's voice, addressing me:

Euan, you will be asking yourself how I have written things only you would know. I understand, because that was the question I asked myself when I was in your position. The simple answer is, we are the same person. I have lived this moment as Euan. I remember the pain, the fear, the confusion. And you will remember it too. You will write it, here, some day. Euan, this is our greatest work. I have grown tired of fantasy, as will you one day. This book tells the truth.

A truth which is, at times, quite terrible. Yet, it is the centre of our existence – the axis around which we revolve. It is our omphalos.

I stopped reading, rose from the bed, paced the room, finger holding my place in the manuscript. He had written beyond this point. Written into my – our – future. Could I bring myself to read on? I began to turn the next page. Then, I slammed the manuscript shut. I leant against the wall, held my wrist up, stared at the brand which peeked out above my cuff. His words had gored me, and now they were embedded, weighing me down.

Connie was at my side. 'What's wrong?' she said. 'Was I bad to show you? He said I shouldn't—' She reached out to touch me as she spoke, and I batted her hand away. She held the arm I had swatted, looked at me, wounded.

'What did he tell you?' I shouted at her.

Her bewildered expression turned to fear.

'What is this?' I hit the manuscript against the wall. 'How did he know?'

In her face, I saw myself change. There was the realisation, that who she had invited into the house was not a friend.

I began to laugh, falling back against the wall as the implications of what I'd read began to dawn on me. I was Malcolm. I had no idea how that was possible, but it was the only way he could have written in such detail about my life. Malcolm was me. A part of me yearned for it to be a sick joke. There was no way, surely . . .

Connie covered her face and said, 'He told me I shouldn't show it.'

'It doesn't matter. Malcolm was murdered. You didn't know that?'

'Stop it,' she said. 'Please. Give it back.'

'He's dead,' I said. 'He's—' And as the words left my mouth, I wondered if I was talking about myself. Had I witnessed my own death?

I began to reopen the book, thinking that Malcolm may have written something that would help me better understand his final moments, but just as I brought my eyes down to the page, Connie threw herself against me.

Reflexively I kicked. She flew backwards, struck her head against the bedframe, lay there moaning.

Ripped back into the moment, I went to her, laid a hand on her back, but she flinched away, looked at me fiercely. The crescents of silver speckles were blurred behind her tears.

I stood, backed away from her, clutching the manuscript to my chest. I had done something which could never be undone. Connie viewed me as a monster. And perhaps I was one.

I left her there, lying on the floor beside her bed, took the manuscript with me as I ran out of Harris's house, across the open ground and back into the shelter of the trees.

On a root stool growing over a thin stream of black water, I sat. Thickets of undergrowth shrouded me as I nestled between nettles, brambles and shocks of rising weeds. I began to pore over the manuscript, stopping again when I reached the present moment. It felt as if the book was following me. Or was I following the book? Everything I had done, everything I would do, was written here. So, did I have a choice? Again, my finger traced the edge of the next page. The page which would describe my future. I stilled.

If I was Malcolm, and he was me, then I knew the circumstance of my own death. I knew my children. I knew my vices and my virtues. I knew my undoing. Did I want to know any more?

A future, perfectly known, is the past.

I stayed there, in that way, finger pressed against the future pages, lost. I recalled what Malcolm had written; that on this land, time is different. So, could it be that the transformation he had mentioned was me becoming him? It felt like a wish granted by a djinn: I had been given my dream of achieving Malcolm's success, but it would not be mine, it would be his, or rather . . . it would be ours.

Lost in thought, I gazed at the waning light which came over the low boughs and thickets. This went beyond my understanding of the world. It defied logic. But, hadn't things beyond understanding always been deemed magical? The ancients thought stars were their gods' way of telling stories. Magic precedes logic. It is older; no better, no worse, and just as real.

It was then that I began to weep, as I allowed myself to change. I realised that my adherence to linear process, to order, had been a way of running from what had happened with Julia, with the war. I had experienced years of chaos and, to survive, had turned wholly to logic. Events were binary things, to be observed. I had removed myself from experience, from the uncanny beauty of life. But now, I held something which could not be explained. I held a magical artefact. My magnum opus.

I wanted to share this with someone, but realised I was alone. Colm, the only one I'd trusted, was an imposter. I remembered what Anwen had said when I'd first arrived : that Malcolm saw us only as characters. He'd known what would befall us – had orchestrated it, even. He'd known that

Colm was a criminal, and had invited him anyway – was it to punish him, or because that is the way this story always plays out? I wondered then if Malcolm had really planned this, or whether it was out of even his control, determined by a greater power. We were all fated to play our roles. And Colm's fate was to be tormented. I thought back to the ferry: Colm and I approaching the island together, outsiders, allied by circumstance. Perhaps his purpose was to remind me of trust's weakness; that to become Malcolm, I could trust only myself.

My future was in my hands, and I felt myself compelled to read it. Again, I had the sense of being trapped in a jar, with Malcolm watching me from above. If I read on, would I have any choice in the unfolding of the future? If I read on, was I sacrificing my free will? If Malcolm and I were the same person, every action I would undertake had already been made by him, and therefore what he had written was the truth. I could not deviate from it. Would I retain my free will by not reading those pages, or was that just wilful ignorance? A way to maintain the illusion of choice? Having these thoughts felt like wading through slutch. So, I followed my instinct.

I turned the page to the future and cast my eyes over the typewritten words. In haste, I shut the manuscript again, but not before I had read Lewis's name. The manuscript said that I would meet him by his cabin.

And I knew it was right. I needed to find Lewis. He had burned down his father's shed, had stolen the letter from my pocket. There was no resistance in my mind, no desire to veer from the path that had been written for me. It was a pernicious desire, to read on, to keep reading until my future was no longer a mystery. But there was something which stopped me. An inner desire for ignorance. I was reminded of what Anwen had told me beside the lake, that she would rather be stupid and mystified than peer behind the curtain.

I stood, rolled the manuscript as carefully as I could, pushed it into the outer pocket of my coat, and continued on through the woods.

I walked as if through a dream. All around me I heard voices, speaking to me from across time. I had been living, until now, in a house with closed shutters – and now they were open, the world was pouring in. I felt watched. The voices were speaking to me. I could see outward, into the twining mass of time, and it could see inward. What sees can also be seen. In the stoop of an alder, I saw the vertebrae of my father's back as he sat hunched over his sewing machine. I heard him calling me over. He turned his eyes to me, peering under his spectacles, asked me what I would do if he was gone.

'I would look after Julia,' I said.

To that, he grinned and answered, 'How will you look after her?'

'I'll protect her from bad people.'

'What if you are a bad person?'

I looked at him, incredulous.

'No one ever thinks they're bad,' he said. 'Remember that.' Then, he pulled the garment from the sewing machine, handed it to me and said, 'I made that for Julia. Tell her to wear it for me when she sees me later.'

The vertebrae cracked and sputtered, and I walked on, through the folding span of time. Fiddlehead ferns began to unfurl, sway, whisper. I stamped up a bank of waving goosegrass, saw a holloway that would take me to Lewis's cabin. But as I walked along, I heard another voice, this time Anwen's. She was younger. 'It wasn't your fault,' she said.

'But if I had acted differently . . .'

'That is no way to think.'

'If only I could go back and change it all.'

'If you did that, we might never have met.'

'We will always meet.'

Her face was in the knothole of a beech, sap twinkling as her eyes. 'The way is set, Malcolm.'

I walked on, pressing the manuscript into my side, paranoid it might fall out. When I neared the end of the holloway, the voices subsided, and all that remained was a monochrome image etched into the light at the end of the path. My father, hanging from a ceiling beam. I'd kept the letter detailing what had happened, how they had found him. I'd lain awake many nights, imagining how he might have looked. Even after his death, he'd made me a victim – to guilt, shame, regret. But now, seeing his grey face, I felt satisfaction. The person I'd been had hid from this feeling; the person I'd become now embraced it.

I pushed through the image, which dissipated as my focus slowly returned to the path before me, leading out into the glade from which the familiar thud of wood being chopped sounded. Lewis was there, as the manuscript had said.

I folded the manuscript, concealing it.

The thud of the axe.

I moved out, to the very edge of the glade, then lingered

there, watching Lewis. He'd lit the firepit outside of the cabin, and amber firelight coated his bare arms. This was the man who had stolen my letter, who had helped murder Jim. Could he have killed his own father?

'How is your investigation going?' he said, without looking up.

A stone had hardened in my throat; I was unable to swallow, to formulate words. Suddenly I wanted to laugh, to fall to the ground and heave up the stone in great convulsions of laughter. The knowledge I now had, of who I was, of who Lewis was, had broken me. The fact that he was speaking to me, as if nothing had happened, was so at odds with what I knew, that it was all I could do to remain quiet. I stared at him, recalibrating. I found my words: 'I thought I told you to stay with Clara.'

'She's fetching the whisky.' He began piling the chopped wood beside the firepit.

I remained where I stood, both hands in my coat pockets. I clutched the manuscript.

'You didn't answer me,' Lewis said, moving back to the chopping block, gathering up the wood. 'How is your investigation? Come on, take a seat. No use skulking in the shadows.' He gestured to the heavy log which was laid beside the firepit.

I moved across the glade, keeping my gaze on him, then lowered myself onto the log. 'I am beginning to realise that my books are nothing compared to reality.'

Bent over, piling lumber into his arms, he looked across at me. A strand of dark hair fell over his eye, and the firelight flickered across his face. 'How can I help? We are partners, after all.'

'You can make that fire bigger,' I said, clutching the manuscript tighter.

'Cold? A dram will help, too. Clara will be along soon.'

'When is the next ferry due?' I asked. 'People need to know about what's happened here.'

'They come a few times a week. The next will be tomorrow morning. Do you intend to leave?' he said.

'Do I intend to leave?' I held the question on my tongue, considered, while never letting my gaze wander from Lewis. 'Would you like me to?'

He stood to his full height, forearms tensing under the weight of the lumber, which he carried and set by the firepit. He placed two logs on the blaze before returning to his axe. 'No' – he circled his finger around the butt of his axe, remaining on his feet – 'I would like you to stay.'

'You would?'

Lewis chuckled and said, 'I've grown fond of you.' He looked up at the sky, which churned like grey sea over shingle. 'It is a tremendous thing, to have a friend. I have had to hide myself for so long, my desires and fears. I'm sure you know; acting is just a method of survival. During the war, I knew what to say, and to whom, in order to escape the worst of it. I, like you, did not survive because of luck.'

'And is this where you tell me you can be yourself around me?'

He shrugged, poked at the blade of his axe with the toe of his boot. 'I understand what you are. We are more similar than you think.' He looked at me with grim curiosity. 'You pretend to be someone else, but in fact, the world has made you dangerous. The thing you want has been denied for

so long, but now you are so close . . . What will you do to
secure it?'

'What do you think I want?'

'You want what my father had.'

I couldn't help but laugh.

'What is it?' Lewis said.

I shook my head, said, 'This is certainly a day I will
remember.'

Lewis narrowed his eyes at me. 'You have something on
your mind . . . Did you find Tilly?'

'I did.'

The air around us stung with anxiety. His arm swung
up in a spasmic motion to the back of his head, which he
scratched slowly while speaking. 'And what did she say?'

I considered my response, glancing to the fire, seeing
it grow as the logs were consumed. I grimaced, then sat
straight and faced him fully. 'Enough,' I said. '"No mystery is
stranger than that we live ourselves." You quoted that at me.'

'And?'

'We both know you took Malcolm's letter.'

He hefted the axe to his shoulder. 'Did I?' There was a
smile on his lips.

'When Clara went to check the telephone, and we were
alone with the body . . . you weren't racked with grief, you
wanted to watch me. You saw me take the letter from under
the ice bucket. And then, during the family meeting, you
stole it from my pocket, along with one of my cigarettes
which you smoked in front of me. For all your merits as
a thief, your weakness is your showmanship . . . So, you
knew that Malcolm had left behind the manuscript, and
with it a great secret. A secret you believed would give you

mastery over time. You ransacked my room, looking for the manuscript. Then, when you found nothing, you went with Clara to your father's writing shed to search for it; and when Jim came upon you both, you helped her murder him. Your father was no longer around to defend him, and you thought there would be no consequence. Just before I arrived, as Clara escaped, you slipped out and got the supplies to burn the shed down.'

He watched me with amusement. 'Are you done?' he said. And when I did not reply, he reached down for a log, set it on the chopping block, split it. The axe lodged in the block. He brought his foot up, set it against the block, pulled the axe free. 'For all you have gone through, you are still very naïve. It's admirable, to have that purity. Perhaps this is why your mystery books have never reached the heights of my father's work: you turn away from true depravity. A great detective must think like a monster, no?'

'What are you saying?'

'That you are right, and wrong. That you have seen everything, but understood only what you can tolerate.'

'You killed Malcolm, your own father, because he would not give you what you wanted. You wanted the estate. You wanted his manuscript. You—'

'You're wrong.' His face had reddened.

'You killed your father.'

'You're wrong!' His voice cracked, and he threw the blade of the axe into the earth. Then, he thumbed the hem of his shirt and spoke quietly. 'You know nothing. Nothing at all.'

'Then, tell me what you know.'

Lewis placed another piece of wood on the block, retrieved the axe from the earth and slung it over his shoulder. He spoke levelly. 'I know that you are a tricky man to shoot.'

There was a moment, shared between us, as our eyes met. An unveiling. He had been there, waiting in the trees, watching his father's writing shed, rifle trained on my back. It had been he who'd shot at me yesterday.

'I know that my father's manuscript held the secret to navigating time.'

I folded my fingers tighter about the manuscript.

'And I know that your right hand has been in your pocket this entire conversation.' He flashed me a smile. 'Take it out,' he said.

I released the manuscript, pulled my right hand free of my pocket.

Lewis watched me hungrily. He slammed the axe down into the wood. 'Take it out,' he demanded.

I rose, but Lewis had already pulled the axe from the stump and was moving towards me.

Before he reached me, I pulled out the manuscript and held it out above the fire.

Lewis stopped, as if gripped by a great hand. He gazed at the papers, transfixed.

'Tell me,' Lewis said. 'Tell me what he's written.'

'You wouldn't believe me. I'm not even certain I believe it.'

'Is it in there? The key to changing time?'

'Perhaps. I've not read it fully.'

Confusion passed over his face. 'Why?'

'It is an account of my life. He's written things only I would know. This novel . . . is no novel. It is my life. I have read up to this moment, and no more.'

Lewis's jaw was slack, and I saw on his face the passage

of thoughts as he came to the same conclusion that I had. 'You . . . you are him.'

'So he writes.'

'But that would make . . .'

I nodded. I was speaking with my own son.

Lewis began to laugh and, as he did, tears welled in his eyes. 'I don't believe it.'

He spoke the words, but there was no resonance to them. We both knew that what had been revealed was genuine. We remained there as this knowledge settled within us.

'Then, it must be real,' Lewis said. 'He had the key to traversing time. We have to read on, to find out.'

'No,' I said.

'Why not?'

'It's not as simple as that. What if I were to read something terrible? I would have to live with that burden.'

'If you know of it, then it can be avoided.'

'But then it would never have been written. Lewis, if I read this manuscript, I lose my free will. I'd live a half-life.'

'You're wrong. Nothing is fixed.' He pointed to the manuscript. 'With that knowledge, do you have any idea what we could do? Do you know what we could change?'

'What would you change, Lewis?'

A shadow seemed to pass through him. He glowered at me, then said with venom, 'Give it to me, if you are too afraid. I will read it for you.'

'No.'

Lewis let the axe fall to his side and stared at me. 'Why did you do it?' he said from the corner of his mouth. 'Why did you have me? You have harassed me from the moment I entered this world. You've made my life a misery.'

The heat of the flame was warming my arms. I was bringing the manuscript down, closer to the firepit. 'I am not him,' I said.

'But you will be. Why don't you remember this moment? Do you know the suffering you will cause me? You will live to be great, but you'll be hated by your own son. Perhaps that's why you have me . . . out of spite. You *want* me to experience this pain.' He held out his hand. 'Give me the manuscript. We can change it all.'

'You don't know that.'

'We have to try. Aren't there things you would change? I know you have regrets. You want this as well.'

Thoughts of Julia came to me once more.

'Read it,' Lewis said. 'Read it and know.'

Could these things be avoided, these events written by my own hand? I thought of Julia, of the war, and of Malcolm; everyone he had damaged with his obsession. Everything I would destroy. And then I thought of his books. Did his greatness require this pain? Could one exist without the other?

'You can change all our lives for the better, if you just read,' Lewis said.

'I can't . . .'

'Then let me.'

I paused, began to thumb the edge of the manuscript.

Lewis stepped towards me, desire in his eyes.

I released the pages, dropping them into the flames.

A great sigh sounded in the boughs of the surrounding pines, in the strata of the rock beneath us, in the waters running through the woods.

Lewis froze, then hurled himself into the fire, trying to

clasp the scraps of blackening paper. He was screaming, raking at the hot cinders, seeming not to care for the flesh of his fingers. I tried to tackle him away, but he pulled me down, pinned my arm to the scalding embers as he reached further into the flames.

Bright pulsing pain came into my arm, and, when I rolled free, I saw that my branded arm, the one which held the mark of the omphalos, was marred with a new burn. The mark on my arm was now identical to Malcolm's. The burn that was given by someone he loved. The person had been Lewis. His son.

Amid the searing pain, I heard time's great fugue turn from dissonance to harmony.

Ignoring the agony, I caught the back of Lewis's hair and hauled him from the firepit, back to the ground beside his axe. He rolled and kicked at me, scrambling to his knees, lurching back to the ashes.

I caught hold of his shirt collar, pulled him to the earth, laid on him with all of my weight pressed on his chest, saying, 'It's over.'

He thrashed, but I stayed heavy, pinning him there as he roared, coughed and, finally, stilled, shutting his eyes and sobbing. His arms were wrapped around me.

When he finally opened his eyes, he looked at me and let his arms fall. They lay limp on the ground. He lay there and stared, as if daring me to understand, to recognise that which I had been blind to. Unblinking, he looked at me. Then I saw it: the silver crescent floating in his iris.

Slowly, I pushed away from him.

Sitting in the dirt, shaking my head in disbelief, I spoke the dreadful truth. 'She has your eyes.'

He began to shake, and with each convulsion came a burst of sobbing. It was quiet at first, but with each moment grew louder and wilder, as if the man's voice were coming away from him, wrenched by a terrible force from his chest, out into the air. He sat up, and, in his face, I saw the similarity between his features and Connie's.

We both got slowly to our feet. I was beside the chopping block, and he beside the fire, which cast a red halo around his dark hair. 'Do you understand now?' Lewis said.

'Your own sister? Why, Lewis?'

The cracked smile was still there on his face. 'Because of you.'

'Me?'

'You made our lives hell. We took comfort in each other. We were all we had.'

I looked down at the scuffed earth, then heard Lewis advance towards me. I turned my eyes to him, and he stilled. I spoke slowly. 'Anwen couldn't stand to have her in the house . . . She was a reminder of what you had done.'

Lewis nodded, with a faraway look.

'But Malcolm wanted her close, so he gave her to Harris. She is the obscenity.'

'And the treasure.' He glared at me, and there was an electricity in his body.

'Malcolm cared for her,' I said. 'Did you know that? While you forgot her, he gave her gifts, protected her.'

'He stole her from us. *You* stole her.' He stepped towards me. He was crying, rubbing the fabric of his shirt again. 'You wanted to know what I would change? Now you know. I would never have let this happen. I would escape with Clara before . . . before it ever went wrong.'

I moved closer to the block, where Lewis had dropped his axe.

Lewis noticed and grimaced, saying, 'What is going through your mind, I wonder?'

'Jim discovered you, didn't he? He found you and Clara together in the shed . . . He saw something he wasn't supposed to . . . and you killed him.'

Lewis said nothing.

'He was innocent. He never hurt Clara. All he ever did was care for this family.'

'I could have prevented that, could have prevented all this, if I had the secret. If I could just go back in time—'

'You can't change it, Lewis.'

'You don't know that.'

'I do.'

'How?'

'Because at some point, I will go back in time. I will become Malcolm. And I wish that you had never been born, Lewis. But somehow, you are still here. Our paths will always lead us to this point, whether we intend it or not.'

There was movement in him, somewhere beneath the surface. It was slow, and dreadful, like the start of an avalanche. His eyes flicked to the axe.

'There is a way to change it,' he said.

He leapt forwards, but I caught the axe before he could. He barrelled into me, knocking the wind from my chest. A tangling of limbs, sweat and dirt. Smoke heavy in our lungs. Breath in my ear and blood on my tongue. We gripped the axe, wrenched until our grips gave out and we fell in a straining mass to the earth, rose again. He fell back, rolled, threw himself at me, and I swung.

A sound left his mouth, worse than a scream. It was a rasping exhale, wet and thick. He fell back and fumbled with the deep gash in his side, touching broken rib and flesh. His gaze turned to mine as I stood there, trembling, axe in hand. I dropped it to the earth. I wanted to back away, to turn and run, but his gaze held me still. There was desperation in his eyes, the look of a man carried along on a current not of his making. He pushed at the dirt with his feet, tried again to rise, but fell flat beside the fire. Blood wept from his side, slicking his arms, his torso. All the while, he did not look away from me.

I thought of what Malcolm had said to me in his study. *Do you want to be great?*

Lewis's lips were moving, making a shape I didn't recognise. He looked afraid.

I fell down beside him, and he flinched from me. I tried to take his hand, but he snatched it back.

There was a noise from the edge of the glade. I looked up, saw a shadow approaching.

Then, Lewis moved his lips again, spoke her name. 'Clara.'

From the rim of slumping trees emerged Clara, holding a bottle of whisky in her hand, oblivious to what had just happened. Slowly, she cast about the glade, then when she saw Lewis lying there, she dropped the bottle.

I watched the subtle play of emotions across her face; at first it was confusion, then fear, and then, finally, horror.

She ran to him, knelt at his side, pressed her hands to the wound at his ribs, pulling back, crying at the thick black blood that spilled across her fingers.

He moaned, and she cooed at him, sweeping his hair back to reveal his face, pallid and vacant. But in that emptiness was not the peace of the departed. Rather, there was pain etched in his features. His lip quavered. He wanted to speak, but nothing would come. The life had spilled from him.

Clara kissed his forehead, his cheek, his lips. In that moment all pretence fell away. We were who we were. There was a freedom there. A putrid kind of freedom that, once brought to fruition, can never be contained: intimate, brutal and, most of all, true.

25

CLARA FOLLOWED ME, SCREAMING my name, asking me why. I walked on. She clawed at my face, pushed me down, but I could not answer her. I rose again, continued walking.

'You murdered him,' she said to my back.

I didn't answer.

'You're worse than us, no matter how much you pretend. At least we cared for each other. You have no one. You're a leech. A demon.'

And she was right. A terrible stillness settled in me and I pushed on.

She let me go. I think she saw the intention in my face, understood what I meant to do.

Clara walked back to Lewis, lay down beside him, held him.

I left my children in their glade, walked into the woods. It was all laid out plainly now; Connie was a daughter of incest. The incest of my own children. Lewis had searched for the manuscript as he believed it contained the secret to traversing time. He believed he could undo the past. But all of this was, ultimately, my doing. It was a loop I had created, somehow. A loop I was trapped inside. Without me, none of this would ever have happened. Malcolm Furnivall would not have existed.

The death, the pain, could have been avoided.

I walked on, found my thoughts returning to Julia. I still felt her with me, drawing me on. In all of this evil, she was there, a guiding light towards the end. I had faith that I would find her.

The land spoke. With old words it wove an ancient spell – a spell I had ignored, fought against. I had ignored it because I could not face the truth it would reveal. It was a spell of divining. It told of my end, and my beginning. Now, faced with the putrid freedom of my real self, I heard the dark magic in the land's voice fully. It was clear, and it was guiding me.

Bog myrtle slunk away from the path, dewy heather fell to soften the way. Like pilgrims, briars bowed their heads as I passed on, over the stones vivid with green moss, through the slutch and fungus-thick web of roots. The dark thrum of the earth's voice was calling me, on to death, to the end of this cycle, to a place without pain, where greatness is dust and legacy wind.

'Will you be there, Julia?' I asked the voice.

'I will,' it answered.

The boughs creaked, the waterfalls laughed, the wind against the cliffs called me on.

'I'm sorry,' I said. 'I should never have left.'

The voice became a kittiwake cry, and I looked up to see, through the canopy of skeletal trees, the white seabirds circling. Above, the sky was bruised and thin. It seemed as if something might push through from the other side.

Now, the wind stung as it whipped the tears away from my face, sent them spinning out over the cliff's edge. Below, the sea crashed. Trails of white foam searched like hungry tongues among fissures in the dark cliffs.

I understood who I truly was, and who I would become. I had killed my own son. His words rang in my mind, about changing the course of things. We were, all of us, woven together in a web of cruelty . . . a web of my making.

Overcome with grief, I left the shelter of the trees and walked out into the brisk evening air, stood by the cliff's edge. The threadbare sky was stained with clouds, streaked with the lines of swarming seabirds.

Was it as Lewis had said? Could it be altered? Could I end it?

I gazed down at the shards of rock below, jutting from churning water. If I were to go on, my life would no longer be my own. It would be Malcolm's. I would become him, somehow. The shame and bitterness would swell in me like a cancer, consuming me and all those about me. I would have to live and accept the rancid freedom in my heart. The savage truth of who I really was.

I toed the cliff's edge, peered down, saw myself falling, torn apart by the stones below. A quick end.

A patch of sky seemed to fray away and there, stark and severe, was the pale face of the moon. *Bolg reothairt*. It shone, in its fullness, across the land and sea, sewing seeds of light throughout the darkness. It was as Jim had said: the full moon had come.

Wind pulled at my clothes, like a youngster, desperate to show me something. It would take me over if I let it. I imagined Julia floating there in the void, tugging at my shirt.

If I fell, I would erase myself. Everything I had worked towards would be destroyed. I would have no legacy, I would not be remembered. I, and my family, would be nothing more than a disgraceful footnote. *Do you want to be great?* That was what Malcolm had asked . . . what I had asked myself. At the time, I did not understand the price. But all things have a price. And now I had paid it, why shouldn't I take what was mine? It had already been written. There was a sacrifice, yes, but wasn't it worth it, to achieve that which I'd only dreamt about? I would have it all. Now, the worst of it was done, and I was free to take that for which I'd worked so hard. My words, these words, would linger in the mouth of eternity. The way was laid out plainly, and I could not veer from it. My story had already been written. I was Malcolm Furnivall.

I stepped back from the edge.

The light of the full moon cradled my cheek, lifted my gaze. Below me, the cities of guillemots stilled, their crying ceased, the waves settled. I made my choice, if it was ever mine to make.

At my back, a voice. 'When you told me, I didn't believe you,' it said.

I didn't turn. Instead, I allowed Harris to come up beside me, stare out over the cliff with me. 'What did I tell you?' I asked.

'When I was just a boy, a man came to this island. A man who said he was from the future. He looked just like you.'

'What else did he say?'

'He asked for me by name. He said we were bound, and would meet again.'

Stony-faced, I asked, 'So, you knew? You knew I was Malcolm?'

'I thought it impossible, even when the evidence was right

before me. But I have watched you, followed closely. I saw you and Lewis in the glade, heard your conversation . . . saw what you did.'

'I didn't want—'

'You don't have to explain yourself. It was written. Just as your death is written. You have witnessed it, and it will always be that way.'

I turned to look at him. 'Who does it? Is it you? Is that what I ask you, when you're a boy . . . to kill me?'

Harris's expression soured.

I had all the answers except the identity of the killer. Although Lewis had reason, I could not bring myself to believe he had murdered Malcolm.

'Does it matter, if all of this is inevitable?' said Harris.

'Malcolm wrote that I would have to find them. It's important. I know it.'

Harris pulled at the silver threads in his beard. 'I should hate you,' he said.

I stepped back, faced him fully.

He was quiet for a time, then he said with a maudlin voice, 'Why don't you throw yourself down?'

'You said it yourself, my end is already written. I do not die today.'

'You came to this island and brought nothing but misery. Do you know the real reason I agreed to live here on this estate?'

'Why?'

'Out of fear. I feared for my people in the hills. I feared his ambition would devour us all. Malcolm knew that, he knew I had made myself his hostage – a sacrifice for my people. And so he did what he did best . . . toyed with my mind. He gave me Connie. He made me party to this madness . . . I love her.' His frown deepened.

'Will you help me?' I asked softly. I could see the torment in his face. He knew Connie's life depended on my survival. If I were to die today, I would never travel back in time, would never become Malcolm. Connie would have never been born. I had trapped Harris with his own affection for my grandchild.

He looked at me with both warmth and resentment. When he spoke, his voice cracked, and he looked to his feet. 'You ask as if I have a choice.'

I reached out, put my arm on his shoulder. 'I can hear it now.'

His eyes widened and he met my gaze.

'The voices in the land, they're clear, calling out across time,' I said. 'You know what I'm talking about, I can see it. I'd ignored them for so long, but now I understand what they want. They only want to be heard. They don't want to be forgotten.'

He looked lost, as his eyes moved from me and up to the moon, which sat like a quartz stone in a churning river. 'To carry on, knowing what you will do . . . what you have done . . . what you will always do . . . I couldn't face that.'

I returned to his side, looking out over the water, up to the bright moon. 'That is why my name will be known, and yours will fade. You will become a voice in the land, nothing more.'

He spoke as if to himself. 'I wouldn't wish for anything else.'

Again, I heard Julia in the wind. I could not make out her words, but the sound of her voice choked me with tears.

I thought of the lunary in Jim's house, the child pointing to the moon, the mention of the changeling, the stolen child. Julia. According to the lunary she would be birthed tonight . . . And the passage revealed by blood. Where could it be found?

'What is the fastest way to Jim's?' I asked Harris.

He bowed his head, sucked his teeth.

An impulse ran through me, and I reached out to him, held him fast, looked him in the eye. 'You know what happens next.'

When he spoke, I could not discern whether it was reverence or fear in his eyes. 'Come with me.' He pushed my hand away, turned his bent back and strode from the cliffs without looking to see if I followed.

We slipped through the secret avenues and holloways, over the moonswept bracken, towards Jim's house. As we went on, I told Harris about my sister, about the lunary, about the prophesy Malcolm had written. Leading the way, he listened with care. On occasion, he turned and looked at me with sorrow.

While we walked, I had the sense that we were being watched. The paths we were taking were imperceptible, and Harris strode with light feet, barely disturbing a branch. He was at home. I began to wonder about his people, who had been here long before Malcolm, who knew these paths too. Was it they who were watching? I peered into the gaps between the boughs, saw something. At first, I thought it was eyes, but when I looked again, it seemed to be the shine on an acorn, or the dried sap seeping from a burl.

'Harris,' I said, 'when I find you, as a boy, do I tell you how?'

'How what?'

'How I travelled. How it is I move from this time to all those years before.'

'You said nothing.'

'And your people . . . they have lived here long?'

'They have.' He brushed a tree with his fingertips as he passed, and the tangled way seemed to part for him.

'If I ask you a question, will you answer honestly?'

He was quiet as he made his way through the wide trees about the forest's border.

'Are they here with us, now?'

He turned on me, set his gimlet eyes on mine. He smiled. 'Jim's house is close. Up through those trees there.'

26

THE DOOR WAS UNLOCKED. It swung quietly open on its hinges as Harris and I stepped inside. The house was empty but humid, and as we moved through the rooms to where I had sat only this morning, I felt Jim's breath in the air, the odour of his body: coffee, sweat, Indian hemp. The floorboards whined. Wind trilled against the roof tiles, pushed against the windows.

'Will you try to change it?' Harris said. He remained in the doorway while I rummaged through Jim's cupboards. 'Even if it's futile, will you try?'

It was my turn to deny an answer.

He stiffened, folded his arms, stayed on the other side of the room. 'You have to try, Euan.'

I grasped the puzzle box which held the lunary. Pulling it free from the cupboard, I turned to face Harris. 'I know.'

He nodded, seeming satisfied with my answer. 'And this lunary,' he said. 'You think it is important?'

'I do. Jim said it was the key to Malcolm's past. It has to have the answer – the keystone that locks this together.'

I slid the panels in the order in which I'd seen Jim do it. There was the satisfying click as the box unlocked, and out came the lunary. My throat was thick when I pulled it from the box and saw the carven girl on the front cover, finger pointing to the full moon. Serene features, languid gesture, she seemed at peace.

I turned to the page with the prophetic words. I read the first line aloud. "'The swollen womb of the spring tide births a changeling, stolen by time.'"

Harris's eyes searched my face. His jaw was set, his brow furrowed.

'This is all linked to my sister. I'm certain she's the changeling that's mentioned. I was convinced she'd died, but . . . what if she was lost? Not in space, but time? I think I can find her, Harris. Tonight, I can find her.'

'Where would you look?'

"'Blood will reveal the passage." There must be a passage somewhere . . . Do you know of any?'

'Plenty, but none revealed by blood.' Then, Harris was at my side. His hand touched my shoulder lightly. 'I know what grief can do to a person.'

I faced him and said, 'What do you mean by that?'

'The girl on the front of the lunary . . . it is Connie.'

'It's Julia, I know it.'

'How long has she been gone?'

'Ten years.'

He looked at me with pity, shook his head. 'Euan, you have to—'

'No!'

I picked up the lunary, pushed past him, moving back through the house, standing outside, holding the book up in the moonlight. I knew that I could find her. Tonight, the night of *bolg reothairt*, she would return to me. She would give me the answers to all of this. She would show me the way through. In the face of the moon, I saw the pattern of her smile; in the wingbeats of the rising rooks, I heard her laugh. Her voice: 'Behind you.'

Harris was standing there, hollow-eyed. His figure was dark in the doorway, but in his hand was the glimmer of a knife. He was pointing it at me. He swayed back and forth and in every sway, a battle was fought within himself.

I straightened, waited for him to decide.

Voice cracking, he said, 'What if I did?'

I answered. 'You never do.'

'But what if I did?'

'Enough. Give it to me.' I held out my hand for the knife.

Harris was shaking. He stepped out into the moonlight. 'I can't go on, knowing that everything I have done, or ever will do . . . was decided by a force not my own. I can't live . . . trapped.'

I considered his words, calm, seeing the fear plain upon his face. 'You are not trapped. If you know the path, you can dance down it; a stranger walks it warily.'

His face slackened, his trembling hand opened, and I was there to catch the knife as it fell from his grasp.

I held the knife in one hand, and the lunary in the other. The light of the moon fell across the page and illuminated the phrase 'blood will reveal the passage'.

Harris stood there in the doorway, head bowed, waiting.

'You understand now,' I said.

'I do.' His gaze was fixed on the knife I now held.

'Our paths are determined.'

He spoke with scorn. 'And I've come to the end of mine.'

My limbs felt foreign, my eyes like heavy stones. About us, the new buds of spring watched in silent judgement.

'Who will take care of Connie?' he said.

I gave no answer.

Pain threaded its way through his body. He gritted his teeth, said, 'Come on.'

I looked down at the lunary in my hand, to the open page, to the empty space beneath the entry.

Instead of the knife, I thrust the lunary at Harris.

Confused, he took it, watched me as I held the knife to my own hand, opened a gash across the crease bisecting my palm. Pain flowered across the tender skin.

'What are you doing?' he said.

I smeared the blood of my hand across the open page, over the empty space beneath the visible words.

Slowly, a new paragraph emerged. Whatever ink with which it was written reacted with the blood, and now, the writing appeared as if scribed by an invisible hand.

'Not a physical passage; a passage of words,' I said, unable to restrain the hysteria creeping into my voice.

We watched the new passage through the curtain of my blood, holding our breath, trembling together. I spoke the words softly.

> Find her at the sunken stones,
> Add your voice to the chorus of the lost.
> To arrive at being all,
> Desire to be nothing.

'The sunken stones,' I said. 'The ones in the lake . . .'
Harris raised his chin. 'You have seen them?'
'I have.'
He grimaced.
'What are they?'

'Old gods. Let them rest.'

'Why?'

'They belong in the darkness. We forget them, as we forget death so that we might live.'

'I have seen them . . . in my dreams.'

Fear was plain on Harris's face. 'These are the dark powers of the earth. Shadows at the edge of old stories.'

'Stories which you believe.'

He stared back at me, desperate.

'I'll find Julia there. I know it.'

Harris's face was white, and his grip loosened on the lunary.

I snatched it from him, read the new passage again. 'She's so close. She is the changeling, Harris. She holds the answer to all of this. You must understand now?'

Harris was quiet.

'What is it?' I asked.

'The more I have come to know you, Malcolm, the more I realise you are just a lonely man entertaining yourself by creating problems.'

'You called me Malcolm.'

'Yes,' Harris said. 'I did.'

★ ★ ★

I ripped out the page of the lunary, dropped the knife and walked back into the woods, making my way to the lake where I had first encountered the sunken stones. My palm burnt from the deep gash I had made, gems of crimson dripped from my fingertips, wetted the earth.

'She's gone,' Harris called from behind me.

I ignored him, moving on, the stink of sweat, sap and blood in my nose. I could hear a thrumming force in the earth, moving like a foetus as the tender hand of the moon stroked its belly. I felt the eyes in the trees watching me. I saw their faces in the lost trails, looming like silver fruits in the gloom.

'You're wrong,' Harris said. 'There is a way out. It can be changed!' But there was desperation in his voice, an underlying doubt.

'She's waiting for me.' I said to myself. The answer was not far now.

The watching faces sang with Julia's voice. They were singing to their old gods, remembering them. Malcolm had reached out into death and brought back Julia. All his years of secret research had been dedicated to this. I would find her, and I would keep her safe. I would bargain with these sunken gods and make a deal. There was nothing I would not sacrifice for her.

Harris's voice dissipated, and I was left alone with the sound of the wind, my breath and the song.

Images of Lewis flashed before me. I saw him lying crumpled and still. My own son. He, like Harris, believed there was a choice, believed things could be different. But we were all borne on by currents, constant and unchanging.

I thought of Malcolm's manuscript. My manuscript. The one in your hands right now. You will never read this far, Euan, but the fact this book exists means that you will travel back in time and become me. This is inevitable. As I write this, I know the end of our story. Or, at least, the end so far. But stories unfurl at their own pace. The game must be played out.

Breaking through the trees, I came to the edge of the lake and found Anwen standing there. She was facing the water and her back was turned to me. Her voice played across the still water; she was humming a melody.

At her side, I saw a patch of disturbed ground, mounded with water-smoothed stones. It was Malcolm's grave. My grave. Though I wondered how she could have moved the body alone.

As I approached, Anwen's voice quavered, but the melody continued – one I did not recognise. It was melancholy and warm, like a last goodbye. She kept her back turned to me, only moving when I laid my hand on her shoulder. She faced me, the moonlight shone across her features and, in that moment, she was gilt in timeless beauty. I saw her truly.

'I found the manuscript,' I said. 'I know.'

She spoke tenderly. 'Well done, my love.' She cradled my face in her hand. Tears ran down her cheek.

'It was you,' I said. 'You killed him. You cut the telephone wire. It was you.'

'We planned it together.'

'Why?'

'It is what has to happen. It is the price of our love. Believe me, there are times I will hate you, will wish we'd never gone down this path. It's why I told you to leave, when you first arrived, even though I knew you wouldn't listen. There is so much pain in our story . . . But that is the price of all of this. It's a price you pay gladly.'

I grasped her wrist, pulled her hand from my face. I held her there, and she was still.

'I wanted to help you,' she said. 'Wanted to help you complete your greatest work. The manuscript . . .'

'I destroyed it.'

'But you will write it again.'

'And I will burn it again.'

'You will. And that is the beauty of it.'

I released her wrist, let her hand fall to my chest.

She moved closer to me. 'You see it, don't you? The pulse of the machine?'

'You killed him as he choreographed. You locked the door as he died, said goodbye . . . then unlocked it once I'd left.'

'And I left through the tunnel leading to the writing shed. Remember this, Euan. This is how it will always be. You will explain it to me when you find me.'

'What did you use?'

Anwen reached back, pulled the hairpin from her hair, which cascaded in a silver sheet across her slim back. She handed me the hairpin, long, black and tapered to a vicious point. To the other end was affixed an emerald, which, when held up to the light, glittered with the pattern of the omphalos. Anwen closed my fingers about the hairpin and looked me in the eye. 'You give it to me when we first meet. A gift.'

I could barely keep the sobs from my voice. 'Do you know it all?'

'Not all. He hid the manuscript even from me. He wanted to protect me.'

I understood, then, why he had given it to Connie to keep: she could not know its terrible significance, would not understand, even if she were to read it. 'Do you know about Connie? Do you know what I do to Lewis . . . my own son?'

Anwen fell into thought. She kissed me just below the ear, then whispered, 'Perhaps next time Lewis will not die?

That is why you will go back. Even though I think you know the answer . . . There are things we cannot change.'

'What about Julia? The lunary said I would find her here.'

Anwen had pity in her eyes. 'Your sister,' she said. 'For a man who saw everything, you have always been blind to the truth.'

'What do you mean?'

She shook her head. Desperately I waited for her to go on, but when she caught my eye, the look of pain on her face only deepened. Gravity welled about us. She held her wary palm against my chest: a brittle leaf. 'She is gone, Malcolm.'

I was still and cold.

She pulled her hand back, held it against her stomach.

'No,' I said. 'It said I would find her at the sunken stones. She is the changeling.'

Anwen said nothing. She waited, watching the realisation occur in me. It came gradually: the 'her' mentioned by the lunary was Anwen . . . She was the one waiting by the stones . . . And the changeling, it was not Julia. I finally understood.

'You see it now,' Anwen said. 'You are the one stolen by time. On this night, you are stolen and reborn. You travel to the past, meet me, and the cycle continues.'

And I knew it was the truth. I was taken by time, cast back into another world. Another life. It was then that I gave in to the weeping, allowed myself to fall into Anwen's arms, cry for all those that I had lost, and all that I would lose. They were confused, impotent tears.

Anwen held me, said, 'You will become truly great, so great you will consume yourself. You and your work are the same . . . I know that when I meet you. I know you will devour everything, and I choose that path. Though it hurts me, though I will fight against it, I know that it is beautiful to be consumed.' She kissed the omphalos burnt into my wrist.

'I can't,' I said. 'It hurts too much.'

'When you tell me for the first time that you love me, you say something I will always remember. You say I am a better artist than you. Why, I ask. You reply that I paint with time. That is what music is, you say . . . You tell me the paintings I make across time's canvas are unlike anything you could ever render. You say that you want me, more than anyone you've ever wanted. Well, I believe we have, together, created the most beautiful painting across time. All you need do now is make the final strokes.'

And all about us, from the shadows in between the trees, figures emerged and watched. Their faces were fissured with crottle and vine. Their mouths hung open, their eyes were burnished stone. They were calling with the voice of the land. Calling for sacrifice.

I wanted it all to end.

The figures in the trees moved. One by one, they came out into the open, long-legged, padding on the forefoot like deer. Enraptured, I watched them converge, picking up single stones from the shore. As their fingers slid across the earth, new buds crested from the black shale, fingerbones dropped away, speared deep, rooted. Carrying their stones, the figures came to my graveside, set them down atop the low cairn. When they had set their stones, they cast their eyes to me. Before I could muster any words, they were moving, herd-like, returning to the trees.

'Who are they?' I asked Anwen.

'Helpers,' she said. 'They buried him.'

Then, as if following the steps to a dance we had always known, Anwen kissed me on the cheek and stepped aside.

I walked slowly, passing Anwen on one side, my own grave on the other. The icy water of the lake lapped at my feet, at my ankles, then my calves. I heard the clamour of the wilderness, the drum of the endless. For the first time, I understood that I was nothing in relation to that drum, just a vehicle for its beauty. The water caressed my stomach, the faces beyond the trees watched serenely. Anwen hummed the unfamiliar song.

With the hairpin in my hand, I walked on through the lake, sinking deeper. When my head was swallowed by the dark water, I looked up through the membrane, saw the full moon spill its light over the surface. It fell down through the water like silt, collecting in my eyes, cascading downwards as I looked to my feet, sinking deeper. I walked down to the drowned stones, breath escaping in silvery bulbs which rose to the surface and bloomed.

The dark figures appeared, pates frosty with moonlight, manes of water weed swaying. Old gods. Another pearly bulb of air escaped my lungs. I went on, body cramping in the cold. I was at the lake's bottom, and rising all about me were the stones, livid with an ancient dark. Their faces were turned to me. In their expressions was nothing I recognised. It was as if I were staring into a void.

For a moment, I turned my eyes to the surface, wrenched my body upwards to reach the cold bright air. Inky sediment rose about me. I floated there, watched by the drowned stones. The moon was flush with the lake, shining fully on its surface. I was behind a mirror. And in that mirror, I saw my life, not only what had been, but what would be. Whether I was trapped, or whether I was free, whether I could change events, or whether this all was inevitable . . . these thoughts spilled from my head, and what was left was an impulse. A desire to surrender. In that moment I felt the pulse of the machine. It was a knowledge that grew in the shrouded place, the place that had existed before language. I stopped thrashing towards the surface. I drank deep the icy water, filled my lungs with the dark.

Sinking, I writhed slowly among the silt and stones. Their pocked hides grew brighter as the moonlight penetrated the black water. Their eyes glowed with cold light. Agony rushed into my chest, tore at me from inside. In the gaze of the old gods, I did not move. I surrendered to the pain. Warmth spread through me, the spasms ceased. My eyes were wide, hardened to glass. And as all went dark, I felt a tremor deep in the earth. The drowned stones spoke.

And I drowned with them.

To arrive at being all,
Desire to be nothing.

It was as I had written.

EPILOGUE

I SAT WITH MY back against the breakwater and waited. Wardie Bay was quiet; on days like these, people flocked to Portobello and left this small patch of sand and pebbles to the anglers. They stood above me on the breakwater, casting their lines out towards the sun-swept skyline of the Western Harbour. Returning was like walking through a memory. Half real seemed the cottages of Granton, which clung to the bay like barnacles. The stone slab of the breakwater was insubstantial. I pressed my fingers against it, half-expecting it to dissipate.

Every few minutes I turned to the gap in the roadside sandstone wall – the one we used to slip through to access the beach. The steps leading down were worn and twisted. I would always leap down them, while she chased me one step at a time. No one passed through the gap now. I wondered if I had mistaken the time.

Nestled in the verge beneath the wall were firepits and shards of glass gleaming bottle-green. There was a mosaic of detritus encircling the bowed saplings which lurched from the crumbling sandstone slabs. The wild crashed against the urban, just as the water met the sand. My breath hitched in my throat when I thought I heard her laugh. I turned again to the gap, realised her voice was in the tide.

Years had passed since I'd become Malcolm Furnivall, and I had never dared come here. I had stayed away, too afraid of the answer to the question: could things be changed? Even then, as I sat waiting, I was unsure what I would do. This was my clearest memory of her, the last memory before our lives were shorn apart and before I realised, fully, what my father had done to her . . . If there was a moment to interfere in the course of history, it was now. Why had I put it off? Because I was afraid of the answer.

Then I saw them. He was a wispy child with wild hair and a lurching run. She was bright-eyed, dark-haired and careful with her steps. Euan and Julia. He leapt down the worn stairs, arms flying out in all directions, landing and laughing, turning back to Julia. She followed, clutching her hobby horse as she went. It scuffed against the rough stones at the end of the bay.

I could have called out. They passed so close to me, I could have touched them. But I did nothing. Instead, I watched, remembering the feel of the wind against my face, the sand against my bare feet. I was with her again. I couldn't interfere – not yet. I was here, again, in this memory – the one which remained in me like a pot-bound root.

After they took off their shoes, Julia galloped across the shoreline, etching lines in the wet sand with her hobby horse. Euan picked up stones, skimmed them over the gentle waves. They didn't see me. Of course they didn't.

I turned my eye again to the wall beside the road. There, a figure, back turned to the beach, smoking and reading the paper. We'd begged him to take us, and he'd reluctantly agreed. Not once did he look out over the water; some men do not allow themselves moments of calm, seeing them as trivial, unworthy of proper attention. I'd learnt that from a young age. He scoured his paper, shaking his head, expelling plumes of bitter smoke.

Howls of laughter pulled my eye back to the children. Euan had pulled thick streamers of seaweed from the foam and draped them over his head, chasing Julia across the shore. She galloped on her hobby horse, over to the breakwater. Just as Euan was about to catch her, she let the hobby horse fall to the sand and leapt away, spinning and laughing giddily. They weaved over to the other end of the bay, Euan chasing, Julia running; and there, lying before me, was the hobby horse.

They circled each other, kicking up mussels and kelp. The tide pulsed quietly. Cirrus clouds lay like wet feathers in the sky.

I remained, fixed against the breakwater, covered by shadow. My eyes were turned to the hobby horse. It was a totem which had fixed itself to my memory of Julia. It held all the joy of this moment. I looked up again at the children, saw Euan skimming stones and Julia walking back towards me.

I did not remember this.

Euan kept his attention on the waves, on the smoothness of the stones, on the wide arcs they traced through the warm air.

Julia moved to her hobby horse, then stilled and caught my eye.

I saw her curious, tender, solemn spirit. She was just as I remembered. I must have scared her, the way I trembled and stared.

'Are you okay?' she said.

I was adrift – no longer an observer of the memory, but a part of it. With only three words she'd melted me.

I came forwards, fighting the urge to run away. Could I save her?

She glanced over her shoulder to Euan, who was still skimming stones.

'I'm just fine,' I said. 'Are you having fun?'

Her hands, which had been buried in her armpits, emerged. She nodded. 'Why are you crying?' she asked.

I looked down at her feet, to the hobby horse.

She took a step back.

I said, 'It's a beautiful day. Is . . . is that your brother?'

Without taking her gaze from me, she nodded again.

'He cares about you. Do you know that?'

'You're funny.'

'Tell me you know it, Julia.'

Her face reddened, and she cocked her chin forwards, shocked that this stranger knew her name. 'I need to go now,' she said.

And tears were flowing down my face. 'Okay,' I said. 'Go on back to your brother.'

She remained there, watching me with a look of curiosity and fear. 'You're alone?' she said.

'I am.' The words resonated through me. A new understanding came: I had always been alone, locked in this cycle. If I told her to come away, that I would save her from our father, it would alter the course of everything. But, as I looked at her, for the first time in many years, I found I didn't care. I could save Julia. If I achieved the impossible, freed myself from the path to which I was yoked, it could be different. I had paid the price of legacy, but, seeing her there,

I realised I was not the only one to pay. I had been selfish beyond belief, Standing there, I covered my mouth and wept into my palm, caught up in the vision of her suffering cycle after cycle. That was the path I had carved. I was complicit in her pain. Knowing I was scaring her, I turned my face away and tried to speak levelly. 'Go on,' I said. 'Go.'

She backed up, stumbled in the sand, turned and ran along to Euan.

I tried to wrap my mind about the chronology: if I saved her, I would not be standing there at the breakwater. I would never have met Malcolm. I would not be writing this now. It was a sequence that seemed eternal. To break it would be to defy the litany of physics.

As I watched her leave, I considered this. Julia ran back to her brother and once again they chased each other, splashing in the foam, laughing. This moment, which would consume the rest of my life, had meant almost nothing to Julia. To her I was a cloud passing on a beautiful day.

She'd forgotten her hobby horse. It lay there, still on the sand before me.

I crouched down and took it, ran my hand along the length of the wood, smoothed towards the neck by her palms. Holding it then, I felt as if I were holding her. I fell back, sat with the hobby horse on my lap, and felt the slender fingers of time fold about me, drag me back to my place in the shadow of the breakwater. There I remained.

I watched my younger self, knowing that very soon he would leave her. He would be called to war, join gladly. Their lives would diverge. He would lose her, for ever. He would never answer the question that would pull at the fabric of his life: what had happened to her? How badly had our father hurt her?

My resolve strengthened. Perhaps, I thought, there was a different physics. Physics, after all, is a language to understand the universe. Might there be words I didn't know, or another tongue entirely? Perhaps one physics might contradict another? If this was true, there might be hope. I could change what had happened to her. I could break from the sequence and learn the first word of a new physics. One that was adjacent and malleable.

If I warned my younger self, I could help him veer from the path. He could make the choice I never did.

His voice rang about the bay, clear and bright. I felt a deep sadness that I would take this perfect moment from him. As soon as we spoke, it would be corrupted. So, for a minute, I watched him and remembered. Remembered a time when I was fully here.

Clinging to the hobby horse, I asked myself again if I could break past this memory's terminus, finally learn what had happened to Julia. Perhaps she had simply run away and lived a life of happiness, far from our father. She may have escaped. I had always held that possibility in my mind. She may have escaped.

But I could do something to make sure. I got to my feet.

Blinking tears from my eyes, I allowed my sight to soften, took in the children wheeling across the shore, silhouetted forms against the sky which became sea which became sand. Through the softened sight, a path emerged; footsteps pressed into the shore. They led towards my younger self.

And I was walking. Holding the hobby horse, I moved back up the beach, following the sight-softened path. I walked into the perfect memory, felt its membrane give.

For the first time, I felt I'd made a choice.

I stopped when I was near him. He glanced across at me as I laid the hobby horse down on the sand, a look of recognition in his eye.

I smiled and spoke the first word of a new physics.

ACKNOWLEDGEMENTS

To Jamie Crawford and Edward Crossan, I am for ever grateful for your belief in my work. To Craig Hillsley, with thanks for your precise and thoughtful notes. To Ludo Cinelli, for your effort and grace. To Noëlle Cobden and the Edinburgh Book Festival team, for your trust and support.

To Will Eaves, Ian Sansom and Tim Leach: the kindest men who not only taught, but demonstrated.

Thank you to Clare Morgan and my cohort on the Oxford Creative Writing MSt, as well as the Warwick Writing Programme.

I will always remember my years working at Blackwell's Oxford fondly. Thank you to the booksellers there, and everywhere else.

To the Watermill Theatre: for a few years, the place I felt most at peace.

To the Low Tide team and the Spartans team, for welcoming me to Edinburgh.

To Jacob Smith: as fine a writer as you are a friend.

To those who have walked with me over the years, there isn't enough room here to elaborate on your profound influence, but know that in writing your name, I am remembering all you've done: Seamus Allen, Theresa Lola, Will Davis, Nia Powell, Paul Hunt, Saksham Garg, Georgina Stewart-Fleming, Heidi Bird, Scott Lilley, Josef Bloomfield, Kat Hill, Emma Easton, Jack Wrighton, Lucy Pulleyblank, Robbie Holland, James Womack,

Amal Chatterjee, Matthew Sperling, Graeme Armstrong,
Jess and Heidi Bell.
And to Mum, Dad and Nathan, with all of my love.